A Novel by J. C. Spencer

This book is a work of fiction. Any references to historical events, real people or real locales are used fictitiously. Other names, characters, places, and incidents are the product of the author's imagination, and any resemblance to actual events or locales or persons, living or dead, is entirely coincidental.

Cover Art by Angela Holmes - Covered-in-Design-Book-Covers

Summary: Katie is a teenage girl trying to fit in to her ever-changing world. While attending a new high school, she encounters a group of "in-crowd" students that have a penchant for picking on "outsiders." To make matters worse, Katie has recently begun experiencing paranormal episodes. As the events of her teenage life unfold, Katie realizes that she can no longer ignore the eminent supernatural powers that exist in her world. Her paranormal dreams become a frightening reality when she faces off in a decisive battle between good and evil and unveils a deep family secret in the process. All of Katie's questions are answered, as she becomes aware of the reality of her dreams, her life, and her world.

ISBN-10: 1494358301
ISBN-13: 978-1494358303

Library of Congress Control Number – 2013923207

Printed in the United States of America

REVISED EDITION

For Grandma Ceil

I love you and miss you
with all of my heart!

Acknowledgements

This book would not have been possible without the love and support of my friends and family. Thank you to my Mom who was my first and best teacher and the person responsible for giving me my love of reading and writing. Thank you for being my biggest cheerleader. A tremendous thank you goes to my big brother, Brad. I am the person I am today because of his love, support, and yes, the torture he inflicted upon me growing up! Bahahahaha! And to Jackson, Matthew, and Emily, who are the most amazing, beautiful, funny, kind-hearted, and crazy children in the world—thank you for the love and support you gave to me while I was writing this book. Katie's journey would not have been the same without your exciting suggestions. Also, a huge thank you to Karen Bazan, without her support and marketing know-how, the world may have never known about Unaware. I would also like to express my appreciation to Shari Bergeron who read my work before it was ready to be read and loved me enough to be honest. A special thank you goes to Megan Simpson-Bergeron whose line edit was an invaluable contribution to this book project. My gratitude also goes to Robin Dooley whose knowledge of character and plot development kept me on the right path. I sincerely appreciate all of the pep talks. And to Deena Bailey and Deb Bordowitz, thank you for enduring the endless stream of book covers that I paraded before your eyes and for your never-ending support.

Thank you all for making my dream of writing a book become a reality.

~ TABLE OF CONTENTS ~

UNAWARE

~ PROLOGUE ~

SIXTEEN YEARS AGO ...

Within every being, there is a battle being fought between the forces of goodness and evil. In the Kingdom of Faery, the struggle between good and evil, light and dark, Seelie and Unseelie continues...

* * * * *

"Daniel," the deep, deafening voice of the Seelie king echoed throughout the shadow-filled cavern. "Bring the girl and the baby at once!"

"No Father, there must be another way," Daniel pleaded, his hands gripping the impenetrable ice bars that held him, Scarlett, and their baby captive.

King Cassius slammed his massive hands against the prison bars. His royal crescent ring chipped the ice. "You are in no position to make requests, foolish boy. You chose to follow your heart and now our kingdom is on the brink of war."

Daniel stood steady, denying his father's order. Queen Elizabeth, the Seelie queen, moved swiftly from one end of the cold chamber to stand beside her husband. Daniel saw her long, green velvet robes dragging across the ground of the cave that had become his dungeon. She reached her thin, aged fingers between the prison bars to take hold of her son's hand.

Elizabeth watched through her pale-yellow eyes the vapor rushing forth from her husband with each breath he forcefully exhaled. Trying to ease the fury that was building inside of her husband and king, Elizabeth placed her free hand on his arm and spoke softly, "Dear, I think you are being too harsh on our son."

Cassius turned to face his wife; he looked as if he would explode. The green and gold robes over his upper torso rose with the expansion of his chest, his full cheeks reddening as his anger built.

"Do you think stopping a war and bringing about peace is a simple task? This deal was born from years of negotiation. Our son is the Seelie prince; it was his obligation to marry Anastasia, the Unseelie princess, not some sniveling human girl. Our plan to unite the kingdoms of Faery and end the war once and for all hinged on his compliance," Cassius bellowed, shaking the frozen bars with his mass and strength.

Queen Elizabeth remained calm with her hand still on his raised arm. "Perhaps it was too great a burden to place on a Fae so young; the boy *is* only twenty-one." The queen fixed her eyes on Daniel.

"The boy knew what was at stake. What happens to the girl and the baby are on his head," Cassius replied, his forest-green eyes cold as the ice around his heart.

"But Father," Daniel dropped his hand from the bar and let go of his mother. He stood with his eyes fixed on his father, but still fear gripped his soul. Denying his father, the king, had meant death for others in their realm. Daniel was readying to offer further protest when . . .

"Silence!" Cassius shouted. "You acted in your own selfish interests. A king must act in the interest of his kingdom. The price for your pardon may seem unbearable to you now, but in the years to come, I assure you, you will see the wisdom of the arrangement I have made."

Daniel grabbed the frozen bars, hanging his head low. "Father, please—" he pleaded, his voice barely a whisper. "Please—"

Unaffected by his son's anguish, Cassius continued, "Anastasia has arranged to raise the prison bars and free you at midnight, Daniel. She has agreed to allow Lucille to take the baby and keep her in the human world."

Daniel raised his head. "But Scarlett will not allow it."

"Scarlett will be sacrificed to assuage Anastasia's pride. That and to free you from the bonds of marriage. Then you, my son, will be united in marriage to Anastasia as was originally arranged. Once the marriage vows are complete, the Seelie and Unseelie will be united again as one race of Fae. And I will preside over the Kingdom of Faery as the one true king."

Scarlett's death was not an option for Daniel. His father dismissed his love for her as a passing thought. Glowering at the king, he could not mask his anger. A lifetime of his father's intimidation paled in comparison to the torment he felt now that the lives of Scarlett and his baby were in danger. A moment passed, then another. Finally, Daniel spoke.

"I won't do it. I won't give up either of them! I would rather die. I—"

"Death is a coward's way!" King Cassius's voice boomed, drowning out Daniel's insolence. "You are royalty. You *will* fulfill your obligation to our Kingdom." His father paused for a second, staring malevolently at his son as if Daniel were a predator threatening to encroach on his prey, rather than his only heir to the throne.

"Dear, please consider—" Elizabeth started.

"Enough! Bring me Scarlett and the baby. Anastasia will be here soon. Our realm cannot afford another debacle."

Daniel looked from his father's cruel, unfeeling face to his mother, searching for her sympathetic expression, but her face bore no hint of empathy or kindness. Elizabeth spoke; her voice dripping with royal authority, "Go now, Daniel. There is nothing left to do but follow your father's command."

Daniel stared, stunned by his mother's demand. "Mother, not you too." He beat his head on the icy prison bars in defeat, incredulity overtaking him. Thin fingers wrapped around his. Daniel glanced up to discover that her expression was firm yet compassionate. His green eyes beheld hers.

Elizabeth glanced quickly at her fuming husband to see that his attention was not directed toward her. Narrowing her yellow eyes at Daniel, she moved her head in the direction of where Scarlett sat holding the newborn baby and mouthed the words, "Trust me," hoping that Daniel would glean the meaning of her cryptic gesture.

Daniel nodded to show his understanding and strode quickly to Scarlett's side. As he approached, she raised her head; her pale-green eyes brimming with tears.

"It is time for Lucille to take the baby," he spoke softly, reaching for the infant who was tucked safely in the light-pink blanket. Scarlett stood and jerked her arm away from Daniel. Long brown-red strands of her hair concealed the baby.

"I will not let you take her from me, Daniel."

"Scarlett, please. It is the only chance she has."

Scarlett turned to face Daniel; her eyes piercing his. "I will not give up my daughter," she said slowly, sitting up straight. Her voice turned feral as she uttered the unthinkable. "If you want to take Katheena, you will have to kill me first," she warned through gritted teeth.

Daniel stood wide-eyed, searching Scarlett's wild eyes for the sweet girl he had married.

"Scarlett, Daniel, stop this at once," Elizabeth admonished in a hushed voice. "You must come to me, now!" She motioned with her hand for them to draw near to her. She had made her way to the side of the ice bars near the young prisoners—far away from the brooding king, who stood waiting for Daniel to comply with his demands.

Daniel and Scarlett moved behind the bars to where his mother stood, Scarlett guarding Katheena like a lioness protecting her cub.

In a voice that only they could hear, Daniel's mother said, "I have a plan, but you will both have to trust me." Elizabeth faced Scarlett. "If you continue with my son in this foolishness, not only will you die today, but your infant will most surely die, also."

"Mother," Daniel scolded.

His mother raised her hand quickly, motioning for him to quiet his speech. She continued, "Sometimes, a mother must make sacrifices for what is best for her child."

"But—" Scarlett started to protest.

Elizabeth silenced her and shoved a handful of herbs through the bars and into Scarlett's hand.

"Eat these. When Anastasia comes to kill you, jump into the black water. She will not follow you into the lake of blackness."

"But, what good will that do? She will only wait until I emerge from the water and kill me then," Scarlett said, confused.

"I did not instruct you to come out of the dark water, my dear. Swim as swiftly as you can through the underwater tunnel beneath the waterfall. It leads to the clear lake outside of this cavern. The herbs will keep you alive as you make your transformation. Daniel will come to you when it is safe."

Scarlett stared dumbfounded at the queen; apprehension filling her mind. She wanted to speak, to ask how everything would work, but she stopped, fearful of the answer that the queen might give.

Elizabeth turned to her son and continued her instructions. “Daniel, when Anastasia raises the prison walls, you will escape through the portal I have created on the south side of the cave.”

“What about Father?”

“When he sees that you have disappeared, he will know my betrayal. He will be furious with me, but I have had many years to learn how to contain his wrath.”

“But what will happen to Katheena, our baby?” Scarlett asked. “Will she go into the waters with me?”

Elizabeth shook her head. “She would not be able to hold her breath long enough to get through the tunnel, Scarlett.”

“What about the herbs?”

“You are a new mother, but surely you know that a baby cannot ingest herbs,” she cautioned with a hint of irritation in her tone.

“Then will she go with Daniel?” Scarlett asked frantically, fear and desperation starting to take over her being.

“A half-Fae child cannot enter the land of Faery until it has acquired the first of its powers, which usually happens shortly after what you humans call ‘puberty.’ Besides, even if there were a way to keep her with us in Faery, Anastasia would surely hunt her down and kill her in our land.”

Elizabeth shifted her gaze from Scarlett to her son. “Daniel, this is the only way.”

He nodded in agreement and cast his stare towards Scarlett. He had spent enough time with her to know that she would never go for his mother's plan unless she knew for certain that Katheena would be safe.

"Tell me Mother, exactly what *will* happen to our baby?"

"The Fae have employed the assistance of a human woman, Lucille. She runs an adoption agency. Human children who are adopted require certain legal documents: termination of parental rights, certificate of adoption, birth certificates. Lucille makes everything look the way humans like. She has been assisting our kind for years. I assure you, Katheena will have a wonderful life. Lucille's people have been very successful at placing children from, shall we say, delicate situations such as these."

Scarlett glanced down the long, mist-filled corridor and saw the outline of an elderly woman standing in the shadows of the dimly lit cave. Her heart raced and her arms tightened around her daughter. The time had come; she had to decide.

She looked down longingly at her sweet baby girl and then regarded the queen.

"But why are you doing this for *me*? You don't even know me, and I have caused so much pain to your family and to your subjects," Scarlett probed, her eyes searching for truth.

Elizabeth stared lovingly at her son and smiled. She turned her gaze to Scarlett and spoke, still in a whisper, "Daniel's father was not my first love. When I was Daniel's age, I did not have the courage to go against my family's wishes; I have never stopped thinking of my first true love. The king is wrong; Daniel will never look back and see the wisdom in his father's arrangement. He will always long for you and Katheena."

Elizabeth closed her eyes and breathed deeply, reminiscing of another time and place. Her eyes opened slowly. She fixed her determined gaze on Scarlett.

"I wish someone had done for me then what I am about to do for you and Daniel now."

"But I can't bear to think of never seeing my precious baby girl ever again."

Elizabeth turned to face her son. "Daniel, give me the stone from the hologram."

He patted his chest lightly trying to find what his mother requested. From the pocket of his threadbare vest, Daniel revealed the stone that he and Scarlett used to make a hologram for their daughter just days before.

Reaching into the folds of her royal coat, Elizabeth pulled a handful of beautiful amethyst crystals from beneath her robe. She took the stone from Daniel and carefully placed it into the middle of the sparkling crystals, closing her fingers firmly around the mass of stone and gems.

Instantly, a light lilac-colored mist swirled softly and slowly around her fist and traveled deliberately towards Scarlett. The mist encircled her head. As Scarlett closed her eyes and breathed in deeply, the magical mist filled her nostrils and vanished within her. When the last of the enchanted vapor disappeared, Scarlett's eyes opened wide.

She stared at the queen, astonished.

Elizabeth smiled and nodded her approval. Looking down, she opened her fingers, revealing a beautiful amethyst stone. She passed the enchanted gemstone through the ice bars. "Give this stone to Katheena; one day it will bring her back to you."

Scarlett stared blankly at the sparkling stone held within the Seelie queen's hand, unsure of her true intentions.

"I—"

"Scarlett, you must trust me," she whispered with each word wrapped in sincerity.

Scarlett stared at the queen, then at Daniel.

A loving smile concealed the reluctance in his eyes. "This is the only way, my love," he tried to assure her, stroking her arm softly.

Scarlett reached out gingerly and took the stone. She tucked it gently into the folds of the pink cloth that was wrapped around the tiny infant; Scarlett pulled back the soft blanket and kissed her baby's rosy cheek.

"Mommy loves you, baby."

Scarlett cradled Katheena close to her own pounding heart. She closed her eyes, took a deep breath in, and held it for a moment, trying to memorize the scent of her precious baby girl.

In her mind, Scarlett knew the truth, but her heart held out the hope that when she opened her eyes, she would discover that all of this was just a terrible nightmare. Still clutching her tiny infant in her arms, she exhaled and opened her eyes slowly.

Scarlett gasped; it felt as if her heart stopped.

A dark faery hovered above Scarlett. Long black robes hung from the evil creature's shoulders and swept down the length of its body. The stench of death emanated from within its very being. Scarlett's eyes saw the malevolent beast first, and then her mind quickly registered the horror that was before her.

A malicious grin spread across Anastasia's face. Scarlett could barely see the Unseelie Princess's once beautiful porcelain skin through the scattered black creases that now plagued her tormented face—a face that had once made Scarlett's heart and mind sick with jealousy made her stomach feel as if she would wretch with a mere glance at it now.

"Ah, there she is. Pretty, pretty Scarlett," she spoke in a high-pitched voice, her eerie laughter infecting every crevice of the dark cavern, sending chills up Scarlett's spine.

Where her eyes should have been, endless black orbs filled the space, and lips bloodied and cracked split her face, her voice foreboding.

"It is time for you to die, Scarlett!"

Sixteen Years Later...

~1~

NEW BEGINNINGS

Whoever said that your high school years were supposed to be the best years of your life never went to three different high schools before the eleventh grade, Katie thought miserably.

She was feeling more like a hostage being transferred against her will rather than a passenger in her mom's car. Katie shifted in her seat and glanced at the passing scenery outside of her mobile prison.

A frigid November wind swept through the almost bare forest, picking the last of the yellow and reddish-orange leaves from the old oak trees. The windows of the car lessened the wind's cry, but its shrill howling sounded more like a wailing woman than a storm.

It must be an omen.

Katie leaned her head against the cold car window as

her mom turned onto Maple Drive. Their new house was just another mile away. In the side mirror, the image of a girl, almost a woman, stared blankly back at Katie through distant green eyes.

Turning away from her reflection, Katie glanced out the window to see the sun suspended high above the horizon; its long, blinding rays pierced through empty branches and the tall pine trees that confined the dusty road. In another month, it would all be covered in snow.

Katie sighed and thought of how much she already missed California. She closed her eyes and could almost taste the salt from the sea and hear the seagulls as they cried above. The car hit a pothole and brought her back to her present reality. *Sometimes, reality really bites,* she thought unhappily.

Their old house with Dad was grand and beautiful, but to Katie, that was a lifetime ago. She and her mom had made many changes since then. This new "home" was what her mom had called a "fixer-upper." Katie remembered thinking fixer-upper must be some sort of code for old, run-down, and definitely not new.

The homes on this street did not compare to the one they had when her parents were married; these houses were older, but to her surprise, each had its own charm.

Her mom turned the car down a long dirt driveway towards an ancient looking, white colonial house that was supported by four large columns. Its huge windows were trimmed with green cobweb-laden shutters, and a wide wooden porch wrapped around the old home. Old wisteria vines, whose flowers had long since died and fallen away, wrapped around the cracked columns, and grasped the second story of the house with their dying tendrils. Katie could see where the paint was chipping and falling off around the ivy-clad walls. Weather and wear had taken their toll on the old house; Katie thought it looked just eerie enough to be a cool place to live.

At least I can check that off my list of things to worry about. Now all I have to stress over is starting another new high school.

Katie tried to be positive, tried to consider what the new school would have to offer her, but the familiar sting of apprehension filled her mind as she considered the customary list of questions that paraded through her mind every time she had to start a new school.

What will my new school be like? Will I fit in? What will my teachers be like? Will everyone be smarter than me, or worse, will I drown in a sea of fools?

Her mom turned off the ignition of the car and announced, "Here we are, our new home!"

Katie took a deep breath and held on tightly to the amethyst stone in the front pocket of her dark purple hoodie. She smiled at her mom, not in a way that could suggest she was overjoyed, but enough to mask her true feelings as she thought to herself, *if only you could understand just how much I wish we could stay in one place, Mom, just you and me.*

Looking away from her mom, Katie tucked a strand of her long black hair behind her ear and pulled on the inside handle to open the car door. Once outside the car, she stood for a moment, readying herself for the next chapter of her life.

Here we go again.

Katie walked toward the latest house that would masquerade as their home.

* * * * *

Katie pushed open the door to her new bedroom and peeked in to get a full view. She let out a deep breath and stepped into her latest blank canvas, completely unaware of what this new place had in store for her. Putting her room in order always gave Katie a sense of peace. To Katie, decorating a new room felt almost like putting the pieces of herself back together after having been disassembled and transported to another place and time. This was their fourth move in two years. She was becoming a pro at turning lemons into lemonade.

After making her bed, Katie searched through the boxes in her closet for her full-length mirror. She leaned it against the brick wall and checked her appearance. Katie pulled her long black hair up into a high ponytail, leaving a thick strand of her purple-streaked bangs hanging in her face. She gave a glint of a smile and raised her eyebrows at her reflection as she tucked the loose hair behind one ear. Katie turned away from the mirror and set her sights on the two large wardrobe boxes next to the closet. One by one, she hung the clothes from the first box and started to open the second one.

"Katie, I need your help down here, now!" Mom's frantic voice interrupted her organizational efforts. Katie ran down the long hall to the top of the stairs. She bounded down the steps and landed at the bottom of the stairs.

Her mom was flailing wallpaper covered limbs as if she were trying to get the attention of a long-awaited rescue ship after years of being stranded on a deserted island.

Stifling her laughter, Katie shook her head back and forth and tsked loudly to show her disapproval of her mom's predicament. Truly, it *was* funny, but Katie was not ready to show her mother an ounce of joy being that her mom was the one responsible for having uprooted her life, yet again.

"Katie, where are you?" Mom screeched at her. "Help me get out of this! I have a pizza in the oven, and your father will be here any moment." All semblance of patience had escaped from her mother's voice. The harshness in her tone rubbed Katie the wrong way.

"He's not my father. He's your husband," Katie retorted.

"I am your mother; that makes my husband your father."

"Step…father," Katie corrected quickly. Her words were dripping with two years of bottled-up anger and resentment.

"I really wish you would give him a chance, Katie. He does genuinely care for you, dear," she pleaded.

Katie shot her a look that said she wasn't buying what

Mom was selling.

"Don't look at me like that, Katie Ryan. You know you would be walking to school if Phil had not bought a car for you."

Katie rolled her eyes and started to turn away. Better that than say what she really thought of the car that Phil had given her.

He couldn't have found a more beat-up, run-down, rusty old car than my Mustang if he had tried. It barely even qualifies as a car.

Katie stopped and looked back. She furrowed her brows at her mom trying to read the peculiar expression that was displayed on her mother's face.

"Why do you always look at me like that?" Katie asked. Her green eyes were filled with accusation.

"Like what, dear?" Mom asked innocently.

"Like I am impossible to understand," Katie said.

Her mom chuckled and smiled lovingly at Katie. "Sometimes I *don't* understand you, honey. Your moods are so unpredictable," she said as she tried to push her brown hair away from her face with her shoulder.

Katie's mouth dropped open in astonishment. *Did she just say that I am unpredictable? Okay, Miss Four Boyfriends and Four New Addresses in Two Years,* she thought, the shock of her mother's statement keeping her from responding.

Whatever.

Katie shook her head and started to leave.

Mom reached gently for Katie's arm. "Ah, a little help,

dear?" she requested, this time in a calm voice.

Mom's smile was genuine and hopeful. Katie could see the tiny wrinkles in the skin around her mother's eyes when she smiled. Katie and her mother had been through many disagreements, but Katie could never stay angry at her mom for long. She knew her mother loved her, especially when that small gleam of light shone in her mother's brown eyes as it did in that moment. Katie reached out and peeled the sticky paper from her mom's back and arms. Together, they walked arm in arm into the kitchen to get dinner on the table.

As her mom pulled the pizza from the oven, Katie set the table with their finest paper plates, plastic knives, forks, and big red plastic cups. Although Phil had already been in the house a month, living and working in the area, he had left all the unpacking to them. The good dishes were still packed away in one of the many boxes that lined each room.

Just as Mom had promised, her husband arrived in time for dinner with his new family. Dinner was pretty much uneventful. Mom and Phil tried to coax information from Katie about how she felt about starting a new school tomorrow; Katie did her best to answer their questions with one- or two-word answers. It was not that she was mad at them or even that she did not like them. Well, maybe she *was* mad at them, and she really did not care too much for Phil. But tonight, her silence was prompted by the fact that she just could not bear to think about starting yet another school.

When it seemed they had finished their inquisition, Katie asked to be excused. She pushed in the wooden chair and turned to leave, but she was stopped by Phil's request. "Katie," he started in a tone that said there would be a demand to follow, "try to have all your boxes put away by this weekend. You don't want to live out of boxes forever."

The nerve of him infuriated her.

"You mean you don't want me to leave my boxes for a month, like you did?" she asked, her frustration masked by the saccharine tone in her voice. She narrowed her eyes at him and turned to leave. She could hear the scratching of his chair as it moved quickly over the hardwood floor. He was standing now, both hands on the table.

"What did you just say?"

Katie turned and smiled wryly, proud of the fact that she had gotten a rise out of him. Her mom placed her hand on Phil's arm.

"Phil, dear," her tone was as sweet as honey, "she did not mean anything by it. Did you, Katie?"

Phil shrugged away from her touch. "Don't get in the middle of this. She will learn."

"Phil, it is our first night in our new home. Please—"

Phil slammed his thin hands down on the table, rattling the silverware and glasses. Mom's sweet demeanor turned to one of shock. Her plastic smile and anxious glare pleaded for Katie to respond respectfully.

Katie stared at her mom for a moment, deciding if she wanted to push the issue tonight. "Actually Mom, I meant what I said."

"Katie," her mom scolded; her tone seemed more

surprised than angry.

"I'm just saying… if I am going to *learn* from Phil, shouldn't he practice what he preaches?"

Phil advanced towards Katie; his wife was tugging at his elbow trying to pull him back. He stood a foot from Katie, his usually pale face turning a deep color of red. "You had better remember whose house you are living in young lady. I can send you back to California any time," he said, shaking his finger in her face.

A triumphant smile spread across her face for a moment as she laughed to herself. Then, her face became a mask of seriousness. As she stared boldly into his cold brown eyes, Katie stepped forward, closing the gap between her and Phil. "Go ahead, Phil. Send me back to California."

Phil exhaled forcefully; his mouth held open as if he were going to say something. But he did not speak. He looked down his nose and glared at her for what seemed like an eternity to Katie. His face was so close she could smell the garlic from the pizza on his breath.

Determined that he would not get the better of her, Katie looked past Phil to address her mom. "Did you hear that, Mom? Phil says he is sending me back to California," Katie said with mock excitement.

Katie's mom rushed to her side and pulled her away from Phil. "Katie, please stop this. Phil is not going to send you anywhere. You are staying here with us. Please stop." Her mom turned to face her husband. "Please, let this go, Phil."

"I will not overlook blatant disrespect from anyone in

my own home," Phil barked. "She owes me an apology."

Katie laughed out loud.

Good luck with that.

"See what I mean? Disrespect," Phil said, motioning to Katie, who stood with her hands on her hips grinning at her mom and stepdad.

"Katie. Dear," her mom urged, eyes wide.

Katie smiled and answered her mom's plea for peace. "Okay Mom, I am sorry Phil was being hypocritical."

Phil started to move towards Katie, but his wife stepped between him and his stepdaughter. Katie turned and stormed out of the kitchen, heading down the long hallway that led to the stairs. She stood on the bottom step and listened to her mom and Phil arguing about Katie's attitude.

He's such a hypocrite.

A small part of Katie felt bad that her mom was left to deal with Phil's tantrum, but no one ever considered Katie's feelings about anything that mattered. Mom and Phil had not asked Katie what she thought about them getting married or the move to Salem. She rolled her eyes at the thought of all the times she had to adjust to new surroundings because of the grown-ups in her world.

Katie stomped up the old wooden stairs, her thoughts coursing chaotically through her mind.

They dragged me across the country to some freakish little witch town, and now I have to start school tomorrow with a bunch of strangers. I have to live with a stepdad I detest, and I haven't seen my real dad in years. Oh yeah, and I think I might have supernatural powers I can't control and don't understand.

When she reached her room, she flung open the door and slammed it shut for effect. She plopped down on her fluffy comforter and lay there for a few moments.

I can't deal with them and their bickering right now.

She breathed deeply and made herself get up. She had just a few hours left before she had to get ready for bed, and there was still so much to put away. Glancing around the exposed brick walls of the room, she settled on the window seat as a display for her large purple and black pillows. Mom had asked Phil to paint the red brick white to brighten up the room, their first of many home improvement endeavors. Katie's two large bookcases made the trip from California intact and were waiting for their usual adornments. She placed them on either side of the huge bay window.

One bookcase held paranormal novels and books on witchcraft. Katie scattered different sized black cauldrons, shiny stones, and crystals that were supported by claw-shaped stands throughout the shelves.

Bookcase number two housed Katie's classical book collection and statues of faeries depicting many scenes. Some were light and sweet; they swam upon pedestals of sea coral and kelp or danced amidst beautiful white Calla lilies. Others were dark and fantastical. The eyes of the dark faeries seemed to hold obscure secrets, and they looked as if they had been bewitched by a spell cast from another time and place. Katie had often considered moving those faeries to her "witchy" bookcase, but opted to leave them instead with their nemeses, the faeries of goodness and light. Their contrasting images reminded Katie of herself, and what people must see when they looked at her. Katie often thought of herself as a walking contradiction.

She was a straight "A" student, with the hopes and dreams of your average American girl: visions of an Ivy League college, a house with a white picket fence, and a modern day knight in a shiny BMW ambled through her mind. But that could not be discerned by others if they glanced in her direction.

Katie's outward appearance gave no indication of the bright, hopeful girl inside. Katie stood five feet six inches; her natural hair color was brown like her mom's, only darker with red highlights. She had dyed it jet black with one thick strand of dark purple highlight added to accentuate the long bangs that swept across her face. Her eyes were green with yellow flecks; her skin complexion was light in the winter and tan in the summer months. Since it was mid-November, her light complexion contrasted dramatically with her dark hair.

On the outside, she looked as if at any moment she might fling open one of her witchcraft books and concoct a potion in one of her many cauldrons. But on the inside, Katie felt more like one of the female protagonists in the classical books she often read. She liked to think of herself as an Elizabeth Bennet, intelligent and quick witted, mixed with a hint of Scarlett O'Hara, charming with a fierce determination.

Katie stepped back from her bookcases and examined

her handiwork. She glanced across the room thinking of what to unpack next. After putting away the rest of her clothes, Katie set her laptop up on her desk.

She wanted to return to the site she had been exploring before she had to pack away her life for this new one in Salem, Massachusetts. Katie quickly typed in the paranormal web address. Since her first paranormal-like incident, Katie found herself drawn to books and websites on witchcraft and other paranormal things. She had kept that incident and the one that followed to herself. Her mom had enough to worry about with her own quest of finding a new man after Dad left without thinking her daughter was a freak of nature.

~ 2 ~

SHATTERED

The day that Katie's father walked out on her and her mother was the day of Katie's first paranormal incident. Sitting in her new room, she shifted her gaze from the screen of her laptop to the dimming evening sky just outside of the big bay window in her bedroom. Her mind dredged up the painful memory.

Although it had been two years, Katie remembered it as if it were yesterday. The fighting had been unbearable; Mom and Dad's voices carried throughout the house. A storm raged outside, but even the thunderous rainstorm could not drown out their shouting. Katie recalled praying for their yelling to end. Then suddenly, as if her prayers had been answered, the shouting stopped. She listened intently for a moment, contemplating whether it was safe to come out from under the cover of her pillow and blankets; it was then that her life was shattered.

The sound of the front door slamming shut reverberated throughout the house. Katie ran to her window to see that her father was walking briskly down the cobblestone walk; his leather briefcase in one hand and an oversized rolling suitcase in the other. With one hand she beat on the windowpane, and the other grasped her amethyst stone as she willed him to return.

"Daddy, no!" she cried out.

She stood horrified and watched as her father left. His car became minuscule in the distance as he sped away from their home, away from her mom, away from her. All that remained was her breath on the inside of the window and the diminishing rain that tapped lightly against the outside. Her breath deepened; both hands were balled into fists at her sides, one still clutching the purple stone.

She turned away from the scene of her devastation and stopped, paralyzed by the pain. Then anger churned within her. She closed her eyes, letting the rage wash over her; it burned her from the inside out. Suddenly, the window that held the pitiful scene of Katie's life exploded into tiny pebbles of glass. Katie turned back suddenly thinking a rock or tree limb had struck the glass. Yet, no evidence of a foreign object existed; in fact, the wind had calmed itself, and the rain had transformed into tiny droplets.

Katie stood and stared at the broken pieces of glass that covered the floor beneath her windowsill. She thought about the obvious symbolism of the broken window and her now broken family.

What have I done? How could I break my window without even touching it?

Gooseflesh started to form on her arms. She couldn't figure out if they were the result of the cold wind that was blowing through the opening that was once her window, or the eerie feeling that plagued the back of her mind insisting that a supernatural force was within the room, or worse, within her.

She stood in a trance and stared at the broken pieces as if the answer to her question would magically appear. Her mom threw open the bedroom door in a panic.

"What happened, Katie?" Mom's startled voice snapped her out of the trance.

As Katie opened her mouth to speak, she knew she would have to lie. "I think a tree branch or a rock must have struck the window. It just… it just broke."

Moving towards her swiftly, Mom wrapped one of her arms around Katie and guided her out of the room and down the stairs. "We can clean that up in a little while. The important thing is that you're all right," her mom said, sniffling softly. "Let's sit in the family room."

Family room, huh, what a joke.

Her mom motioned for her to sit next to her on the fluffy brown and white striped couch. Her mom took a wet tissue from her pocket and dabbed her moist eyes. It was obvious that she had been crying. She looked so pallid and frail.

Katie had always known it was her father that was the

head of their household, and that her mother found her own self-worth in the fact that she was the wife of a lawyer. What little inner strength her mom had seemed to have vanished when her father walked out the door.

What is she going to do without Dad? She's going to need me more than ever now. It must be killing her to keep from crying in front of me.

Katie swallowed her own hurt, angry feelings, stifled her snide remarks, and gave her mom her undivided attention.

Her mom spoke, "We need to talk, Katie. I have something I have to tell you, sweetie."

* * * * *

Katie shook off the grip of the painful memory.

I can't deal with this now. I'll have to deal with it later.

Her thoughts turned to all that would be expected of her for the fourth time in two years. Tomorrow would be a big day: another new school, another group of kids to figure out, and who knew what else would await her in the morning.

~ 3 ~

A PIECE OF THE PIE

When Mom married Phil, she promised me this time would be different, but I don't see the difference. Every time Mom gets a new guy, I get to be the new dork on campus.

Katie made the two-mile drive to the new school; the GPS on her phone announced, "Turn right in 200 feet. Then, your destination will be on the right."

As she drove around the corner, Katie spotted the school on the next block. The traffic leading to the parking lot was at a standstill. There, before her eyes, was an accurate depiction of teenage society. They were all present. The jocks, sporting lettermen jackets, blue jeans, and expensive athletic shoes were on the grassy area flanked by the school's cheerleaders. The "raw raws" were wearing short skirts, ponytails, and matching tennis shoes.

Another group of kids, all of whom were either

holding or sitting on instrument cases, occupied the opposite end of the lawn. Neither group dared to cross the invisible line that separated the two social groups.

Carefully placed out of immediate sight was another piece of the social pie. Boys with shoulder-length hair, concert T-shirts, and pants that were too tight rode skateboards down a row of stairs that led to the vacant side entrance of the school.

Katie supposed that she would find the bookworms inside the library once she got inside. The library had always been the perfect spot to hide away during those first few trying days at a new school. In the library, everyone had their nose in a book; they did not worry about what others were wearing, what they were talking about, or whom they were sitting by. If someone was to speak to her, she would be in her element, the world of fiction.

The stopped traffic began to creep along again. As Katie was about to edge forward, she spotted a group of girls standing opposite the skaters that mirrored her own fashion sense. Other students called girls that dressed like that Emo or Goth, but she did not think of herself as Emo or Goth. She simply liked her clothes dark, and her hair cut in a fashion that allowed it to cover a good portion of her face.

She felt the butterflies begin their ritual dance in her stomach as she rolled into the parking lot. She could hear the faint sound of the morning bell calling the students to begin the day.

It's now or never!

Katie checked her look in the mirror. She brushed her

long bangs over her left eye and tucked a few strands of dark hair behind her right ear. It was time to get inside and get the day over with.

Once inside, the scene was very familiar. The halls sang the chorus of a typical high school. The peripheries of the hall were cluttered with girls huddled together, sharing secrets that they would inevitably betray by the end of the next class period. Boys were giving each other high fives, checking out various girls, and talking about the plays they would run at the game after school. Students hung on to open locker doors as they contemplated which books to grab, finished text messages, and crammed unneeded items into their lockers. The stop and go of the traffic in the middle of the hallways made it difficult to get to class on time.

Although Katie knew the answer, she could not help but wonder, would this school be any different?

Could I be part of the "in-crowd" again? Is it too much to hope for?

When she started her freshman year two years ago, she was a different individual entirely. Mom, meaning well of course, liked to remind her of how popular she was back then.

"Why can't you just be like you used to be, Katie?" she would question sweetly and smile.

Katie wondered if her mom was actually so out of it that she really thought Katie wanted to be a dork or a social outcast. Did her mom believe people chose to be unaccepted by their peers?

What Katie wanted to say was, "Because nothing is the

same as it used to be, Mom. You've made sure of that!"

Of course, she would never speak such cruel words. Her mom would probably crumble into pieces if she were to hint about how difficult her life had been since the divorce.

Three high schools by the eleventh grade were too many, and now, two and a half months into her junior year, she was starting her fourth new school.

At least I know the drill. After about a week of feeling like a social outcast, I will suddenly sprout a small group of fellow social outcasts as friends and begin to feel a little less out of place.

Although she had come to terms with the fact that it would never feel like her home in California, life would be bearable again.

I just have to get through the first week, but it is the first week that always feels like torture.

~ 4 ~

THE TORTURE ZONE

Katie looked anxiously from one side of the hall to the other looking for her class. She glanced again at her schedule to make sure she was going in the right direction. When she looked up, her eyes were met by deep pools of blue. The blue eyes belonged to a tall, dark-haired, very hot-looking guy. Much to her surprise, she realized that he was smiling at her.

Although she was caught off guard, she smiled shyly back at him. Suddenly, his eyes shifted, and she heard him say, "What? No, I am listening."

He was talking to a girl with long, strawberry-blonde hair. The girl craned her head to look past him to see what he had been staring at. Strawberry Blonde's dark brown eyes were daggers.

If looks could kill.

The girl flipped her hair and turned back to face the boy that had been smiling at Katie. As if she had practiced the move a million times, Strawberry Blonde wove her arm through his and dragged him down the hallway, away from Katie.

The scene made Katie giggle to herself. That girl looked ridiculous herding him away from the presence of another girl. Katie thought of how ludicrous it was to try to stake your claim on another person. Then she remembered that she too had felt a little possessive of her old boyfriend, Sean. She hoped she had not made a fool of herself the way that Strawberry Blonde had, but before she could get lost in the past, she quickly pushed the thoughts from her mind.

As Katie continued through the hallway, she reached inside the pocket of her black jacket. There, she felt the heat radiating from the stone. She had always wondered if the stone were an entity that possessed an internal energy, or if the warmth simply came from her. Perhaps it was all in her imagination. She ran her fingers carefully over the rough edges and gingerly stroked the smooth surfaces. The familiarity of its features calmed her nerves as she entered her first academic class, English.

Since it was mid-November, the class had already read through a third of the eleventh grade reading list. Katie found the list, along with a map of the school, and a copy of her class schedule in the welcome packet that the office gave her earlier that morning.

Of Mice and Men, *The Great Gatsby*, *The Scarlet Letter,* the list went on. Mr. White, the English teacher, interrupted her perusal of the list when he called the class to attention and put the spotlight on her.

"Katie, we have a ritual in our class. Every new student must give a mini autobiography. Go ahead, we're all ears."

"Um… um…" Katie stuttered as she searched her mind for her well-developed vocabulary but came up short.

"Her name is Um-Um," a strawberry-blonde girl from the side of the room cackled just loud enough to be heard by Katie but unnoticed by Mr. White.

Where did she come from?

It was the girl from the hallway. Katie got a better look at Strawberry Blonde. Her long hair was even more beautiful than Katie first thought. It was peppered with spiral curls and little wisps that framed her face. She was the kind of girl teen magazines placed on the cover with a perfect smile, flawless skin, and salon styled hair that flowed unnaturally as if the wind were always blowing around her. She was the kind of girl that always had a date and a ton of friends.

The group that surrounded her joined in her haughty laughter. Katie glanced from one side of the room to the other trying to assess just how many students the snotty girl had wrapped around her little finger.

A dark-haired girl from the back of the room chimed in, "Maybe it's short for Dumb-Dumb."

More laughter followed, and Katie felt as if she wanted to bolt out of the door and never return, but she was determined not to give them the satisfaction.

Oblivious of what, or whom, had provoked the

laughter, Mr. White tried to calm his students. "Settle down, now. Give Katie a chance."

She took a deep breath and let it out slowly. She closed her eyes to gather her thoughts. Grandma Ceil always said, "This too shall pass."

When Katie opened her eyes, they were all staring at her anxiously as if they were waiting for her head to explode.

"My name is Katie Ryan. I grew up in California; my family just moved here," she explained. She could feel her heart beating faster as she looked around the room at each of the blank faces staring at her.

She fumbled for what to say next.

What exactly does this teacher want me to tell them? Should I share how my family has not been the same since my parents divorced? Would they want to know that my mom had cried herself to sleep every time one of her boyfriends left, and how my mom never seemed like herself again until she had a new man? Did they really want to know about Mom's second boyfriend's drinking habit, or number three's inability to remain faithful to my mom? Perhaps the gossip-hungry group would revel in the fact that I haven't seen my real father in two years.

By the time she decided just to stick to the surface facts, Mr. White had interrupted her internal dialogue and demanded to know her favorite novel.

"*Pride and Prejudice* by Jane Austin," she blurted out, thankful that he had made her job easy for her. Katie loved talking about literature. She would much rather talk about a book or the motivation for a character's actions than try to explain something, anything about herself. It was not that she was incapable of telling her own story. It was simply that she did not feel others would care to hear it.

"And your favorite character is?" he questioned.

"It's a toss-up between Elizabeth Bennett and Mr. Darcy," she shared. Before she could explain why, she heard the screech of Strawberry Blonde's mouth from the other side of the room.

"Did you get in a fight with a can of purple spray paint or something?" This time even Mr. White heard her sardonic inquiry.

Katie turned towards her and started to think of how to answer. Her grandma Ceil had always said, "If you can't beat 'em, join 'em." She would join Strawberry Blonde's little game and beat her at it if she could.

"Yeah, I… well… I…" again her words failed her. *One point for Strawberry Blonde*, she thought chagrined, shaking her head at her lack of response.

Where is my wit when I need it most?

"Why does she stutter like that, Mr. White? Maybe you should ask the question again, s-l-o-w-l-y this time," suggested the dark-skinned boy next to Strawberry Blonde, drawing out the word slowly as if Katie could not understand him.

He was sitting, but Katie could tell by the way his legs did not quite fit under the desk that he was tall. His hair was wavy and dark, and his eyes were hazel. If it weren't for the fact that he was rude and arrogant, he would be kind of cute. Too bad he was obviously a jerk.

To his left sat the hot, blue-eyed guy from the hallway. Katie could not quite read his expression. One minute he looked like he was laughing with the rest of Strawberry Blonde's followers. The next, he glanced from one side to the other as if he were trying to see if anyone was watching him.

Katie could swear he mouthed something to her, but she could not quite make out what he said. The bell rang and everyone sprang out of their seats to exit the room.

The students gawked as they pushed past Katie trying to be the first one out of the classroom. She closed her eyes and sighed.

That definitely did not go very well.

Mr. White tried to appease her and apologized for the behavior of his students "They don't usually act like that," he offered looking at her through dandruff dusted glasses.

Great, then it was just me.

She forced a half-smile as she made her way to the door. *One class down*, she exhaled; there were only six more to go.

The next two classes passed uneventfully for Katie. It was time for the dreaded lunch adventure. The cafeteria was separated much like the grassy quad area outside the school. Every group had their own section of the lunchroom; long rectangular tables created imaginary barriers keeping each group to itself and the outsiders at bay. There did not seem to be a place for her yet. Even the girls that dressed like Katie did not seem very welcoming. She did not let it worry her though. It was only the first day. These things took time.

Her stomach growled which reminded her that she had other important things on her mind, like food. Once in line, she glanced around to scope out the scene. She discovered one of the girls in the "Goth" group staring at her. The girl did not even try to hide the fact that she was watching Katie.

Katie waited for some expression that suggested the girl wanted to talk to her, but she waited in vain. Goth Girl's attention was diverted by a boy that approached her table. The lunch line started to move; Katie's cue to move along.

She ordered a burger, fries, and grabbed a carton of milk from a large stainless-steel cooler as she passed the register. She purposefully walked past the Goth group again to see if maybe there would be an invitation to join them. The girl that caught her attention earlier was gone, so Katie carried her tray to the grassy area outside where the kids with instruments were seated earlier, before school.

As she glanced to her right, she discovered that beyond the area was a long, paved slope that led to a small pond surrounded by reeds and Calla lilies. Poised in the middle of the pond was a spectacular stone fountain embellished with alternating amethyst and quartz stones that created a ring around its upper ridge. An immense gray stone arbor jutted out from the water's edge and encircled the entire pond. The stone arbor was supported by pillars that were dispersed every few feet; they reminded her of columns that she saw in pictures of Greek or Roman ruins in her Ancient Civilizations class at her last school. Mini turrets, like those from a medieval castle, stood sentinel atop the center of the arbor that faced the grassy quad area. The bright afternoon sun revealed cracks and scratches in the surface of the gray stones that stood out from under the ivy that wrapped around the columns and towers.

It was amazing, and yet it seemed to be very much out of place. Katie wanted to get a closer look at the beautiful arbor surrounding the pond. As she ventured down the walk towards the structure, she heard voices. Her adventure would have to wait for another day. She experienced enough of *those* voices to last her a lifetime, or at least for the rest of the day.

As Katie turned to make her escape, she heard another voice.

"Stop! Let go, Destiny! Don't do it!"

Katie turned back and started in the direction of the pleading. Before she took two steps, she stopped dead in her tracks. The Goth girl from the cafeteria was amidst the group from English class.

The strawberry-blonde girl and cute but arrogant guy were there along with four others. The Goth girl looked very much out of place, and she definitely did not look happy. Strawberry Blonde had a vice grip on one of her arms. The dark-haired girl from English, who Goth Girl had just called Destiny, held Goth Girl's other arm and demanded she hold still. Destiny towered over Goth Girl. There was something in Destiny's hand. Katie could not quite make it out.

She struggled with the decision of turning away.

This is not your business; just keep walking. This

encounter will not lead to me making friends.

Then she heard Strawberry Blonde's shrill voice, "Hold still. We just want to give you a little tattoo!"

Tattoo?

Katie found herself heading towards the girl in trouble. As she approached, but before she could startle them with the element of surprise and gain the upper hand, Strawberry Blonde noticed her.

"Hey guys, look who decided to join our little tattoo party," she said in an overly sweet voice. "Darrell, did you bring an extra pen? We have another victim, um, I mean customer."

Darrell was the tall, good looking, African American guy from English class. Destiny, who Katie now saw was holding a pen, had already used the sharp end of the pen to poke a hole in Goth Girl's arm. She was trying to fill the small wound with the ink from the open end of the pen, but all she succeeded in doing was to smear the trickles of blood and ink across Goth Girl's arm.

"I only have the safety pin we were going to use on her ears after we finished the tattoo. Hey, maybe Dumb-Dumb would like a piercing today," Darrell said as he looked around the group for approval. "What do you think Christy, do you think we should pierce Dumb-Dumb's ears?"

So that is Strawberry Blonde's name, Christy.

Katie glanced to the side and saw the hot, blue-eyed guy among Christy's clan too. One by one, she recognized all of Christy's faithful followers from English class as the circle of psychos closed in around her and Goth Girl.

This is like a scene from a bad afterschool special.

"I'm thinking we should pierce her tongue; it might help with her stuttering problem!" Christy offered.

Darrell walked towards Katie eagerly with a small pin in hand.

Suddenly, the hot blue-eyed guy spoke up. "Uh, I think we might not have time for all of this, guys."

"Don't worry, Brian. We'll give her the express piercing treatment," Christy reassured him through her chortle.

The group broke out in laughter, all except Brian. He stood there anxiously rubbing his forehead. His face was a mask of worry, or was it fear that Katie saw?

If these were his friends, and he was scared, she knew she should have been frightened. Her body quickly registered that fact, which made the hair on the back of her neck stand on end. Her attention was diverted from Brian to Darrell as the sting of his grip was becoming more persistent.

Katie glanced to her left and could see that Goth Girl's face was streaming with tears. A scary realization plagued Katie's mind.

These students are crazy; there is no telling what they are capable of. This is going to end badly, and Goth Girl and I are going to have the scars to prove it.

Katie's worry turned quickly to anger. She could feel the familiar rage begin to boil within her. She closed her eyes and let the feeling wash over her. Suddenly, her concentration was interrupted. Out of nowhere, Mr. White and the chubby principal, Mr. Blackstone, came rushing down the hill.

"What's going on down here?" Mr. White demanded.

"Oh, we were just helping Cherene," Christy explained.

"What, are you crazy?" Katie interrupted. "They were trying to torture us."

"Katie, is it necessary to be so melodramatic?" Mr. White asked—not giving her time to answer before continuing. "I think if we all keep calm, we can solve this little problem."

"Little problem? Seriously? You weren't even here," Katie insisted.

Principal Blackstone interrupted Katie. "Christy, go on and explain," he said as he placed a gentle hand on Christy's shoulder.

It was in that moment that Katie knew how the situation was going to turn out.

Christy looked smugly in Katie's direction and continued her impromptu lie. "Cherene was so upset and said she wanted to hurt herself. We just couldn't leave her alone." She wrenched the pen from Destiny's hand and held it up for Mr. Blackstone to see. "Look, she had already taken the pen and tried to cut herself."

"Ah, I understand now. From where we were standing, it looked as if you might be holding her against her will," Mr. Blackstone asserted, letting out a sigh of relief.

"Seriously, Christy? Are you crazy or just pathological?" Katie asked in disbelief.

"Please, let us handle this," Principal Blackstone insisted.

"Well, we *were* holding her," Destiny chimed in. "But she wanted to hurt herself, and we had to hold her back. You know how the girls like Cherene like to cut themselves."

"Is this true, Cherene?" Principal Blackstone queried.

Cherene stood as still as a statue. Except for the tears that were running down her cheeks, there was no sign that she was, in fact, a living breathing person.

Principal Blackstone took her lack of response as an admission of guilt. He placed his arm gingerly around her shoulders and guided her toward the school.

"Wait, this is not right. You don't have the facts," Katie pleaded loudly as they were leaving.

Mr. White stood in front of her, his arms crossed in front of him, looking through his dusty spectacles at Katie shaking his head back and forth, his mouth twisted in disgust.

Katie's eyes widened; her mouth dropped. She could not believe what was happening.

"Don't you care about the truth, Mr. White?" she asked softly with expected defeat dominating her every syllable.

"Katie, sometimes people see things from one perspective and jump to conclusions. You don't look like you were being tortured, and Cherene just looked plain confused. Sometimes people make rash decisions when they're confused. Girls like you and Cherene see things differently than the rest of the students." He pushed his glasses up and continued speaking. "I think when you give this some more thought, you will see it as they do," he said patting her on the head as if he were trying to calm an upset child.

Girls like me and Cherene.

Even the teachers of the school bought into the stereotypes.

This day is just too much.

Katie blew off her last few classes and returned to her house. Mom and Phil would still be at work. There would be no one to question her about *her perspective* or grill her about why she chose not to stay in school. Katie wished her father were here. He would know what to do. He always knew how to make her feel better.

What is the use in wishing?

It's not like she had a magical fairy godmother watching over her.

This is reality, and sometimes reality really bites!

~ 5 ~

THE TRUTH HURTS

After ransacking the kitchen for chips and bean dip, Katie decided it could not hurt to try to call her dad; it was years since they last spoke. Maybe he would want to talk to her as much as she needed to talk to him. She fumbled through her nightstand drawer and found her diary. Stuffed in the back of the purple and black striped book was a paper that had her dad's cell number on it. She dialed the number. She heard the tone of the first ring, closed her eyes and took a slow, steady breath in.

Please let him answer. Please Daddy, answer.

The ringing continued.

Come on, pick up Dad.

Then she heard his voice.

"Hello, this is Mark; I can't take your call right now. Leave a message after the…"

She hung up before the finality of the beep could choke all the hope from her heart.

Katie grabbed her laptop and plopped down in her oversized black Papasan chair. She tucked her feet off to one side and glanced towards her "witchy" bookcase. The old wooden shelves were filled with books on witchcraft, faeries, and other paranormal phenomenon. She tapped the space bar to wake up her laptop and began reading the information on the paranormal website she had been perusing before the dreadful cross-country move from California to Salem.

Katie had been scouring books and online sources on paranormal beings since she shattered the window with her mind two years earlier. She had ruled out the idea that she was some sort of zombie or vampire. She certainly did not prey on humans, and the thought of sucking blood from anything, especially a human being, made her want to hurl.

She did find her supposed power to be consistent with the powers of some witches. However, most of their powers were derived from spells. Katie was confident she had never cast any spells, so she found herself investigating the Fae.

The words of the webpage were scripted like the images of a horror film. The letters were dark red and seemed to trickle down the page like blood flowing from an open wound.

"The Battle of the FAE Courts!"

She scrolled down and began reading the description of the battle between the two courts of Fae, in other words, faeries. These were not Tinker Bell type of faeries. They had immense power, were quite crafty, and the evil ones took pride in the three D's: debauchery, destruction, and deception. The article read:

The two courts of Fae are the Seelie (light and good) and the Unseelie (dark and evil). It is believed that they were once united, but as with many powerful ruling systems, there was dissention in the ranks. The once unified group of Seelie Fae became torn in two. Those Fae that wanted to overthrow the powers of the Seelie Court were discovered, and they were banished from the Kingdom of Faery. They were cast out and forced to live in the wastelands of the Otherworld, also known as the Shadow Lands. The outcast faeries were branded traitors and became labeled as the Unseelie Fae.

The two factions of Fae spent countless years battling one another, fighting over power and territory. Over time, the courts of the Unseelie were as corrupt as they believed the original courts of the Seelie had been. After many years, members of the Unseelie race wanted to reunite with their Seelie brothers and sisters.

In order to unite the two kingdoms, a marriage was arranged between an Unseelie princess and a Seelie prince. Once united, the Unseelie would be allowed to return to the Kingdom of Faery and join together as one race of Fae: the Seelie.

However, a terrible incident happened on the eve of their wedding causing the Unseelie to mistrust the Seelie once again. They swore never to believe in the goodness of the Seelie again. The Unseelie princess never wed, and she spent the remainder her life swearing to avenge her broken heart. It is said that she still searches for the one that was lost to her.

* * * * *

Interesting story, but it said nothing about their powers.

Katie was looking for something related to mind control. She thought her own powers were triggered by intense emotions.

The first paranormal incident happened when she was caught between extreme anger and tremendous sadness over her father leaving.

The second incident happened at a soccer match during PE when Katie became very angry at one of her teammates. She had to spend a whole week in detention after that mess.

I have to find something related to supernatural activities provoked by emotional reactions.

She continued making one Google search after another.

Nothing. I'll never find what I am looking for.

Katie grabbed the wireless mouse and clicked the shutdown button. Then, she slammed her laptop shut and laid her head back in the chair.

Katie heard a car engine and a door slam shut. She jumped up and stripped off her school clothes. She threw on her nightshirt, grabbed her pajama bottoms, and fumbled to get them on before whoever came home early made their way up the stairs. Before she could crawl into bed to feign ill, her mom's husband was banging on the door.

"Katie, are you in there? I'm coming in."

She tried to protest. "Wait, I'm…" but true to his word, he burst through the door.

"Oh, thank goodness, you're okay. The school called and told us about the 'cutting' incident. I was so worried when they said you left early. I was afraid of what I might find when I got here. We need to call your mom right away and tell her you're okay." He shoved his hand in his front pants pocket and pulled out his cell phone. "We were both out of our minds with worry."

Katie rolled her eyes. "Phil, chill out."

"Chill out?" His voice was a mixture of shock and outrage.

"It's not that big of a deal. Just chill."

"Just chill out. What kind of response is that? Where I come from, something like this is a very big deal."

"You don't even know what happened, Phil."

"I know enough," he said, his words plagued with authority.

"Really? Grown-ups always think they know everything, but really, they don't know anything."

"I know you got into trouble at school, on your first day no less. I know you and another girl were cutting. I know you ditched several classes and left campus without permission or letting anyone know your whereabouts, and now you're standing there telling me to chill out?" Phil shouted.

"Ah, and I thought you were so concerned, Phillip," she taunted.

Phil drew a deep breath in; his eyes grew to be immense. They looked out of place, like dark steel marbles bulging out of his small head. His pale, little fists clenched at either side; he was turning red. His ruddy face looked like it would explode.

He turned abruptly and stormed down the stairs.

When he was halfway down, Katie shouted, "Good talk, Phil! Let's NOT do it again sometime soon." She chortled to herself, elated by the fact that he was infuriated.

The sound of his retreating feet on the stairs stopped, and Katie could tell he was running, probably two steps at a time back up the stairs.

"How dare you. How dare you speak to me in that manner." His face was so close to hers Katie smelled the mint of his chewing gum. "Wait until your mother hears about this. I knew you would be nothing but trouble. I told your mother we should have left you in California with your father. Too bad he wouldn't answer our calls."

Phil stopped his rant abruptly; his face displaying the mistake of his own speech. He breathed deeply and stood speechless.

"No, don't stop now, Phil. Let me have it! Tell me how you *really* feel about me!" Katie screamed throwing her hands up in the air.

"I've said too much," Phil offered remorsefully taking a step back.

"No, you think?"

"I did not mean what I said, Katie. Please, let's just talk about this later," he bargained as he reached for her shoulder.

She shrugged away from his touch.

"That's okay. I don't need to talk later. In fact, I don't need to talk to you *ever* again!" she exclaimed.

"Katie, I…" she put her hand up to stop his words. Her eyes were threatening to well with tears. She had to end this immediately. She would not give him the satisfaction of seeing that he had hurt her.

Taking a deep breath, she placed a smug smile on her face, turned on her heel, and retreated to the bathroom. Katie slammed the door for effect and barely made it to sit on the edge of the bathtub before she burst into tears. She heard the click of the bedroom door as Phil left her room. When she knew he could not hear her, Katie slid to the floor and began sobbing.

Hours passed by. Katie did not know how long she had sat on the cold, tiled floor of her bathroom, but when she came out her bedroom was nearly dark. The curtains were still open, but all the natural light was gone. Evening stars cast a faint glow across the bed, illuminating her thick down comforter and fluffy pillows.

All she wanted to do was crawl into bed and sleep, but she could hear Mom's voice downstairs as she talked to Phil. She decided she had better go see what kind of punishment they had conjured up.

As Katie approached the stairwell, she could see that they were in the newly wallpapered foyer trying to speak quietly. By the time she got halfway down the stairs, they looked like they were yelling at one another, but only harsh whispers could be heard. They must have heard her steps because they both stopped talking and looked her way at the same time. Katie stopped on the stairs and waited for the hammer to drop.

Immediately, Mom burst into tears and ran halfway up the stairs to embrace her. She was sobbing and holding on tighter than she ever had before.

"Oh Katie, when I got the news, I was so worried." Mom pulled away, both her hands still grasping Katie's arms. She spoke her voice soft, "Honey, why? Why would you think of hurting yourself?"

"Mom, I didn't."

"Sweetie, denying it won't make it better," she explained as she gently pushed Katie's long, black hair back and away from her face. "You know we love you no matter what. We just want you to get help."

Katie pushed her mother's hands away from her and stepped up a step to allow some space between her and her mom.

"No, you don't understand, Mom. I really didn't. This girl, Cherene, was being harassed by a group of kids. I went to see if I could help her, but then they were going to hurt me too."

Her mom lowered her head, causing her brown hair to

hang in front of her eyes as she spoke, "I knew I shouldn't let you read all that paranormal stuff and dye your hair black. This is my fault. Grandma told me not to let you experiment with all that voodoo." She paused for a moment, looked up at Katie, and inhaled deeply. "She's never going to let me live this down now. She'll probably say, 'This is what happens when you let your children have too much freedom.'"

"It's not voodoo, Mom. And I didn't even try to cut myself. As usual, you've got it all wrong," Katie said, shaking her head in disbelief.

Mom was looking back and forth between Katie and Phil. Katie waved her hand in front of her mother's face trying to get her attention. "Hello. Did you even hear what I said, Mom?"

What is the point of talking when no one is listening? And why is she so concerned about what Grandma thinks anyway? Doesn't she have a mind of her own?

After the day she experienced, this drama was more than Katie could take.

I have to get away from here.

She pushed past both, grabbed her coat and purse from the brass hook by the door, slipped on her Crocs, and left the house. She could hear Phil shouting from behind her.

"You'd better come back here young lady. You're not eighteen yet. You will follow our rules if you're going to live under our roof."

"Let her go, Phil. You're making the situation worse," Mom pleaded.

Katie glanced back for a moment as she was getting into her beat-up Mustang and saw her mom tugging at Phil's arm, trying to pull him back inside the house and out of Katie's line of sight. At least her mom knew enough to know that he would only make things worse. They always made things worse.

The men that she brought around Katie each tried to discipline her. It was as if they hoped that they would win the "Non-Father, Father of the Year Award" if they could just control, in other words fix, that out-of-control teenage daughter of hers. Katie knew that nothing they had to offer was going to fix what was wrong with her.

She thought about that for a moment. What was wrong with her? She was smart, funny, nice, and more than one boy had told her that she was pretty. What was wrong with her was everyone else.

She did not ask for any of what had happened to her.

I didn't ask my dad to leave or tell my mom to need a man more than she needs me. I didn't ask for kids at school to treat me like I am a leper. There is nothing wrong with me. I don't need any of them.

~ 6 ~

ALL'S WELL THAT ENDS WELL

Katie drove along the empty roads for what seemed like hours. The clock was better at keeping track of the time than her; only twenty minutes had passed when she saw the light on at a little ice-cream shop. Katie knew she could not do anything to bring her dad back, but somehow, ice-cream seemed to make things better.

There was an empty stall right in front of the glass wall that made up the storefront. Katie glanced down and realized that she was still in her pajamas, but the coat covered enough to allow her to look presentable. Lots of kids even wore pajama bottoms to school. The comb that she kept in her glove compartment came in handy for occasions such as this. As she ran the comb through her hair, she spotted Cherene, the Goth girl from school. She was behind the counter serving ice-cream to a family of four.

Cherene looked different. Her hair was up in a high ponytail instead of long and brushed into her eyes. Her grayish-blue eyes stood out from under the blue and pink striped hat; Katie could see them from where she sat in her car. The hat Cherene wore matched the pink, blue and white striped uniform top which was more flattering to her than the layers of black on black she wore at school. A bandage that covered a two-by-two square of Cherene's arm drew Katie's attention; it reminded her of the events from earlier that day.

When Katie walked into the parlor, Cherene had just finished handing a double scoop of pralines and cream to a little girl that could not have been more than six years old. Cherene glanced up and started to say, "Can I help you?" but stopped mid-sentence when her eyes fixed on Katie and registered who she was.

"Hi Cherene, I didn't know you worked here."

"Four years now, since I was thirteen. My parents own the shop; apparently, they didn't think child labor laws would apply to their own child," she said with a twinge of sarcasm as she smiled at her mom and dad who were standing further down the counter.

Her dad, a tall, muscular, African American man, wrapped his arm around her mom's plump waistline and announced, "We aim to please."

Her mom smiled up at him and then back at Cherene. Her mom was much lighter than her pecan-brown father. A dark blonde bob framed her face and accentuated her welcoming smile. Cherene's complexion was mocha, a beautiful blend of her mother and father, but her eyes were her mother's. After seeing Cherene's mom, Katie wondered if Cherene's hair was really that dark. Maybe she dyed hers too.

Katie's gaze moved from Cherene's parents back to the ice-cream encased in a glass-covered freezer in front of her. "So, what do you recommend?" Katie asked, smiling at her schoolmate.

"We have a special deal on banana splits tonight: buy one and get one for free," Cherene suggested.

"I don't think I should really eat two of anything, even if it does have bananas," Katie said.

They both laughed.

It was the first time since Katie arrived in Salem that someone besides her own mother thought she might be mildly amusing. She had not made such a good impression at school earlier.

Cherene looked at Katie, contemplating something. She squinted in Katie's direction and cocked her head to the side. "Well, if you could wait a few minutes, I'll be getting a break, and I could eat the other one. Just so you wouldn't feel guilty, of course." She smiled from ear to ear.

Katie nodded and smiled back. "Of course, we wouldn't want me to feel guilty or anything."

They stood there for a moment, just smiling.

This feels like the beginning of a friendship, and I could really use a friend right about now.

Before the moment could turn awkward, she turned on her heel and went to sit down at a small round table near the corner of the shop. The time passed quickly; before she knew it, they were sharing ice-cream and conversation.

"I couldn't believe it when you stopped and came over to see what was up with Christy and her posse today."

"I almost didn't, but when they said, 'tattoo,' I knew they were up to no good. What were you doing out there with them anyway? Not to be stereotypical, but they really don't look like your type of friends."

"It's funny that you would say that because in elementary school we were all great friends. It was not until junior high school that things changed."

"So, what did they want with you?" Katie questioned.

"Christy was mad because she copied off my paper in US History. I wrote down the wrong answers to throw her off. She got an 'F' on the test."

Katie laughed so hard that ice-cream threatened to come out of her nose. "That's perfect! How did she find out you played her?"

"She figured out that I had changed all my answers because I ended up with an 'A.' Plus, everyone knows that I would *never* get an 'F' on anything."

"Well, if you ask me, she got what she deserved."

"You and I know that, but Christy doesn't take kindly to being made to look like a fool. She had to have the last laugh. That is why she sent Darrell into the cafeteria to persuade me to come outside."

"Didn't you know it was a setup?"

"When a guy like Darrell says, 'Come here, I'd like to

talk,' you don't ask why; you just hope for the best and go with it. I mean seriously, have you seen the guy? He's hotter than hot!"

"Good point. I would probably have gone for a long walk off of a short pier too, or in your case, around an arbor, if he had asked me to, too."

Cherene looked at her perplexed. "Around an arbor? What arbor, Katie?"

"The one surrounding the pond with a fountain in the middle of it," she reminded Cherene.

"At school?"

"Of course, silly. The one you were standing next to when they were trying to tattoo you. Did they ink your brain or something?"

"Um Katie, I think you're confused. There isn't a pond, a fountain, or an arbor at our school," Cherene corrected in a baffled tone.

Katie thought for a moment. That was odd. She distinctly remembered seeing the arbor that surrounded the pond. There was no doubt about the fact that a beautiful fountain stood in the middle of that pond. At this point, she had two choices: appear crazy or confused. She chose the latter.

"Oh, yeah, yeah, you're right. I am thinking of my old school. Today was so traumatic; I'm not thinking straight."

"Whew, I was going to say," Cherene responded, sounding relieved.

As Cherene prattled on about being worried about

Katie's mental stability, Katie's eyes glossed over as she contemplated the possibility that Cherene did not see what she saw so vividly earlier in the day.

This is starting to totally freak me out.

It was one thing for Katie to personally experience what she thought to be "paranormal" activity when she was alone, and there was no one else to verify or deny the happenings. It was a different matter entirely for her to have seen something when another living, breathing person was present yet the other person did not see anything at all.

Was she going crazy? Was she under too much stress? Was there a fountain and pond at her last school? No, there definitely was not a pond at the last school. She feared that she must be losing her mind. She closed her eyes briefly and shook her head to clear her mind of the peculiar thoughts.

"So, how many nights a week do you work here, Cherene?"

"I only work Saturday through Tuesday."

"Maybe we could get together afterschool on Wednesday. You could give me the lowdown on all the teachers and students. I don't want to walk into another tattoo party if I can help it."

"Absolutely," Cherene said grinning from ear to ear.

As Katie drove the deserted road back to her new house, she caught herself singing to a song on the radio and smiling.

Today turned out to be a good day after all.

~ 7 ~

PYROMANIAC

By the time Katie got home, Mom and Phil were sleeping. She tiptoed past their room and down the hall to hers. Katie quickly showered and threw on her pajamas. It was too late to do more Internet research on the Seelie and Unseelie Courts, but they were on her mind. When she fell asleep, her dreams were filled with Fae, both good and evil.

* * * * *

Katie emerged from a wooded area to a clearing; a stone fountain with amethyst and crystal stones encircling it stood out in the middle of a large lake. She blinked to clear her vision. She could not believe what she was seeing.

Around the outskirts of the fountain, faeries of all varieties hovered, floating daintily above the water below.

They wore beautiful, luminous, flowing gowns, and crowns of gold and gossamer; each emitted a sparkling light that was almost blinding.

It looked as if they were holding some sort of council. They appeared to be laughing and exchanging friendly chatter. Without warning, the faeries were interrupted by a dark, ominous cloud and a clap of intense thunder that sent shock waves through the water; the fountain shook and threatened to be reduced to rubble.

Out of the blackness of the storm arose a strikingly beautiful, yet dark creature. She had long black hair that blew back away from her face revealing her brilliant onyx eyes and the well-defined lines of her extraordinary face. She too emitted a glow, but hers was tainted black around the edges.

In an overly dramatic gesture, she waved one hand and caused a huge wave to crash down upon half of the faeries leaving the others to scatter quickly to the perimeter of the lake.

Then, the evil faery spoke, "You cannot hide her forever. I will find her, and when I do . . ." Suddenly, a flash of bright white light struck near the dark faery, and she vanished in a puff of darkness as quickly as she had come; her menacing laugh hovering over the cloud-covered lake. Katie stood alone in awe and disbelief; the wind from the storm blew her white gown and sent a chill through her body.

Katie had the sensation that someone was near, watching, waiting. She spun around trying to survey her surroundings. In the distance she spied a lone image. It was the image of a tall, thin man in a dark trench coat; like the faeries she saw earlier, he was floating above the ground.

He made a motion with his right hand for her to come towards him. As if she were under a spell, she obeyed his command and drew near to him. His face was pale but welcoming. His eyes were a deep green with light yellow flecks around the edges. Something about his appearance was familiar to Katie. As she stopped before the mysterious being, she spoke softly, "Who are you? Do I know you?"

His mouth twisted into an impish smirk. "Of course, you do, my dear. I am—" he stopped his speech. "I... I have been sent to teach you about your powers."

"You know about my powers?" Katie asked.

"You have only just begun to scratch the surface of your powers. Among other things, you have all the elements of nature at your disposal, my dear."

"Elements of nature?" she questioned.

"Fire, water, wind, and earth," he announced as if it were common knowledge.

Katie contemplated this new information. She had powers to shatter windows and make objects move. What if this being were right? What if she had other powers as well?

"Are you some sort of oracle?" she asked, not quite believing her ears.

"It is not important what I am; it is more important that you know what you are," he answered.

"Then tell me more about these 'among other things, powers,'" she challenged.

"Among other things, powers?" he asked, confused.

"You said, and I quote, 'Among other things, you have all the elements of nature at your disposal.' I can imagine what the elements of fire, water, wind, and earth might be about. I would like to know about the other powers," she asserted folding her arms in front of her and cocking an eyebrow.

His dark green eyes danced with pride as he eyed this tenacious teen. "All right. First, I will teach you how to transport your body. Listen and close your eyes."

Katie was not exactly sure what he meant by transport her body. Usually, she just walked from one place to another. If she wanted to get somewhere in a hurry, she drove her car. Although she wanted to ask a million questions, she chose instead to follow his directions.

Katie closed her eyes. She could hear his deep, convincing voice fill the chilly night air.

"Focus on the opposite end of the forest. Do you have a spot in your mind?"

Katie nodded in agreement.

"Now, let the warmth of your powers wash over your whole body. Imagine your whole being vanishing from where you are now and reappearing in the place in which you have focused all your energy."

Katie held her eyes tight and tried to conjure the feeling of warmth that would wash over her each time her magic had happened. She envisioned herself vanishing in thin air and making her body reappear across the room. She felt the warm sensation envelop her entire being.

* * * * *

"Beep. Beep. It's six a.m., and the weather today is going to be cloudy with a chance of thunderstorms in the early afternoon."

Katie hit the snooze button on her alarm clock. Something nagged at the back of her mind though she could not quite put her finger on it. She glanced at the amethyst stone sitting on her nightstand. It sparkled in the morning light. The dream returned to her mind: the fountain with the stones, the faeries, and that menacing laugh.

She thought for a moment longer. Then she remembered the dark male figure. He had called to her, and she had followed. Katie tried to recall his face; she had the sense that she knew him, but his identity evaded her. A shiver ran down her spine. Katie tried to shake the creepy feeling that found its way into her being.

The disturbing feelings reminded her of the unsettling conversation she had with Cherene at the ice-cream parlor. Cherene had not seen the fountain in the pond or the arbor at school. Yet, Katie had seen the same fountain twice now, once at school and again in her dream. It had to be real.

Maybe Cherene is trying to play me for a fool. She seems so genuine though. There must be a logical reason why I saw the fountain and she didn't. Cherene just can't be a phony.

She made a mental note to check for the pond at school later that day and reached over to turn off her alarm before it could sound again.

Katie resolved to get to the bottom of the mysterious fountain without losing her new friend in the process. With a new mission in mind, she rolled out of bed and got ready for school. As she dashed down the stairs, she could hear Mom and Phil in the kitchen.

Katie decided it would be best if she avoided their drama, so she grabbed her things and left the house before either of them could see or hear her.

*****

Once inside the walls of her new high school, the events of the previous day flooded Katie's mind. She had ditched the rest of her classes after the tattoo debacle during lunch the day before, so she did not get a chance to see if Christy and her group would say anything else to her.

Katie stood outside the door biting her bottom lip as she considered how many days she would have to miss class for them to forget that she was the target of their insanity.

There aren't enough days in the year to make that happen. I guess I have to go to class and face the music.

Katie reached for the knob on the door and paused for a moment before going in.

Mr. White was writing notes on the whiteboard when Katie entered the class. She hurried past him and sat in a seat farthest from where Christy and her gang sat the day before. She was one of the first to get to the class and thought it would be wise to at least pretend she was doing something important; maybe they would not notice her.

Katie thought about hiding behind her backpack or putting her head on the desk with the hood of her sweatshirt pulled over her entire head. That might make her look like a coward. Worse, it might give them proof that she was dark and depressed like girls that cut themselves.

Christy and her band of idiots came into the class as the bell rang. They ran right past her to their seats without making any comments.

Good, they haven't seen me yet.

Mr. White turned around from the board and passed out a paper that detailed an essay contest. It read:

WINTER CAMP ADVENTURE CONTEST

Do you like camping? Do you enjoy snow hiking, skiing, zip lining, songs around the campfire, smores and more?

We have a winter break solution for you.

Cost of Camp: $300.00

Three Camp Scholarships Will Be Awarded

For The Most Original and Outstanding 5,000 Word Essay

Katie was intrigued. This was only her second day, but she decided that she could definitely use a break. Every new school brought challenges and obstacles, but this was the strangest school of them all. The bullies at this school took the cake. Then there was the whole fountain issue. Katie had never imagined large structures and bodies of water at any of her other schools. She made a mental note to herself to check out the fountain status at lunch. She stashed the flyer in her backpack and took out her notebook.

Mr. White was about to lecture; Katie breathed a sigh of relief. There would be little cause for interaction.

Maybe Christy and her crew will forget I exist.

Katie kept up with the notes for a while, but her mind started to wander. She thought of her Fae research, topics for her essay, the fountain, and what Cherene and she would talk about tomorrow.

Then her mind drifted back to the homecoming game of her freshman year. The first few months of her freshman year were blissful. Her parents were still married, she went to school with the same group of friends since elementary school, and she had been voted freshman homecoming princess.

* * * * *

The stadium was filled to the brim with students, parents, and alumni. Katie's high school team was playing their cross-town rivals, but the home team was favored to win because of their awesome wide-receiver, Sean Whitman, who just so happened to be Katie's guy. The energy in the stadium was electric.

The court nominees were waiting to enter from the side entrance; each girl was poised on the back of her designated convertible. Katie's dad's boss lent them a '65 candy apple red convertible Mustang which had been restored to mint condition.

Katie's dress was a strapless black gown that had a fitted bodice and a full skirt. The black and white striped bow on the back draped halfway down the dress and was spread out to the fullness of the skirt. She held a bouquet of red roses which matched the color of the car. Katie's hair was high on her head with tendrils of curls falling and framing her face. She felt like a true princess.

The crowd erupted into a frenzy when Sean ran sixty yards for a touchdown, and the whistle blew. This was it, halftime.

"It's show time!" Katie's dad said as he glanced back and gave Katie an approving smile. The music pounded in her ears. Cheers from the crowd were intoxicating as her father drove through the dirt track that lined the football field. Katie could see friends waving and yelling from the stands as her car made its way around the stadium.

Each nominee took their place on the podium and waited as the announcer began naming the court princesses. Katie looked out into the sea of faces and saw all her friends as they cheered her on. She could hear shouts and screams from the girls calling her name and boys hollering and waving their fists in the air to show their support. It seemed like a lifetime that the crowd was incited; Katie could not stop smiling. She was living every girl's dream.

A hush fell over the crowd as the announcer said, "Representing the freshman class, Katie Ryan." Suddenly, the stadium erupted again in shouts. Flowers flowed from the standing crowd and showered over her and onto the podium. She scooped down and picked up a whole bouquet worth of flowers and raised her hands to the crowd to show her appreciation! More cheers. She thought the moment would never end.

Of course, it did end as each girl received her own accolades when her name was announced. Finally, the homecoming queen was crowned, and their dates joined them on the podium. Sean's eyes were gleaming with pride and what? Serious like? Dare Katie hope… love? Puppy love, maybe. Regardless, it was a look of adoration.

The boys won the game; the celebration continued in the school's gym which had been transformed into a wonderland. Strands of lights hung across the ceiling creating a gazebo of light overhead. The tiny specks of light from each bulb were magnified off the hundreds of silver and iridescent balloons that flooded the top of the building. Streaming down the walls were long sheets of fabric lit with tiny, twinkling lights that highlighted the sheer gossamer drapes.

The queen's court assembled on the stage and awaited the official crowning and the infamous dance that would follow. Katie remembered feeling so joyful, yet so very nervous. She had never danced a slow dance with a boy. And Sean was quite a boy.

The lights dimmed, and the music began to play. As if the night was not already perfect, Sean stood up and bowed in front of Katie, making a dramatic sweeping gesture with his hand and requested the honor of the dance with her. She placed her hand in his, hoping he couldn't tell how nervous she was.

Sean led her almost to the center of the dance floor. He turned toward her and nodded his head. Taking her in his arms, he led her through her first dance. Katie remembered thinking that she would treasure the memory forever. She did not know then just how short the moment would be.

As the song ended, Katie and Sean continued to sway from side to side, glancing into each other's eyes. Sean stroked the back of his hand gently along her cheek, leaned in and pressed his lips to hers.

* * * * *

Katie's daydream was interrupted by a folded piece of paper that struck her temple. She looked around in the direction from which it came. Of course, it was someone from Christy's clan. Katie contemplated whether or not to open it. On the one hand, she really wanted to know what they wrote on the note. On the other hand, reading the note would give them the satisfaction of knowing that they had gotten to her. Katie knew that the "mature" thing to do would be to let it stay where it was and ignore it. That is what her mother would tell her to do, "Be the bigger person, Katie."

Maybe that was how they handled things back in her mom's day, but this was today, and today, letting something like this go would seem weak. The last thing she needed was to appear weak to this band of idiots.

Katie scooped up the paper, unfolded it slowly, and stared in disbelief. Who could be so cruel and childish at the same time? The words were pure hate. Taking a deep breath, Katie closed her eyes to calm herself. Her hand automatically reached for the stone in her pocket, but her attempt to calm herself was not working. She felt it again, anger building within her body. Suddenly, the paper burst into flames; Katie flung it to the ground.

The other students stared, mystified as they watched the ignited paper burn on the floor of the classroom. The boy next to Katie stomped on the paper and put it out before anything else caught on fire.

Katie stared at the charred remains, her eyes wide as she shook her head back and forth. Whispers from Christy's corner diverted her attention. She considered the voices and turned to find that everyone was looking at her like she was some sort of aberration.

At least they'll think twice before sending any more notes in my direction.

"Katie," Mr. White snapped, "go to the office, now. You have some serious explaining to do."

~ 8 ~

LITTLE WHITE LIES

Katie pushed past two boys that were standing near the exit and glowered at Mr. White as she left the class. She slammed the door, closing herself off from the chaos that was building inside the classroom.

Katie flew around a corner and stopped abruptly, her eyes surveying the silent, sterile hallway. She leaned against the cold steel of a nearby locker and slid slowly down to the floor. Her heart felt as if it were trying to break through her chest. Katie took deep breaths, her mind racing through the possible outcomes of her latest paranormal incident.

If I go to the office, I will be expelled or at the very least, suspended. If I don't go, the trouble could be worse. There is no way Principal Blackstone will not hear about this. I should just go and take my lumps, but Mom is going to be devastated. How will this look to her new "friends" at the country club?

"Always take responsibility for your actions, dear. Whatever is supposed to happen will happen. It will all turn out in the end." Katie could hear her grandmother's voice inside her head.

But how can I tell them that I made a piece of paper spontaneously combust? They will probably put me in a straitjacket. Your rules apply in a normal world, Grandma. I wish I could tell you what is happening to me. You would never steer me wrong.

Katie closed her eyes and could almost feel her grandmother's arms around her. She imagined the feel of laying her head on her grandmother's shoulder, and Grandma's small, loving fingers running through her hair.

Katie knew what she had to do.

It is not exactly what you would do Grandma, but I am going to have to improvise. I know you will understand when you hear about it, and I am sure you will hear about this fiasco.

She pulled herself up off the cold tiled floor and began the long walk to the office. Before she even rounded the last corner, she heard Principal Blackstone talking on his radio, "No, she did not come this way. I am on my way to find her now. Call security for backup."

Security? Do they think I am going to blow up the whole school now? Maybe taking that five-minute break to clear my head was not such a good idea.

Katie started to turn in the opposite direction and

hightail it out of the school, but she heard that familiar, grandmotherly voice in her head, "Katie, do the right thing. Do the right thing, and you can't go wrong." Resigned, Katie sighed and marched forward to uncover her fate.

When she rounded the corner, she realized that the principal's back was to her. He must have turned in the opposite direction. She shouted out to him, "Mr. Blackstone, I am so glad I caught you. I was just on my way to your office," she said as sincerely as she could.

The principal seemed startled. He turned in every direction, scanning the hall for backup.

Hello? You are three times my size. Are you seriously scared right now, or is this an act to make me appear more dangerous than I am?

"Mr. Blackstone, I was on my way to tell you what happened in Mr. White's class."

"Katie Ryan, I was just looking for you," Principal Blackstone spoke. "Are you…uh…are you all right?"

"I am fine, but there was an incident in English class. Mr. White said I should come and explain to you what happened," Katie said in the most innocent tone she could muster.

Principal Blackstone looked from one side of the hall to the other. It appeared as though he was trying to decide if he should deal with me—a dangerous student—without help from security. After a moment of silence, he cleared his throat. "Why don't you come with me, Katie? We can discuss this in my office."

They walked single file through the secretaries' desks, past twelve large, gray-colored file cabinets, and entered Mr. Blackstone's glassed-in cubicle at the back of the large office.

"Have a seat, Katie."

Rather than have the principal grill her, Katie decided that she should talk first. It would seem like she was in charge, reporting the incident, rather than defending herself in an inquisition.

"I was taking notes in English class, and the next thing I knew, a piece of paper dropped on my desk. I started to pick it up, but it was on fire. It startled me, so I flung it on the floor trying not to let it burn me."

"Is that so?" Mr. Blackstone asked, his eye raised high.

Katie nodded.

"That is interesting because I have a referral from Mr. White that says you lit a piece of paper on fire in the middle of his lecture."

Darn that man! He had his back turned. How would he even know what happened? Figures he would take the side of the popular people.

Katie could feel herself becoming very angry. The familiar rage was churning inside.

Keep your cool, Katie. Take a deep breath. This is not even your fault. They started this; you just finished it. It won't do your cause any good if you blow out the windows in the principal's office.

Katie placed a pleasant smile on her face and continued, "Mr. Blackstone, I mean no disrespect towards Mr.

White, but he was lecturing when this happened. He had turned around to draw a diagram on the board. Maybe he just assumed that I lit it on fire, but that's impossible."

"Impossible?"

"Well, I don't even have any matches. How could I light the paper on fire without any matches?" Katie questioned batting her eyelashes and smiling as if she were the angel of innocence.

"Well, I am going to have to have security check you as well as the hallway for matches."

"Of course, that sounds reasonable," she responded, trying to sound mature and rational.

Principal Blackstone left the office; it seemed like forever before he returned. When he did, he had an awkward look on his face.

"Well, it looks like I have to let you go."

"Excuse me?"

"Mr. White corroborated your story that he was in fact lecturing with his back towards the class, drawing something on the board. The other students said they saw the paper on fire while it was in your hands, but everyone except three students said that they did not see you with any matches."

"Let me guess who the three students were: Christy, Darrell, and Destiny?"

"The names do not matter, but it seems that no one was willing to implicate anyone as the paper thrower, and all the students that sit around you said they did not see you with matches. They just said you were holding a paper that was on fire which backs up your story. Plus, our security officer said he did not find any traces of matches on you or anywhere from your desk to this office."

"No one checked me for matches," Katie almost blurted out, but she caught herself in time.

Mr. Blackstone nodded in the direction of the door. Katie turned in her chair quickly; her curiosity piqued.

A tall, skinny security officer was standing in the doorway. He was wearing a pale-grey uniform and matching cap. He tipped his hat at Katie and gave her a sheepish grin. Katie narrowed her eyes at the peculiar individual; she was certain that she had seen him somewhere before. Unable to place him, she glanced back at Mr. Blackstone.

"So, I can go then?" Katie questioned, leaning forward towards Mr. Blackstone's large desk with an impatient smile on her face.

"You are free to go," Principal Blackstone answered.

Katie stood up and turned to walk out of the door. Just as she turned the handle, Mr. Blackstone said, "And Katie, I think it is only fair to tell you that I am going to be keeping a close eye on you."

She smiled tentatively, a small source of frustration making its way to the surface. "Of course, Mr. Blackstone, I would expect nothing less from such a conscientious and fair principal," she said, her words dripping with sarcasm.

Walking briskly towards the exit of the office, Katie's elation at avoiding trouble was overshadowed by the fact that her frustration was quickly turning to anger.

Why did he have to add that last part? I am very well aware of the fact that I am on the principal's radar. You don't have to announce it as if I were an idiot. Just because I look different doesn't mean I don't have a brain in my head. Why can't the world refrain from judging people by their outward appearances?

Katie flung open the office door intending to escape from the madness of school, but she was bombarded by the last remaining students that were trying to make their way to their classes. She pushed past kids as she headed towards the side exit of the school. Katie stopped dead in her tracks. Standing right in front of her were Christy, Darrell, and Destiny. If looks could kill, they would all be dead. The hatred was palpable. Katie glared at the trio through squinted eyes.

"You got off the hook this time, freak. Next time you won't be so lucky!" Christy said through clenched teeth.

The anger that had started to heat up in the office was now at a boiling point. Each word Katie said came out with an incredible force, "Oh, I don't think there will be a next time, Christy."

Christy cocked her head to the side and glared at Katie. "Miss Super Freak thinks she's tough now. We'll show you what we do to freaks that don't know their place."

The bell resonated throughout the halls, but even the piercing sound could not break the stares between Katie and Christy. Darrell tugged on Christy. "Christy, the teacher is coming. Let's go," he whispered with urgency.

"Alright, everyone get to class now; the bell already

rang," a peppy, bright-eyed young teacher announced into the hallway as she ushered Darrell and Destiny inside. Christy was the last to enter.

As Christy crossed the threshold, she turned towards Katie and whispered—her voice low, dripping with hatred. "This is not over, freak."

The door slammed shut behind Christy, leaving Katie standing alone in the hallway. She stood motionless, hands clenched at either side, seething, each breath like the ticking of a bomb that was about to go off.

~ 9 ~

BATTLE LINES

Katie ran down the empty corridor and out the double doors intending to head straight for the fountain. Storm clouds brewed in the sky above.

The eeriness that surrounded Katie reminded her of the dream she had the night before. She circled around the grassy area expecting to see a dark creature hovering above, ready to strike. There was not any sign of the menacing being. Katie turned, as if in a trance, and walked towards the hill that led to the pond, to the fountain, and to her sanity. She stood atop the hill and glanced down. She released a deep sigh of relief; there before her eyes stood the ancient image from yesterday.

So, it is real. I'm not insane. But what explanation is there for how the paper spontaneously combusted into flames?

Katie remembered her bedroom window and the other paranormal episode too. There had to be an explanation.

Part of her dream from the night before forced its way into the back of her mind. "You have all the elements of nature at your disposal," the mysterious male figure revealed to her in the dream.

Another thing to uncover. Who was the man from my dream? He said that I have the powers of the earth, wind, fire, and water. That might explain the note that burst into flames.

Katie remembered her original quest and started making a mental list of all the unexplainable events she had to expose: shattered windows, flying balls, secretive fountains, combusting paper, portent dreams, and sketchy men in black trench coats.

I can only deal with one mystery at a time.

Katie walked towards the arbor; it was just as she remembered it. The ivy weaved its way around the columns and over the top. She reached up to touch one of the verdant leaves but was interrupted by an anxious voice.

"Katie, Katie, where are you going?" It was Cherene, almost breathless as she ran towards Katie.

"I just had to get out of there!" Katie answered.

"Everyone is talking about what you did. Why did you light that paper on fire?" Cherene asked, flipping her dark hair away from her face with her hand.

Katie could have asked herself the same question. What made her light the paper on fire? Better yet, *how* did she light the paper on fire without a match? It was mind boggling. The others must think she used a match to ignite it. She guessed it was better they think that she was a pyromaniac than some sort of paranormal freak. She wanted more than anything to tell Cherene what was happening to her, but she could not be sure Cherene would keep her secret or even understand what it was that she was going through.

"You should have seen what they wrote on the paper; you would have torched it too!" Katie responded.

"What did it say?" Cherene asked. Her gray-blue eyes were wide with curiosity.

"It's just too terrible and embarrassing. Can we just forget it?" she snapped, her eyes threatening to expose the depth of her sorrow.

Katie wanted to tell her best friend. She needed someone to talk to about what was happening to her. Her mind wandered back to the ice-cream shop, the night Cherene had told her that the pond and fountain did not exist. How would Cherene explain the appearance of the pond and fountain now that they were both standing next to them?

"Sure, we can forget it," Cherene said. "Do you want to grab a bite to eat?"

"I don't care what we do as long as we get away from here." Katie turned away from the pond to leave and heard Cherene rambling.

"Good, I know a shortcut to the parking lot. Come this way." Cherene turned and began walking in the direction of the pond. Before Katie could warn her, Cherene was walking across the pond. Katie shook her head and blinked her eyes. The pond and the fountain, even the arbor, all disappeared before her eyes. Katie stood very still, shocked at what she had just witnessed.

Cherene turned back. "Aren't you coming? The administrators won't see us if we go through this meadow." She laughed and motioned for Katie to follow as she traipsed through the open field. Katie walked behind in a trance as Cherene led them through the meadow to the cars in the parking lot.

What just happened? Am I insane? Either Cherene is a prophet that walks on water, or I am seriously losing my mind.

Katie did not want either option to be true. They emerged on the other side of the meadow and clambered up the hill that led to the parking lot. Katie glanced back towards the meadow, hoping she would not see it, but there it was; the fountain stood sentinel in the middle of a small pond, surrounded by the beautiful, antique, ivy-clad arbor.

Katie looked again and saw a familiar figure running across the pond…no, meadow. A boy was running across the meadow.

This is getting creepy. Is it a pond, or is it a meadow?

She started thinking she might need to see a doctor. The occurrences of paranormal activity and mysterious visions were becoming more frequent. The question was, would she see an eye doctor for glasses, a psychiatrist for a straitjacket, or maybe she needed a brain scan for a huge tumor pressing on the rational part of her brain?

As the figure drew nearer, she realized who it was. It was Brian, Christy's friend Brian. Mr. Blue Eyes was heading in her direction, and she did not have a clue what he wanted from her. She took a deep breath and waited for him to make his way up the hill.

"Katie, what are you staring—" Cherene stopped midsentence and came to stand by Katie's side. She did not need to say any more. The answer to her question was jogging up the hill to join their ditching party.

Out of breath, Brian said, "Cherene, I didn't know you were here, too. Katie, I need to talk to you."

"What do you want?" Katie questioned without a hint of feeling in her voice.

"Well, it's kind of a private issue. Can we go somewhere and talk?" he asked, running his hand through his dark hair.

Katie thought about his question. Blue Eyes wanted to talk to her. The last time one of Christy's friends tried to get Cherene "alone," it was for dubious reasons.

"Brian, if you have something to say, just say it," Katie said, trying to sound indifferent.

"Here?" he asked, shifting his blue eyes from one girl to the other.

"Where else?" Katie said. She stood with both hands on her hips seeming unaffected by his plea for privacy.

"Maybe we can go somewhere, away from school."

Katie looked at Cherene. They nodded at one another, seeming to agree in that nonverbal way that girlfriends do. "We were going to get a bite to eat. If you want to follow us, we can talk there," Katie said.

At least they would be in the place of their choosing, and they would be in public. Katie thought it was a safe bet.

"Okay. I'll follow you. I'm parked over there." Brian shrugged his head in the direction of his car and jogged towards it.

Cherene and Katie left in Cherene's car and Brian followed.

"What does he want to talk to you about?" Cherene questioned.

"I don't know; I was going to ask you what you thought he might want."

"Well, I'm not an expert, but all the other students were talking about the fire; maybe he wants to find out what happened back in class."

As if he had a right to ask about what happened. He was sitting right in the middle of the group that sent the evil message hurling in her direction.

"If I don't want to talk about it with you, I certainly don't want to talk about it with him."

Cherene cleared her throat. "You know, I know we have only known each other for a few days, but I feel like, with the whole Christy thing, we kind of have a connection. Maybe you don't feel—"

"No, I feel it too," Katie replied before the moment could pass.

Cherene smiled and said, "I'm glad I am not the only one. I would kind of look like a dork over here spewing out all this mushy stuff!"

"Yeah," Katie added, "like…awkward!"

They both laughed.

Cherene continued, "So, if you ever need to talk, I'm here. Okay?"

"Okay. *If* I need to talk, I will let you know." They settled into a comfortable silence for the next few minutes of the drive to the local sandwich shop. Katie wished she could tell Cherene what the note said. The thought of it made her stomach sick.

There had been "mean girls" at her other schools too, but these chicks took the cake. If she did not know better, she would think she had offended one of them in a previous life. Katie considered the thought for a moment. Maybe she should not be too quick to dismiss the idea. With everything that had been happening to her, past lives did not seem too distant a reality.

Brian pulled into the spot next to them at the sandwich shop. Katie glanced out the car window to find him staring at her. She did her best to smile nonchalantly, but his gaze continued. She stared back at him for a moment and considered why he might be looking at her like that. Did she have food in her teeth? No, she had not eaten yet. There was only one way to find out what was going on inside that brain of his.

Here goes nothing.

They exited the cars at the same time. Brian rushed to grab the door to the restaurant before Cherene or Katie could open it. Katie did not expect him to be such a gentleman.

Stay focused, Katie.

They settled into a booth with their lunches. Brian broke the uncomfortable silence. "So Katie, are you sure there isn't somewhere private we could talk?" he asked, eyeing Cherene.

"Just spill it, Brian," Katie said as she bit into her club sandwich.

He looked at Katie with uneasiness and narrowed his eyes at her. "About today," he started.

Katie rolled her eyes and sighed. Her aggravation was obvious.

Brian shifted in his seat and looked around as if someone was going to slip him a script with just the right words scribbled on it. He took a deep breath and continued, "I just didn't want you to think that Christy is cruel. Most of the time, it starts out as a joke. Then it's like she flips a switch, and the innocent pranks turn dark and all wrong. When it is over, she's like a different person."

"Are you seriously going to sit there and defend her to me?" Katie asked, leaning forward, glaring at Brian.

"No. I'm not defending her. I just didn't want you to think—"

"Why do you care what I think?" Katie snapped.

"Because I think Christy and her group have stepped over the line."

"You think?"

The bite of her words made Brian flinch. "Katie…I—"

"What Brian? Just say what you have to say and be

done with it."

"You seem like a cool girl. You don't deserve what she's trying to do to you."

"So, if I were a different kind of girl, I might deserve her cruel . . . what did you call them? Jokes?"

"Yeah, well no. Katie, this is not coming out the way I wanted it to."

"Look Brian, I am not a fool. You are part of Christy's little group, so that puts you and me on opposite sides of this battle. In fact, aren't you two dating?"

"I am not on Christy's side, and no, we are not dating. Besides, it's not a battle."

Katie narrowed her green eyes at Brian as she spoke. "Oh, let's be very clear Brian. This *is* a battle. And from where I am sitting, you are not on my side."

"Right," he said hanging his head down for a moment. He looked up at her with defeat in his blue eyes. "Okay, Katie. Don't say I didn't try." Brian grabbed his coat and got up to leave.

"Trust me, I won't say a word to you," Katie said watching him walk towards the glass door.

Brian paused for a moment as if he were considering one final plea. He started to turn and face the booth that Cherene and Katie occupied.

"Bye, Brian," Katie said dismissing him. Her cold words ended his dilemma.

The frigid outside air rushed in as he left the sandwich shop without another word. Katie watched as he sped away in his car. wishing it had gone differently.

"Well, that did not go very well," Cherene said, licking the mustard from her fingers.

"Yeah, thanks for the encouraging words, friend."

"You didn't need my help. You handled him just fine on your own," Cherene asserted as she dried her hands on her napkin.

"What game do you think he is playing?"

"Beats me. You are talking to the girl that took a walk straight into an ambush just because Darrell spoke to me. I am the last girl that should be evaluating people and their motives."

"Still, I wonder what he wants. This is not the first time he has tried to contact me."

"Maybe he likes you," Cherene said, raising her eyebrows up and down.

"You mean like Darrell liked you? That's all I need."

"That's cruel, Katie." Cherene looked away from her friend and stared at the table.

Katie opened her mouth; the shock of Cherene's hurt response kept her from speaking at first. She reached out and placed her hand on Cherene's arm. "I'm so sorry, Cherene. That did not come out like I meant it," Katie corrected, her tone softer, sincere.

"Oh, you mean like how what Brian was trying to say did not come out the way he meant it?" Cherene countered raising a brow waiting for her to reply.

Katie removed her hand from Cherene's arm and sat

for a moment staring at her friend. "What? Why are you taking his side?" Katie asked, shaking her head back and forth in disbelief.

"I am not taking his side, Katie. I'm just saying maybe you should give the guy a chance."

"But he's with *them*."

"Yes, but he is trying to let you know he doesn't approve of how they are acting."

"Well, maybe he should be telling *them* that he doesn't approve of their actions, not me."

"Well, he kind of did, didn't he?"

"What do you mean?" Katie asked.

"Remember when Christy's minions were trying to torture us? Brian told them not to," Cherene replied.

"Actually, if I remember correctly, his exact words were, 'Uh guys, I don't think we have time for this.' That is not exactly a declaration of disapproval."

"Seriously, Katie?" Cherene said, shooting her friend a disapproving smirk.

"I am just saying; he did not say he was morally opposed to their actions." Katie defended her position, her resolve weakening with each word she spoke. "It was more like he saw a time management issue." She saw that Cherene was not buying any of her story. "Alright, alright, I see what you're saying."

"Thank you." Cherene smiled and let out a small screech of triumph.

Katie stifled a laugh, shook her head and rolled her eyes. “Let’s get out of here. I have to get home and start on my camp essay if I am going to get away from this crazy place.”

~ 10 ~

SECRET AGENT

Katie arrived home to the sound of muffled voices in the den. Creeping down the hall, she stopped just before the doorway.

"Do you think she suspects?" Mom asked.

"How would she even have a clue?" Phil whispered.

"What did you do with the paperwork?"

"Relax. Grandma Ceil sent it overnight in the mail yesterday. I'll take care of everything when it arrives," Phil assured her.

A list of questions flooded her mind. Were they talking about her or someone else? What was the paperwork for? And why so secretive?

Katie did not like Phil, but he seemed to be more stable than the other losers her mother had brought home. After all, he did buy her a'65 convertible Mustang; it might be old and rusty, but it was still a car. A true loser could not afford an extra vehicle unless he was selling drugs or stolen goods. Katie thought about that prospect for a moment. He did not seem like a druggie.

Besides, wouldn't I have seen the signs by now?

Phil and her mom had been dating the longest of any of her mom's other boyfriends. Plus, he had proposed and stuck around for a wedding.

Katie racked her brain for a pattern. How long had it been before the first guy after her dad had started showing signs that he was bad news? Dad left in October, and Mom introduced guy number one, David, to Katie a month later. At first, he seemed like a good guy. He dressed in a suit and tie and went to work in a high-rise office building each day. By January though, it was obvious that he liked booze more than anything else.

Katie sighed as she recalled the Valentine's Day dance that she and her friends never made it to because David, in his drunken state, picked a fistfight with her boyfriend, Sean, before the dance.

To Mom's credit, she did leave David, but Katie's reputation at school was ruined. People either felt sorry for her or wanted nothing to do with her. Sean's parents did not press charges against David, but he did break-up with Katie. It was almost a relief when a month later Mom met boyfriend number two and moved them to a neighboring town.

The memory was hideous and painful but scanning the files of her past might help her get to the bottom of what her mom and Phil were talking about. David showed his true colors in about two months. Mom's second boyfriend lasted about four months before he had to be discarded, too. Mom and Phil had been dating for six months before they got married.

Wouldn't I have noticed if he had a hidden vice—besides just being a hypocrite and a general pain in my backside?

Katie thought about calling Grandma Ceil to find out what paperwork they were talking about. She wondered if her grandma would even tell her. She did not want to put Grandma in a bad position, or worse, have her own grandma lie to her. No, Grandma would not lie. Or would she?

Whatever it was that her mom and Phil were hiding, she was not going to figure it out tonight. She would think about her options another day and make plans to expose Phil later.

Katie decided she was done playing Nancy Drew for the moment and retired to her room for the evening. She must have been beat because she fell asleep as soon as her head hit the pillow. She dreamed another dreadful dream about being near an ominous creature in the mist.

* * * * *

Katie stood within the dark, wet cave. The cavern walls were smooth and slippery from the damp night air. Thick grey fog rolled into the entrance of the cave. A dark figure advanced from the opening towards her. The mysterious creature moved gracefully but held the stench of death within her being. Her long black robes trailed behind her, as she moved swiftly, without hesitation. Katie's breath caught as the woman's face was revealed. Her brilliant, onyx eyes bore through Katie. Strands of her long, black hair blew wildly in the cold air.

"Ah, I have finally found you. I knew you would come eventually," she taunted, her words giving way to her menacing laugh. Katie shivered from the cold air and the paralyzing fear that was overtaking her body.

Although Katie was frightened, she could not help but be intrigued. It felt as if she had waited so long for this moment. The anticipation almost outweighed the fear. Katie drew nearer to her, but quickly wished she had not. The intense being's dark eyes began to glow, creating a blazing heat that burrowed deep into Katie's chest.

The rays singed her skin and delved deep into her ribcage. Extreme pain grasped her heart, refusing to loosen its grip. Katie stared, panic stricken. Complete horror plagued her mind as she realized that her heart was motionless and at the mercy of the evil being's eyes of death.

* * * * *

Katie woke with a gasp and sat straight up in bed. Beads of sweat gathered on her brow. She heard that if you died in a dream, you would die in real life. She pondered that for a moment and thanked God that she had woken up before she drew her last breath in the frightening dream. She turned on her TV for some company and her iPod for some tunes. She had to relax before she'd be able to sleep again. Her mind drifted back to the conversation that Mom and Phil were having earlier.

I need to get my mind off this drama. Next thing you know, I'll be having dreams about my mom and Phil selling drugs out of our garage and stolen stereos from the back of my beat-up Mustang.

Too afraid to go to sleep, she decided to get up and start on her essay. She had to get away from her life. The perfect escape would be the winter camp. Two weeks without Mom and Phil and Christy and her gang sounded like heaven. It would have been easier if a topic was given for the essay. She always did better with writing prompts.

The instructions had asked for an original creative writing essay. That could be about anything. She would have to make something up. She thought she could steal a topic from someone else's work on the Internet; then her conscience got the better of her.

I am better than that.

She contemplated writing about her crazy life.

No, too personal.

Katie imagined a movie producer making a full-length feature film about the wild dreams she had been having since she moved to Salem. Maybe the house was haunted, and it was affecting her dreams.

That's it.

She settled on writing about a haunted camp with faeries and wicked magic. If that did not get the attention of the judges, she did not know what would.

She set up her laptop and began creating a magical world that could be unbelievably believable. She had read enough on the supernatural and paranormal to write a documentary. Add those "facts" to the dreams she had been having, and the essay might not be as difficult as she first thought.

Katie began writing and the words just flew out of her mind and onto the screen. Before she knew it, two hours had passed, then three. By the time she finished, the sun was creeping up over the horizon bringing the dawn of a new day. She printed her final draft and headed off to school.

She was confident in her ability as a writer and thought that the world of her dreams might just be more livable than her own reality.

~ 11 ~

BOOKS AND BULLIES

Three weeks had passed since Katie submitted her essay, and she had not missed a class since the burning note incident in Mr. White's class. It was not that the problems with Christy and her friends stopped; rather, Phil had laid down the law; any ditching reports and Katie could kiss her Mustang goodbye until after winter break. The car was not all that. In fact, it almost qualified as junkyard status. However, the car was Katie's ticket to freedom, and it granted her access to visit with Cherene as much as her mom would allow.

She and Cherene were becoming fast friends. Katie felt like Cherene was the best friend she had ever had. They agreed on all the important stuff: guys, friends, makeup, hair, fashion, most movies, and almost all books. When their ideas differed, they simply agreed to disagree.

Katie drove by Cherene's house to pick her up for

school. They had been taking turns driving each other to school since the day after the infamous "fire" incident. The girls agreed that there was safety in numbers, plus they saved on gas and could use the extra money to add to their winter wardrobes. If Katie won the essay contest, she would need a heavy winter coat, boots, and a sleeping bag for camp.

Her mom had not gotten a job since moving to Salem, so Katie did not want to ask her for money. Katie could probably get Phil to agree to buy the supplies, but she did not want to be indebted to him for anything. She made a mental note to herself never to have to rely on the support of a man. Katie watched Cherene as she bounced down the driveway. Cherene threw open the door and jumped in.

"What's up?" Cherene said.

"You look happy!"

"I am. My mom and dad agreed to pay for me to go to the winter camp," she revealed.

"Yes! That's awesome!"

"Now all we need is for you to win that contest, and we'll be set for a cool two-week vacation."

"No parents, no school."

"No Christy!" Cherene added.

"Yeah, no Christy! That sounds like heaven."

"When will you hear about the essay contest?"

"I'll know by the fifteenth of December. I'm getting kind of nervous. What if they don't pick my essay?"

"You're nervous? If they don't choose your essay, I'll be going to camp alone. I don't even like camping! I am only going because you're going."

The girls laughed at the prospect. Then Katie's mind turned to the essay she had written. The "paranormal" content reminded her of her own brushes with the mysterious. She was grateful that there were no more "incidents" in the last few weeks.

Maybe things are looking up.

Katie turned up the song on the radio. They sang along to the words they knew and mumbled through the words they didn't. Katie tapped the beat on the steering wheel while Cherene wiggled in her seat dancing to the rhythm as they approached the school's parking lot. Nothing had changed since the first day that Katie had arrived at the school. The grassy quad area was still segregated by the distinct social groups of students; everyone seemed to know their place and did not dare challenge the already established social system. Katie and Cherene were proof of what happened when you tried to buck the system.

The morning passed without event. Cherene and Katie hung out with Cherene's friends in the cafeteria during lunch. They took a quick trip to the girls' restroom to check out their hair before returning to their classes.

"Meet you at the table by the parking lot," Cherene shouted as she bolted out of the door of the restroom.

"See ya," Katie answered as the door swung shut. Katie freshened up her dark purple lipstick and ran her fingers through her black hair. She loved the way the lipstick shade matched the purple streak in her hair perfectly. She turned her face to see her hair from either side. Pursing her lips in a pouty expression, she looked in the mirror and considered her appearance.

Her father had told her she was the most beautiful girl in the whole world. A lot of good being pretty did her; Katie had not seen her father since the day that she saw him leaving. Tears threatened to spill from her eyes and ruin her mascara. She tried to shake off the feeling, but the familiar anger began to boil inside her. Katie reached for her stone.

She stared in the mirror and spied the open door from the stall behind her. She narrowed her eyes and thought of how good it would feel to slam the door shut with all her might. Before she could finish the thought, she was interrupted by the sound of a metallic, stainless-steel door hitting against the frame of the stall.

Katie turned around in a flash. Staring at the door, she peeked under to see if someone had slammed it shut. The stall was empty. She glanced towards the open door of the stall next to the closed door she had just shut with her mind. She focused on her anger, again feeling it roil within her. Concentrating on the second door, she willed it to slam shut too. Bam!

I did it! I did it again!

Katie whirled around as if she were looking for someone to tell her good news. She raised an eyebrow and scanned the restroom for something else to manipulate. She turned towards the large, rectangular bathroom mirror that was secured above the four-faucet, porcelain sink. The memory of her shattered window took residence in her mind.

Katie breathed in deep and fixed all her energy on the image of a spider web of broken glass cutting through the smooth mirror. The sound of the glass cracking shocked Katie. A large shard of glass fell to the sink and shattered into several small pieces. She gasped and jumped back into the door behind her.

This is amazing. I didn't imagine it. There is no doubt about it. I have the power to move and break things.

Her internal celebration was interrupted by the sound of the bell.

Darn. I must have lost track of the time.

She was late to class, but nothing could subdue her delight. She had powers. She did not know how or why, but she did not care. She had powers.

Katie chortled to herself and started out of the bathroom. If she cut across the north end of the cafeteria, she could get to her next class in no time. Before she got all the way out of the bathroom, she heard Christy's high-pitched voice. Katie retreated a little into the bathroom, leaving just a crack of the door open so that she could see and hear what was going on in the cafeteria. Christy was being her usual cruel self.

Christy and Destiny had picked a different victim; this time it was a freshman girl that looked like a little pixie. Her hair was cut short and spiked all around. If she weren't so tiny, she might have passed for a metal head. She wore a black spiked dog collar around her neck and one to match on her wrist. The tips of her blond hair were peppered with bright pink and light purple. She looked like a headbanging faery.

Who am I to judge?

Katie marveled at the image of the tiny creature before her. Her first thought was to help the girl, but she quickly remembered how her attempt to help Cherene had gone so very wrong. She held her ground and thought for a moment.

How can I help her without getting in the middle again?

She took in her surroundings. The girls were surrounded by dirty tables and a few stragglers who were taking their sweet time finishing their lunches. Then Katie spied a display of books next to the bathroom. A wicked smile spread across her face.

Katie studied the scene. Christy and Destiny were pushing the small, waiflike girl between them; their snotty laughter reverberated throughout the almost empty cafeteria. A small crowd began to gather near the girls. Katie had to act fast. She looked at the display of books near her and allowed her frustration to overtake her, empathizing with the feeling of helplessness that the girl must be feeling. Katie's eyes narrowed and her thoughts focused; suddenly, a book slid across the floor and hit Destiny in the foot.

Destiny looked down startled. "What? Who threw that?"

Christy glanced at her friend but could not be bothered to stop bullying the pixie-like girl long enough to see what was wrong with Destiny. Destiny grabbed the girl's arm,

"You're going to pay for that; you little. . ."

Katie saw a tray of unsold milk cartons and thought those looked a little less damaging than hardback books. She willed a carton of milk to fly into the middle of the girls; this time it hit its mark, square in the middle of Destiny's back. She whipped her head around to see who hit her. Before she could enlist Christy's help, Christy was yelping from the smack she took on the back of her head.

The small girl did not waste any time; she ran away before they could get their bearings, leaving the bullies standing in a shallow pool of milk. Katie stepped out of the bathroom quietly and tried to slink away unnoticed.

Christy and Destiny surveyed the onlookers. Destiny turned and spotted Katie just as she was passing the stand with the books. She tapped Christy on the arm. "Check out the freak," Destiny said as she pointed in Katie's direction.

"You!" Christy screamed. Katie kept walking. She thought if she ignored Christy, she would give up. No such luck.

"Katie. Stop right there," Christy demanded as she and Destiny stormed towards Katie.

Cornered, Katie turned to face her accusers.

"What?"

"What? All you have to say is what?"

Katie let out a bored sigh trying to feign disinterest, "What, Christy?"

Christy grabbed Katie by the arm and shoved her into the stand of books. "You think you're going to throw books and food at us and just walk away?"

Katie looked past Christy and Destiny; a small crowd of students were watching, but none of them stepped forward to defend Katie. "I didn't throw anything at you," she said, reaching her free hand into her pocket to hold her amethyst stone. A surge of energy rushed through her being.

Destiny reached for Katie's hand and shouted, "What are you doing? What's in your pocket?"

Katie loosened her grip on the stone and slipped her hand out of her pocket. Opening her hand, she held it out for Destiny to see. "I don't have anything," Katie said forcing her face into an emotionless mask as she looked up at her tormentor.

Christy and Destiny moved closer to Katie, their normally pretty faces looked ugly, distorted by their intimidating scowls.

Katie scanned her surroundings hoping to find a way to make her escape. She knew she could not use her mind to make the books or milk hit Christy and Destiny again; that would prove their case that she was in fact the one responsible for striking them earlier.

Katie's glance found its way into Christy's oversized purse; there were two glass bottles of iced tea. Katie channeled her energy towards the bottles; thoughts of the bottles bursting, and the tea spraying everywhere flooded her mind, but nothing happened.

Katie panicked. What had happened to her powers? Why couldn't she make the bottles explode? She could feel her own heart start to race; a thousand images flashed through her mind all at once. All of them involved Christy and Destiny pummeling her to death.

Christy and Destiny towered over Katie. Christy pinned her against the wall by her hair while Destiny held her hands down. Her grip was almost unbearable. Katie tried to move her arms, but Destiny was much stronger than her.

"We're going to make you pay little freak," Destiny threatened. Katie could feel the heat of Destiny's breath in her ear; her words cutting like a knife.

Overwhelmed by panic and anger, Katie tried to focus her thoughts on the bottles again. She closed her eyes and used all her inner strength to concentrate on that one single act. Katie felt the sting of the back of Christy's hand on her face. Feelings of complete anger overshadowed her fear. She tried to free her hands to strike back at Christy, but Destiny's grip was like iron.

Katie's rage boiled inside. She fixated her energy on the bottles in Christy's purse once again. In her mind, she commanded the bottles to explode. *Explode, explode, explode*, she repeated through her mounting anger. Her thoughts became screams within her own mind demanding the glass to detonate, until finally she let out a snarling growl like that of a wild animal caught in a hunter's snare. Katie screamed out loud, "NOW!"

Katie heard the explosion, a warning siren before the storm. Lukewarm liquid filled her nostrils. Christy and Destiny released Katie from their grip at the same moment.

Their screams echoed through the cafeteria as they tried to shelter themselves from the shards of glass that were raining down on them like shrapnel in a war zone.

Katie slipped past the two girls and saw that Christy was holding her eye.

"She hit my eye. I can't see!" Christy screeched.

Katie saw Mr. Blackstone making his way down the hall that led to the cafeteria. Despite his heavy stature, he was rushing to get to the squalling girls. Katie bolted in the opposite direction, knowing full well that she would be blamed for yet another episode with Christy and Destiny.

She pushed past a few students; only those that were very late were still in the hallway. She thought of leaving campus but remembered Phil's threat. She needed to keep her car privileges, but then none of it would matter if she were suspended for fighting.

Katie decided to go to her class and hope for the best. She was not in her seat two minutes before Mr. Blackstone's husky image appeared in the frame of the classroom door. Katie could hear Christy's shrieking from behind him.

"In there. Katie is in there, Mr. Blackstone."

"Mr. Mathis, I need to see Katie in the hallway," Mr. Blackstone requested.

"Of course," Mr. Mathis, the art teacher, answered. "Katie, you are wanted in the hallway," he said in a formal tone.

Katie smiled innocently at Mr. Mathis. He was a kind old man. She enjoyed his art class and was surprised that she felt so bothered by the prospect that he might think badly of her. He closed the door behind her and left Katie to fend for herself with Mr. Blackstone and her tormentors.

"Katie, why don't you make this easy on all of us and tell me the truth about what you did to Christy and Destiny in the cafeteria," he began in a calm, but stern voice.

"Well, Mr. Blackstone," she began, "I would tell you the truth, but you wouldn't believe it." As hard as she tried, she could not keep the sarcasm out of her voice.

"That little tone of yours is not helping your case young lady."

"See, I told you she would deny it, Mr. Blackstone," Christy asserted.

"Actually, I didn't deny anything."

"So, you admit it then?" the principal questioned with a sense of hopeful triumph in his voice.

Katie turned away from Christy and looked at Mr. Blackstone, her face a blank mask. "I didn't deny anything, and I didn't admit to anything either."

Mr. Blackstone's frustration became evident. His face twisted in a scowl; he reached out to grab Katie's arm. As she felt his huge hand clamp down around her upper arm, she could sense the anger gathering within her body.

She narrowed her eyes and returned his grimace with a defiant sneer of her own. "I would not do that if I were you," she warned. Anger's familiar temper began to boil and threatened to unleash its fury. She reached into her pocket and felt her amethyst stone.

Seeming startled by her veiled threat and the menacing look upon her face, Mr. Blackstone heeded her warning and let go of her arm.

"You'd better just come with me then, Katie. We'll handle this in the office," he announced, his calm, stern voice returning.

"Whatever," Katie said, resigned to the fact that she did not stand a chance. As they walked through the hallway to the principal's office, Katie could see the onlookers staring from the windows and doors of the classrooms as the parade of principal, popular girls, and Goth chick passed by. Katie could already hear the whispers from the students that gathered in doorways as they were passing by.

"Did you hear how she hit Christy?"

"I heard she threatened the principal."

"Someone told me she was a descendant from the Salem witches."

"I bet they kick her out of school."

"I don't think we're safe with her kind here."

The whispers went on and on. None of them bore anything close to the truth.

Katie had been through some tough times at the other schools she had attended, but none had reached this level of drama. For a moment, she thought life would be easier if she were to be kicked out of school. She was smart enough to finish school at home, but then what college would accept her?

She had dreams of becoming a teacher or maybe even a lawyer. Who would she teach with a criminal record? Maybe she could teach at the local prison, or she could be an in-house counsel for fellow inmates. She could start up a peer-prisoner mediation group. Her anxious thoughts were taking control again. She had not even been accused of a crime, but Katie was already planning how she would spend her prison term.

Mr. Blackstone led the girls towards his office. "Christy and Destiny, you sit in these chairs and wait outside until I call you in. Katie, come inside my office now."

She followed him inside letting out a sigh of defeat as she walked through the threshold. Katie glanced out the three large windows that looked out over the quad area as he made a call to security. "I am having security bring in the tapes of what happened in the cafeteria. This will all go smoothly if you will just admit to what you did, Katie. The tapes won't lie."

"Yeah, not like people," she whispered under her breath.

"What was that?" Mr. Blackstone questioned.

"Nothing."

They waited in silence until there was a knock on the door. The lanky, light-colored security officer tried to look official as he came into the room. As he popped the DVD into the principal's video player, the officer stole a glance at Katie and winked.

What was that? Either he knows my secret and is one of the paranormally insane too, or he just hit on me. I don't know which is worse.

He fast-forwarded the DVD to the part that showed the

scene of the cafeteria. The image slowly came into focus. The top of a dark-haired girl's head and a few snippets of wild, strawberry-blonde spirals filled the screen.

"Can you zoom out a little?" Mr. Blackstone queried.

"No, this is it. Someone may have tampered with the lens on the video camera," Officer Weird Winker explained. "There is usually a panoramic view of the cafeteria from this camera."

The officer turned towards Katie and gave a queer smile. She looked sideways in his direction, trying to decipher his cryptic message.

A red flush crept up Mr. Blackstone's neck until inch by inch it covered his whole face. "What about the other cameras?" he asked, desperation plaguing his voice.

The weird officer shook his head back and forth and twisted his mouth into an apologetic grimace. "Sorry Mr. Blackstone, the other cameras have been down since last week. The maintenance team has been working hard to restore their functionality, but these things take time, you know."

An odd sensation coursed through her body. Studying the officer more closely, Katie realized *he* was the source of the strange feelings adrift in her veins. It was not just the weirdness of having the old man wink at her, there was more to this person who stood before her making excuses to the principal on her behalf. She felt as if she had encountered the officer somewhere before. His eyes reminded her of someone, but before she could fully realize who it was, her train of thought was interrupted by Mr. Blackstone's voice.

"Well, without the proof of the tapes, it looks like it's your word against theirs, Katie," Mr. Blackstone said as he pushed away from his desk and stood up. Katie sat, wide-eyed, waiting for his final word. "I am warning you. I'm keeping my eye on you, Katie Ryan."

Katie smiled looking up through innocent green eyes. "I can go then?"

Mr. Blackstone's chest expanded with the deep breath he forced himself to take before nodding—her cue to leave. As Katie walked past Christy and Destiny, she could feel their eyes on her. She heard Mr. Blackstone's deep voice behind her, "Christy, you know I knew your father since we were boys."

"Yes," Christy said batting the lashes of her brown eyes.

"He would not want you to be involved in this nonsense. You can't continue to be in the middle of every incident with girls like Katie. I can only look the other way for so long. Eventually, the excuse of what happened to him will expire. Please, let this go, Christy," he begged.

"But, Mr. Blackstone. I didn't—" Christy started.

Katie turned back to see Mr. Blackstone's hand set firmly on Christy's shoulder. "Christy, I said what I needed to say. You have been warned. You girls go back to class."

He gave her a little push and turned towards his own office door. Christy frowned at Destiny and shook her head.

Looks like Miss Popularity is not happy with Mr. Blackstone's lack of loyalty.

A triumphant smile spread across Katie's face as she continued to walk out of the school's office and back to class.

Katie arrived back to Mr. Mathis' art class a few minutes before the end of the period. She pushed open the heavy wooden door and stopped for a moment. Mr. Mathis and a few students were gathered around a canvas of a nearly nude oil portrait. The teacher was trying to describe the piece of artwork that was displayed, but the immature students, mostly boys, were laughing and cajoling each other about the true inspiration for man's love of art. The rest of the class stood about talking and waiting for the bell to ring.

Katie shook her head at their nonsense and made her way through the boisterous group to retrieve the books she had left under her seat when Mr. Blackstone pulled her from class. As she made her way through the room, all conversation stopped. She could have heard a pin drop. Katie eyed the students, waiting for the worst. The school bell pierced the silence of the crowd, and on cue, as if someone had hit play on a video, the students returned to their raucous behavior and rushed out of the room.

Katie tolerated her last two classes.

After school, she went to the usual spot to wait for Cherene. Katie's mind was filled with worrisome thoughts about what Cherene might say about what happened. Cherene was cool, but she was not stupid. In the short time that they had spent together, Katie had learned enough about her friend to know that she was not a troublemaker. Deep down, she was not dark and brooding like her exterior. She was a lot like

Katie with hopes and dreams and a grade point average that could get her into a great college, maybe even with a scholarship.

Maybe it is time to come clean. Maybe I should just tell Cherene what has been happening to me. She's not going to buy some concocted tale where I am an innocent victim again. At some point, she's going to start believing that I am an out-of-control teen, a derelict, or worse, a psychopath. I can't afford to lose Cherene's friendship. She's the best friend I've had since the eighth grade. The truth, I have to tell her the truth.

Katie glanced at her watch. It was thirty minutes past the last bell. She pulled out her phone and called Cherene. The call went straight to voicemail. She hung up without leaving a message. She did not want to sound pathetic, and the way she was feeling right then, she couldn't help but sound like a wounded puppy.

Although she was trying to remain optimistic, Katie could not help but wonder if Cherene had ditched her. After all, Katie was Cherene's ride home. Her fingers flew deftly over the keyboard as she texted Cherene and told her to call when she got a chance. The truth would have to wait.

Katie drove home with the car windows down. She turned up the heater for warmth and blasted the radio, hoping it would drown out her negative thoughts. The frigid December air stung her cheeks and blew her black hair wildly around her face.

Why does everything have to be difficult? Why can't I

just be normal? Why can't I have my old life back? Things weren't perfect, but at least my parents were together, and I had more friends than I could count. Now, I live with Phil, a man I barely know, and if I am lucky, I will be able to salvage a friendship with my one and only true friend.

As Katie turned down the dirt drive to her home, she rolled up the windows and tried to pretend everything was normal. She walked into the house and bolted straight up the wooden stairs to her room. She threw her book bag on the bed and pulled out her math book. She did not want to face her mom's inquisition. Katie knew if she looked like she was working on homework, her mom would not bother her with unnecessary questions.

Mom's delicate hand rapped on the door, the sound almost too soft to be detected. Before Katie could tell Mom she was busy, she opened the door and peaked her head in. Katie stayed focused on her math book as her mom entered the room.

"Katie, I thought I heard you come home," her mom said in a hopeful tone. Katie looked up with eyebrows raised, but she did not say a word.

"Oh, I see that you're doing homework." Her mom sounded disappointed. "I'll just come back later to talk."

"Kay," Katie mumbled, holding a pencil between her teeth as she looked back down at the math book that was spread out on the bed.

Katie's mom shut the door, and immediately the guilt of ignoring her mother set in. Katie started to get up to see what it was that her mom had wanted, but she fell back on the pillows at the top of her bed.

I can't talk to her now. She will never understand what I am going through. She would probably just remind me about how popular I used to be and tell me to do what I did back then to make friends.

Her mind returned to her present situation with Cherene. Cherene still had not called or texted. Katie decided that Cherene probably just needed a little time to process what happened. She could give Cherene time to consider what she knew, and then she would tell her the truth.

Katie closed her eyes and drifted off to sleep. She slept through dinner and all her favorite television shows. When she woke, the clock read one-thirty a.m. Her thoughts went to Cherene. She grabbed her phone to see if she had slept through a call or text from Cherene. No missed calls. The only text was one from Mom asking if Katie was coming down for dinner.

Cherene did not call or text. She must hate me. I need to talk to her, now. If I wait until tomorrow, it may be too late. I gave her time; now I need to give her the truth.

~ 12 ~

CLARITY

"Clink. . . Clink. . . Clink." Cherene woke to the sound of little pebbles hitting her window. She jumped out of bed and scurried to the window. She glanced at the clock on her antique, white nightstand. It was two in the morning.

After clearing a small hole in the lightly frosted glass, she peered through the window. There on the snow-covered ground stood her new best friend, Katie.

Cherene raised the bottom windowpane; instantly, the chilled night air rushed in and took her breath away.

She pressed her face against the icy screen. "What are you doing?" she inquired in a loud whisper so that Katie could hear her.

"Let me in!"

"Do you know what time it is?"

"Let me in before I freeze to death!"

After a moment, Cherene agreed and ran down the

stairs to let Katie in out of the cold. She opened the sliding kitchen door which led to the backyard. Katie bounded inside the warm kitchen and pulled off her hat, coat, and gloves before Cherene could say a word.

She threw her arms around Cherene's neck. "Thank you, thank you! It was so cold out there!"

"Shush. You'll wake my parents. Come with me down into the basement. We can talk there. My parents won't be able to hear us."

Katie followed, grateful that her friend had been there to let her in. She did not know what she would have done if Cherene did not wake up, or worse, if she refused to let her in. After what happened yesterday afternoon, she knew there was a possibility that Cherene would not want to have much to do with her anymore. The news of what had happened with Christy and Destiny probably made it all the way around the whole school before the end of seventh period.

Katie had searched for Cherene after school. When she did not find her at their usual meeting place, Katie feared the worst. She imagined that Cherene had heard that her new best friend was a paranormal freak and had run screaming for her life. The fact that Cherene had let her in her house gave Katie hope.

They walked down the thinly carpeted stairs to the musty basement. It was colder down below the main part of the house, but it was still warmer than being out in the snow when it was twenty-five degrees outside. As they emerged at the bottom of the stairwell, the girls turned to the left and entered a cozy room. Plush dark maroon carpet filled the small space, and wood-paneled walls surrounded. Katie thought it was either a den or a library. An immense bookcase spanned the length of one of the walls. Opposite the bookcase, there was a small loveseat and an end table that held one dimmed lamp. The room was warm and welcoming. Katie hoped Cherene's attitude would be as well.

"Okay, tell me what's going on, Katie," Cherene blurted out as if she had waited a lifetime to say the words. Her voice suggested that she might not be very understanding after all.

Katie paused. She had rushed over here, prepared to tell her friend everything. Now that the moment presented itself, she could not think of how to put her thoughts into words.

"I…I don't know where to begin, Cherene."

"Why don't you start at the beginning? That is where a 'normal' person would start," Cherene said. Her tone was borderline sarcastic, just as Katie feared it would be. Cherene had been tainted by the rumors that must have been circulating around the school.

Katie exhaled her fear. "Okay. I am going to tell you everything, but you must promise me one thing."

"Seriously? You're making demands?"

"It's not like I'm threatening you, but what I am about to tell you is very damaging. I can't have the rest of the school knowing the truth about me."

Cherene took a deep breath, considering her words.

"Let me put it this way, Katie. The whole school thinks you are some sort of psycho, teenage derelict with anger management and impulse control issues. At this point, you're making the rest of us 'Goth' chicks look like cheerleaders. It can't get much worse than it already is."

"I know. It's just hard for me to tell you this. I haven't told anyone what I am about to share with you."

Katie contemplated the events that had transpired. After school yesterday, Cherene had ditched her. Katie figured Cherene had vowed to herself to walk away from their friendship altogether. After all, if what everyone was saying about Katie were true, Katie was a ticking time bomb. Even though Cherene looked like a girl that lived on the edge with her dark clothes, black hair, and tons of piercings, Katie was sure Cherene did not have a death wish, and who would want to ruin their chances of going to college or having a good life after graduation by calling an out-of-control, paranormal freak, friend?

She probably only let me inside so she could tell me she doesn't want to be friends anymore.

Katie looked at Cherene for just a moment and then hung her head in defeat.

Cherene broke the awkward silence, "Just say it Katie. If you haven't broken any major laws, I think we can still be friends."

All Katie heard was, "We can still be friends." She picked her head up, her eyes sparkling with hope.

"Make me a deal, please." Katie paused and motioned

with her finger for Cherene to wait before she spoke. "Let me finish, and then you can say yes or no."

Katie smiled impishly hoping to break through her friend's new tough exterior.

Cherene cocked her head and raised her eyebrow. "What's your deal?" she asked.

"Even if you decide you don't want to be my friend after I tell you everything, can you promise not to tell anyone what I am about to tell you?"

"Well, what if you admit to me that you killed someone?"

"I haven't killed anyone."

"What if you say you stole someone's baby?"

"I didn't do that either."

"What about drug trafficking?"

"Cherene!" Katie blurted out and quickly lowered her voice when she remembered how late it was. "I did not do anything bad, not like that."

"Okay, then tell me what it is."

"Promise not to tell?"

"Fine, I promise."

"Say it."

Rolling her eyes, Cherene droned, "I promise not to tell another living soul what you are about to tell me even if I decide not to be your friend, which I probably won't."

"Okay. Here goes nothing."

Katie's heart was pounding. More than anything, she wanted to tell Cherene what she had been experiencing. On the other hand, she was pretty sure that Cherene would choose to end their friendship once she had all the information. Katie was not ready for their friendship to end, but things came to a head earlier in the day. She knew she had to come clean with Cherene.

"I am…I am a…I am a…a…"

"Katie, just say it."

"Okay. I think I am a paranormal being." Katie let out a huge breath and waited for Cherene to run from the room.

Cherene stifled a laugh. She looked at Katie with a peculiar expression: a cross between incredulous and mildly humored.

"So… you think you're a… what? An alien?"

"Ah, no. I mean that I can make things happen, like magic."

"So, you're telling me you're a magician?"

"Not exactly."

"I don't get it," Cherene said with a hint of frustration in her tone.

Katie breathed in deeply and took her time to exhale hoping she would gain the nerve to divulge her deepest secret. "Let me start at the beginning." Another deep breath. "Sometimes when I get angry, things around me break, or burst into flames, or go flying across the room."

"So, you're saying you do have anger management and impulse control issues?"

"No. Well, I guess that is part of it. When I get upset, those things happen, but I am not touching the objects to make them move, or turn to flames, or break into pieces before my eyes. It is like my mind makes the things happen, like magic or a spell."

Cherene looked astonished. As Cherene considered this new information, Katie fidgeted with her fingers as she waited for her friend's response. Cherene grinned mischievously; the sparkle in her eyes revealing her excitement. "A witch! My best friend is a witch!"

Katie breathed a sigh of relief. Cherene did not look mad or scared of her.

"I am not sure what I am. I have been doing a lot of research on paranormal beings, but I don't quite fit into any one category," Katie explained.

"So that day that the paper caught on fire in class, you're saying that you did not have a match to light it?"

"Exactly."

"Wow! That is amazing. Can you do it whenever you want?"

"Before today, the incidents have just happened randomly when I was angry. Today was the first time I made something happen by choice."

"What else can you do?"

Katie laughed at her friend and looked at her with a new appreciation.

This conversation is going way better than I thought it would. Cherene doesn't seem mad at all. In fact, it seems like Cherene thinks my paranormal status is kind of cool. I should have come clean to her weeks ago.

"The second time it happened, I was at another new high school. We were in PE class. Of course, the teams were divided the way that everything in high school is separated. The 'in-crowd,' made up of school athletes and pretty girls, were on one team, and I was on the outcasts team, made up of well . . . you know."

Cherene nodded in agreement. "Yeah, yeah, I know. Go on."

"So anyway, one of the other team's players had elbowed me a bunch of times, and she pushed me every time I got near her. I kept looking at the referee, who was one of 'them,' hoping she would call a foul, but she never did.

"The next time the player came near me, I bumped into her by accident. The ref called a foul on me and gave her a penalty kick. That sent me over the edge. The next thing I knew, the soccer ball mysteriously rose from the ground in front of me and smacked the referee in the face."

"That is too funny, Katie," Cherene said through her laughter.

"I thought that it was funny too, but the penalty kick cost my team the game. If I had had any real friends on my team, I might have gotten some high-fives for letting the ref have it. As it was, I became the outcast of the 'outcasts.' I think I got my PE grade lowered for unsportsmanlike conduct, too."

"Ouch, that hurts," Cherene said.

"I didn't know how I had managed such a feat. The ball never even touched my cleat. Luckily, no one else had focused too intently on my footwork, or lack thereof, or I would have been found out for the paranormal freak that I am!"

"This is amazing. It's like something you read about in a novel."

"That's me, a regular old character!"

"What was the first incident like? In fact, I want to know all about all the incidents," Cherene demanded.

Her friend's enthusiasm made Katie smile from ear to ear. She told Cherene about the first incident, and the ones that happened at school the day before.

"This is awesome, Katie!" Looking around the room from one thing to another, Cherene asked, "Can you make one of those encyclopedias on the bookcase move over here?"

Katie scanned the room, her impish smile lit up her face. "I have a better idea." She closed her eyes and focused all of her attention on the throw pillow on the far end of the couch. Cherene looked quizzically at Katie. A moment later, the pillow hit her in the back of the head.

Cherene gasped and both girls laughed out loud.

"Quiet, we'll wake my parents."

They spent the rest of the hour giggling, sharing stories, and plotting supernatural revenge on Christy. Cherene could hear the faint chime of her mother's grandfather clock in the upstairs hall. It was three o'clock in the morning. The girls made their way from the basement to Cherene's room upstairs. It was much warmer than down in the basement and the thick, lilac comforter on Cherene's queen-size bed was calling them to rest.

Before she went to sleep, Katie texted her mom back telling her she was sleeping over at Cherene's house.

~ 13 ~

BETTER LEFT UNREAD

Katie and Cherene woke up six hours later to the alarm clock. Cherene had promised her mom she would fill in for one of the workers at the ice-cream shop in the morning and work her regular shift later in the afternoon. Katie offered to help her friend at the shop.

When Katie woke up, she saw her mother had responded to her text with information. Her mom and Phil were getting up early to go to a wedding a few hours away and they did not expect to be back until later Saturday evening. Katie grinned while reading the text.

Good, there will be no one to give me the third degree when I stop by the house.

The girls took Katie's car back home so she could shower and change into fresh clothes before they headed to the shop. Running up the stairs to the shower she shouted back to

Cherene, "Help yourself to some breakfast."

"Okay."

While in the shower, Katie thought about how the events of the last twenty-four hours fit into the other anomalies that plagued her life. For the past two years, since her father left, she worried that she was some sort of a freak of nature. She thought that something was terribly wrong with her, but she could not be certain if it was real or if it were all in her own mind. Katie *still* did not know what she was or how she came to possess supernatural powers, but there was no longer any question about it; she had powers.

She wondered what other powers she possessed. Had she already experienced the scope of her magical abilities; were her powers limitless, or would they someday run out? Katie decided to be satisfied with what she knew and search for more answers another day. She was content in the knowledge that she could exercise control over her powers. Most of all, she was ecstatic that Cherene still wanted to be her friend; things were definitely looking up.

She turned off the shower, wrapped a towel around her head and threw on a robe. Katie ran down the stairs and into the kitchen. "Hey Cherene, what did you get for us to eat?"

"Um, Katie, I think you'd better come in here," Cherene said, her voice full of concern.

"What's up? Whatever it is, it can't ruin my day."

"Oh, it's just that I found this envelope here."

"Yeah, so. What is it?"

Unable to contain her excitement, Cherene grinned

from ear to ear and jumped up and down hitting Katie in the head with the manila envelope.

"You won! You won! We're going to camp!"

Katie's mind was trying to register what it was that Cherene said. She swiped the papers from her and read through them zealously, looking for the words. . . there they were, in bold black letters: **"YOUR ESSAY HAS BEEN CHOSEN AS ONE OF THE WINNING ESSAYS."**

Katie read the words slowly and looked up at Cherene. Cherene jumped into her arms. Each girl performed her own celebratory dance around the kitchen as if Katie had just won the lottery. For Katie, a two-week reprieve from the pressures of home and school felt like the lottery.

She tossed the notice on the table and ran over to the desk in the corner of the kitchen searching feverishly for a pen. They had let the time get away from them and should have already been on the road. Katie still needed to get dressed and leave Mom a note telling her where she was going.

"What are you doing?"

"I have to leave my mom a note," Katie said.

"Can't you just text her, Katie?" Cherene asked.

"I'll text her too, but Mom is always misplacing her phone or letting the battery run out when she is at a big event. I have to cover my bases because she will have a fit if she comes home from being gone out of town and doesn't find me."

"Okay, but hurry. I have to get to work."

Katie scurried back up the stairs and threw on some khaki pants and a white polo shirt. After pulling her hair up in a messy bun, she seemed to float down the stairs and back to the kitchen. She scanned the marble kitchen counters for a stray pen but did not see one. Katie shuffled the papers on the built-in kitchen desk again and opened and closed the drawers quickly, looking for something to write with.

Unable to find a working pen on the desk, Katie bolted down the hall and into the study. She did not usually go into the study since it was where Phil did all of his work. She made her way over to his desk. There was not anything to write with in plain sight, so she cracked open the top desk drawer, reached in and grabbed a heavy, gold-lined pen.

Okay, I've got the pen, but where is his paper? I can't very well scrawl a note in the mahogany wood like a caveman.

She pried his desk drawer all the way open and shuffled through the documents, looking for a little blank piece of paper.

She thumbed through pieces of mail, a flyer for fly-fishing, an old photo of Phil with his dad, and then she stopped. Under her right hand was a pale-blue paper with an official, golden seal on the bottom of it. Katie lifted it out gingerly, being careful not to disturb the other mail. She could not believe what she saw before her eyes.

It was a birth certificate but not her birth certificate. The name of the mother, father, and the little girl were all foreign to Katie.

Paper clipped to it was a certified letter; Katie read the

words across the top: Official Transfer of Parental Rights. It had Katie's first and last name, but where the names of her biological mother and father should be it did not have *her* mother and father's names. It had the names of two strangers.

This can't be right. It must be a mistake.

"Katie, hurry!" Cherene shouted from the kitchen.

Katie looked from the open door of the den and back to the desk. She was torn between wanting to investigate further and the sick feeling of never wanting to lay eyes on the papers again. She knew Cherene was not the patient type. Katie replaced the document exactly as she had found it.

As she shut the drawer, she stood for a moment; part of her wished she had not seen it all. Just when she thought she had almost conquered her mountain of uncertainty, an avalanche of doubt threatened to overtake her. She felt a sick sense of suffocating anxiety.

Pull it together, Katie. It's probably not what you think. You always think the worst.

Katie took a deep breath and steadied her thoughts.

I can't deal with this right now. I'll have to deal with it later.

She tried to lessen her worry by reminding herself that she had become a pro at dealing with the unknown. She had spent the last two years waiting for her father to come home, not knowing if or when he ever would.

Maybe that is why he has not come back. I am not even his daughter.

Katie shook the unwanted thought from her mind.

It is just too terrible to believe. It would explain a lot though.

Katie resolved to bury the undesirable information.

Her father, being a lawyer, had always taught her to wait until all the evidence was in before making a decision. Jumping to a conclusion at this point would be like sending a jury to deliberate the fate of a defendant's life with only one side having presented their case. Katie rationalized that she did not have all the facts. In fact, she did not even know if what she had were facts at all.

Maybe it was a sick joke, or maybe she had misread the document. She did not have time to look at it again. She would deal with it later. Right now, she had to go to work with her best friend. She scanned the wastebasket beside Phil's desk for a discarded piece of paper. She tore a small scrap of paper from an unwanted envelope and scribbled a quick note on it.

Why didn't I just do this before?

Katie walked back down the hall to the kitchen and pinned the note to the stainless-steel refrigerator with a magnet.

"Finally," Cherene said, exasperated.

She must be too obsessed with getting to work on time to notice that my world is crashing down around me. I guess it is for the best; I don't want to try to explain one more reason why I am a freak.

Katie grabbed her coat and car keys and slung her big black purse over her shoulder. "Let's get out of here," she said, her tone riddled with agitation.

Katie rushed towards the back door. As soon as Cherene made her way through the threshold, Katie slammed the door shut behind them forcing her key into the lock and turning it as quickly as she could as if she were trapping an evil demon within the walls of a haunted house rather than a piece of paper in her home. As if sealing the unwanted document inside would erase the fact that she had held it with her own hands and read it with her own eyes.

Katie knew she would have to deal with her demons eventually, but for now, she wanted to keep them locked away where they could not grasp ahold of her heart and tear it apart piece by piece.

~ 14 ~

WINTER CAMP

"Bye, Mom!" Katie smiled and waved as she turned away from her mom and rushed towards her best friend. Cherene met her with an excited smile, and the two girls made their way to the entrance of the bus. Once on board, they walked to the back of the bus to ready themselves for the two-hour ride. Both girls donned their earbuds and rested their heads against the pillows they had brought from home.

The city scenery outside the bus windows changed to snowy foothills and then to incredible, white-capped mountain peaks.

Cherene nudged Katie's arm. "Are you glad we're finally outta there?"

If only you knew.

Katie gave a manufactured grin. "I thought this day would never come! I can't wait for camp!" she said, feigning excitement to conceal the fact that she was still reeling from the information she had found inside of Phil's desk almost two weeks earlier. When Katie had tried to go back to look at the documents again, she discovered that someone had locked the drawer. Desperate to uncover the truth, she had tried to force the lock open with a paper clip, but the lock did not budge.

Katie sunk her head back into the soft pillow. Music filled her ears, but it could not drown out the worrisome thoughts that raced through her mind.

First, I find out I'm a freak of nature. Every time I go to a new high school I become more of a social leper, and now I might not even really be Katie Ryan. I wish I never had to come back to this awful place.

Cherene grinned back at Katie; she seemed to be unaware of her friend's internal dilemma. The girls returned to their shared silence. Katie turned her phone over in her hand and thumbed through her contacts. The picture of her sweet, gray-haired grandma stared back at her.

Maybe I should call Grandma Ceil. Surely, she wouldn't lie to me. Especially if I tell her I already know the secret, she might not feel like she is betraying Mom's confidence.

Katie scrolled up through the list; her dad's blonde hair and blue eyes caught her eye.

Blonde hair, blue eyes, and Mom has light brown hair and brown eyes.

Her unwelcomed thoughts were interrupted by the force of the bus jolting forward and back again. Katie's eyes found Cherene's familiar face. They beamed at one another excitedly.

"We're here!" they said in unison.

The girls followed the group of bus riders to a fence that was lined with the campers who had either driven themselves or had parents that insisted on bringing them to camp. Katie was glad Phil had talked her mom out of driving her to camp. She was sixteen for goodness sakes. She did not need her mommy chaperoning her trip to camp.

Mom only relented because Phil and Katie made a compromise. Katie would ride the bus to camp; thereby saving face in front of the kids she would be spending the next two weeks with. Mom and Phil would pick her up at the end of camp when there would not be any damage that could be done to her reputation.

Katie had thought it was odd that Phil had taken her side. She began to wonder if he had a "cool" side, but then settled on the reality that he probably just did not want to be bothered with taking *and* picking her up.

The counselors stood before the group of teens and instructed them to break into two groups: guys and girls. It was a simple enough request, but the protests of the campers could have been heard across the frozen lake.

"Are you serious?"

"We're all almost seniors. This sucks!" The chorus of discontent rang throughout the snow-covered forest as the teens shuffled reluctantly and found their place with either the boys' or girls' side of the line of camp counselors.

“Oh, look at that counselor over there,” Cherene boasted, pointing in the direction of a hot-looking guy. He was old enough to be a counselor, but still young enough to make the teenage girls gawk.

“Too bad he can’t be our counselor,” Katie added.

Cherene nodded in agreement. “I know, right?” Both girls giggled and looked around for their next topic of conversation.

Before they could settle on another hot guy for their approval, the head counselor, Oliver, clapped his hands together to get their attention. The campers looked in the direction of the noise. Oliver stood with his fists at his waist and his elbows held outward, which made him look more formidable than his short stature would normally allow. A light breeze blew his short, brown hair away from his face, making it stand on end.

“Can I have your attention, please?” Oliver began. “Cabin selection is about to start. Each counselor will read the names of the campers that will be in their cabin. You will go with your counselor and take your personal belongings with you to get settled in. Chow time is at five o’clock; last cabin in does the dishes.” Oliver cupped his hands together and smiled like a Cheshire cat.

Katie and Cherene looked at each other their eyes wide, silently wishing for the same cabin. Two female counselors called their groups and left. A short, athletic girl with dark, almond-shaped eyes stepped forward. Her black hair was cut in a sassy bob, longer in the front than the back.

Dark strands fell just below the line of her chin; she brushed a few stray pieces away from her mouth and said, "My name is Meagan Kim."

She began calling names, one by one, "Lauren, Sharylin, Cherene." Cherene grabbed Katie's hand; Katie closed her eyes and squeezed back tightly as the two listened for the rest of the cabin mates. "Kareisha, Riley…"

Please say Katie, please say Katie…

"And… Katie."

"Yes!" they said together. The girls grabbed their bags and headed off, up the snow-covered path towards their cabin. Excited chatter and laughs filled the air. Katie scanned the scene trying to take it all in. The branches of the tall pines were heavy with snow; the ground was covered with a thick blanket of soft snow that looked as smooth as glass. It was obvious that the last set of campers had respected the beautiful, natural landscape by sticking to the thin, white trail that had been carved out by the footsteps of those that had traveled the path before.

The path meandered through the tall pines, past several other cabins, and around a small, snow-covered hill. A small sized, wooden cabin stood at the base of the other side of the hill. The front porch was freshly shoveled and looked like a brown canvas dusted with salt. Smoke rose from the stone chimney of the mini lodge.

Meagan turned to face her charges for the next two weeks. "Here we are; it's your home away from home."

All the girls rushed towards the heavy, wooden door

pushing their way into the cabin. Once inside, Katie saw that the room was small but cozy. Twin-size bunk beds were set up against three of the walls. The fourth wall supported a bunk bed with a double-size mattress on the bottom and a twin bed on top. A red brick fireplace occupied the space adjacent to the big bed. Different sized pinecones were scattered on the mantle between three wooden frames that displayed portraits of nature.

I wonder who you have to bribe to get the big bed.

Knowing it was most likely for the counselor, she threw her rolled up sleeping bag on the bottom of the bunk opposite the big bed. Katie turned in a circle searching for the bathroom. It was not in plain sight.

"Uh, where's the restroom?" she asked.

"Oh, didn't they tell you?" Meagan inquired.

Katie looked puzzled.

"The cabins don't have inside plumbing. Walk to the bottom of the trail. The bathrooms are down by the lake."

Katie cocked her head and raised her eyebrows in disbelief.

"Seriously?" Riley asked. Her blue eyes were wide with disbelief. Riley was a little taller than Katie. Her dishwater blonde hair was pulled back into a long pony; it swished side to side as Riley turned her head from one group of girls to another, her blue eyes searching the cabin for girls who were as astonished as she was at the prospect of no indoor plumbing.

"You've got to be kidding," Cherene chimed in.

"This *is* the twenty-first century, you know!" Riley added, still astounded at Meagan's disclosure.

The room quickly became a hive of angry hornets. Agitated voices filled the small space, but Meagan did not lose her head.

She jumped up on the edge of the double mattress and announced, "Girls, girls, it's just a little snag! Look on the bright side; we're the closest of any of the other cabins."

Meagan's bubbly voice calmed some of the agitation, but the air still rang with a chorus of discord. Long sighs and groans threatened to overtake the room. Meagan jumped off her bed and pulled a huge bag from the top of her dresser drawer. She held the bag up high, the bright colors catching the frustrated campers' attention. Meagan shook the bottles of nail polish, cotton balls, and lotion out on her bed.

"Who wants to do manicures and pedicures?" she asked smiling at the girls with bright eyes that could not be denied.

The girls fought for the colors they wanted and settled down on their respective bunks. Cherene and Katie got the black polish and set to work on touching up their nails. Calm settled over the group and small chitchat could be heard.

Their spa time was interrupted by the ringing of a loud bell.

"What's that?" Lauren questioned, startled. Lauren shared the bunk to the left of Katie and Cherene. What Lauren lacked in stature, she made up for with her wit. She wore her long, dark hair away from her light brown face in a headband which accentuated her big brown eyes.

"Oh, that's just the warning bell for chow time," Meagan reassured her.

"Chow time? What, do they think we're dogs or something?" Cherene asked laughing at her own joke.

Katie joined in their innocent banter, "No, that is probably what they call the food because it looks like dog food."

"Let's just hope it doesn't taste like dog food," Lauren said.

The girls finished polishing their nails. Some fanned their toenails to help the polish dry quicker. Nobody wanted to be late for "chow" time.

When the last of the polish was put away, Meagan opened two of the windows to let the room air out. The girls filed out of the cabin and headed down the small, snowy path towards the mess hall.

As they approached the dining area, they were met by many other campers with the same goal in mind: not doing the dishes. Each group of cabin mates pushed to get through the door and rushed towards the table with the name of their cabin on it.

Katie and Cherene settled into their spots at the table with the other girls in Meagan's cabin. The noise of the crowded hall quickly faded as Oliver, the head counselor, banged on a big skillet with a metal spoon. "It looks like we have one table missing. Jackson, take Matt with you and find out where the girls in Chatty Patty's cabin are," he ordered.

"You got it, boss!" Jackson yelled in Oliver's direction. Jackson grabbed Matt by his collar and said under his breath, "Come on Matt, we don't want to keep the commander waiting."

"Someone should tell this guy he's a camp counselor, not a drill sergeant," Matt added as the two left the mess hall.

Oliver continued, "Okay, while we're waiting for the last group, let's get the rules of the mess hall down. First, just because it is called a mess hall doesn't mean we want it to be left in a mess. Each cabin will take a turn cleaning off the tables, but as I said earlier, the last cabin to their table will do the dishes after each meal. Second, and I hope this goes without saying, no food fights. Finally. . ."

"You can't make me do the dishes!" a loud voice yelled from outside; its echo resonating throughout the mess hall.

"I know that's right," another voice screeched. The sound of it made Katie cringe.

It couldn't be. How could this be happening to me? What did I do to deserve this?

In the doorway, to all of Katie's dismay and horror, stood Destiny and Christy.

"Yo D, Yo C…waz up?" another familiar voice echoed from the crowd. Katie craned her neck to look three tables behind her.

This cannot be happening.

She closed her eyes and sighed deeply. There was no mistaking that voice; it was him.

Where did he come from? And how did I not see him before now?

Darrell jumped out of his seat and was making his way towards Destiny and Christy.

The three friends exchanged fist pounds and hugs, so caught up in themselves that they were oblivious to the fact that they were disturbing the entire mess hall. Katie glanced over at Cherene; the two exchanged knowing looks.

My arch nemesis and her two faithful sidekicks. Are they stalking me now?

Katie hung her head and ate her meal in silence.

After dinner, the campers made their way back to their cabins. To kill time before campfire, the girls sat around talking and making leather lanyards from long strips of colored leather.

"Are you okay?" Cherene inquired.

"I just can't believe it. I came here to get away from them. I think I want to go home."

"Oh, no you don't. How am I going to explain to my mom and dad that I no longer want to study the amazing scenic art displayed in this majestic, snow-laden forest?"

Katie let out a laugh and could not help but smile. "Is that the reason you gave for wanting to come to camp?"

"Yep."

"And your parents bought that?"

"I guess so. I think they secretly wanted to be rid of me for a couple of weeks anyway," Cherene speculated.

"Don't say that."

"No seriously, they are having their twenty-year anniversary in a couple of days. They were probably planning on having my aunt come and stay at the house with me while they went on a second honeymoon or something. I just saved them the trouble," Cherene explained.

"That makes sense, but I still want to go home. I came here to get away from them."

"Maybe they didn't see you yet!" Cherene offered trying to be as optimistic as she could when faced with the fact that their nemesis and her evil sidekicks just crashed their two week reprieve from the drama at school. Katie rolled her eyes and gave Cherene a doubtful look.

"Who didn't see who yet?" Sharylin interrupted.

Katie and Cherene looked at one another, wide-eyed. Katie contemplated whether she should divulge her secret to this new girl.

Sharylin's mannerisms made Katie think of her as a Mini Meagan. Although their outward appearances contrasted drastically, their small stature and cheerful personalities matched perfectly.

Anyone as sweet as her couldn't possibly betray someone.

"There are some girls and a guy here from my school," Katie answered.

"Who?" Sharylin asked. Sharylin was almost a whole head shorter than Katie. Her shoulder-length blonde hair framed her face, making her bright blue eyes pop.

"Did you see the girls that showed up to dinner late

and the guy that came running up to them?"

"Oh, them," Sharylin responded.

She knows them. Maybe I shouldn't say any more. I don't need to end up with more enemies.

"They are terrible!" Sharylin exclaimed. "They have been here every year that I've been here, and I've been coming since I was six. They used to be nice, well sort of. The last couple of years though, they have been wretched."

"Wretched? How?" Lauren asked.

"Last summer, there was a boating incident. A boy fell out of a canoe and the staff couldn't find him. One of the campers discovered him hiding up in a tree, stripped down to his underwear. No one could prove anything, and it was not even a case of his word against someone else's. He could not even talk for a whole month. When he finally spoke, he would not tell anyone what happened to him."

"That doesn't prove it was them, though," Kareisha stated.

"You're right, but they were the last ones to be seen with him on the lake," Sharylin explained.

"Still—" Kareisha started.

"They were all in the same canoe, Kareisha."

"Oh," Kareisha said and looked down at the wooden floor of the cabin.

"I can't believe it. That's sick!" Katie said, shocked and disgusted at the prospect of what they could have done to make someone not talk for a whole month.

"Sick nothing, that's insane," Lauren chimed in.

"Forget background checks for counselors, they need to fingerprint the campers," Riley asserted.

Katie considered that for a moment.

What do I really know about any of these people? For that matter, they don't know me either. In fact, what they don't know about me could hurt them. Geez, I don't even know all about me. Maybe everyone has some deep, dark secret they're trying to figure out and at the same time trying to appear normal to the rest of the world.

Katie looked around the room trying to determine what each of their secrets might be.

What would Grandma Ceil tell me to do?

"Look into their eyes, Katie. Then you'll know the truth," Grandma had once told her.

Katie studied Sharylin's eyes. They were the prettiest blue eyes she'd ever seen, except for her grandmother's eyes, of course. Her grandmother's eyes had a brilliant twinkle of light that welcomed everyone.

At first glance, Sharylin's eyes seemed to shift from baby blue to dark blue, but the longer Katie looked at Sharylin's eyes they seemed to be transforming into dark, shadowy orbs.

Katie cocked her face a little to the side, almost entranced by Sharylin's morphing eyes.

Her eyes are dark and mysterious—not trustworthy. But I don't understand. She looked so nice at first.

"It is what is on the inside that counts," Katie could hear her grandmother's voice inside her own head.

Katie snapped herself out of her trance and shifted her eyes from one side to the other. Katie could hear that the conversation had gone on without her. The girls were laughing and chatting about crazy campers.

"One year, when I was fourteen, my best friend fell for one of the guy counselors," Riley was saying.

"Can you say cradle robber boys and girls?" Lauren asked no one in particular.

"It wasn't like that," Riley corrected. "The counselor was a junior counselor, so he was sixteen."

"Information that would have been helpful a minute ago," Kareisha, the tall, caramel-skinned girl declared as she glared at Riley through dark green accusing eyes.

Laughter erupted throughout the small cabin.

Rolling her eyes, Riley continued. "Anyway, as I was saying, she fell for this counselor. My cabin mates and I planned a crazy trick on them."

Great, just what I need. Another Christy in my very own cabin. There must be something in the DNA of blonde-haired girls that makes them act cruel.

"So, you're a bully then?" Kareisha said, her tone more accusation than question.

"No, it was a funny joke, and my friend laughed more about it than we did."

"Yeah, right!" Kareisha argued, her chocolate-brown spirals brushed her shoulders as she shook her head back and forth in disbelief.

"Do you want to hear what happened, or do you plan

on playing the morality police for the next two weeks?" Lauren asked.

"I'm not the morality police. Although, some people act like they might need some help in the morals area," Kareisha retorted, looking down her nose at Riley and Lauren.

Lauren shook her head as she rolled her eyes and turned to take Riley's hands in her own. "Go ahead, Riley, some of us have a sense of humor here. Tell me what happened."

"I want to know too!" Katie and Cherene chimed in together. They looked at each other and smiled. Kareisha sat back on her bed, pretending not to listen. Sharylin and Meagan listened from Meagan's bed as the two of them thumbed through the teen magazines that were spread out on the open sleeping bag.

Riley continued, "Okay, so the two of them were supposed to meet in secret on the dock after lights out. We dressed up one of the guys from another cabin in my friend's dress. We walked him to the dock and hid. When the counselor got there, he immediately put the moves on "her." Before the counselor realized what was happening, he had hugged and kissed our guy friend who was disguised in the dress."

"No way!" Lauren laughed, "That's classic!"

"You're too funny Riley!" Katie said.

At least she's not a bully. A little harmless fun never hurt anyone.

A stifled laugh came from Kareisha's bunk. "That *is*

funny, Riley!"

Riley glanced at Kareisha and said, "I knew you would see the humor in it! It was all everyone could talk about for the rest of the week that summer." Riley pulled Kareisha off her bunk. "Grab your coat. It is going to be cold at campfire tonight."

"I'll be sure to keep on your good side, Riley. I would not want to be your enemy," Cherene added as she pulled on her hat and gloves.

"Come on girls, let's get to the campfire!" Meagan directed. As she opened the cabin door, a light wind and tiny snowflakes pushed their way inside.

~ 15 ~

DARK SHADOWS

The girls were the last group to arrive at the campfire. All the other cabins sat surrounding the huge bonfire. Behind the fire, a large, half-moon shaped, concrete stage had been built. Oliver was parading around in a bear costume.

He was banging on a drum that looked like a picnic basket and yelling for everyone to be quiet. It was hard to take him seriously in that getup, but eventually, one by one, the groups of campers settled down and gave him their full attention.

Katie glanced around to see if she could see Christy and her clan. She heard them before she saw them. "Hey Yogi, what's in the picnic basket?" Darrell's booming voice interrupted the silence, and the whole group of campers erupted in laughter.

Katie shook her head in disgust. Even though the

comment was a little comical, she would not allow herself to laugh at Darrell's attempt to demean the head counselor.

"It'll be your campfire privilege if you shout out like that again, son," Oliver countered.

"Man, I'm not your son," Darrell started, but his comment was interrupted by the head counselor's admonishment.

"If you know what's good for you, *son…*" the crowd broke out in oh's and ah's, "simmer down now, simmer down," Oliver instructed. "If it's alright with all of you, I would like to start this campfire before morning light."

The crowd calmed down. Katie was listening to Oliver, but she felt as if someone were staring at her.

Oh great, they've seen me. Now, I will be their target.

She looked to the area where Darrell, Christy, and Destiny were sitting. None of them were looking at her, but she could not shake the strange sense that someone was watching her. She changed her focus from the dreadful trio back to the stage.

Oliver continued, "After the ghost story, the counselors will have a skit to share with all of you. Please treat others as you would want to be treated. No talking when someone else has the stage."

Oliver looked around to see that everyone was still at attention. "Without further ado, I'd like to introduce Sharylin. She's been coming to camp for years and years, and she'll share her version of the 'Cavern Escapade.' Sharylin, the floor is yours!"

The campers clapped and gave Sharylin a warm welcome. Her blonde hair was bobbing from side to side as she walked up the stairs and across the stage. Some whistles came from the audience.

She raised her hand and waved to the crowd. "Thank you, thank you!" Her bubbly voice rang out throughout the group. "If you'll settle down, I have a story for you!"

The group quieted quickly, interested in what she had to share. Sharylin closed her eyes, breathed in deeply, and when she opened her eyes, a dark shadow appeared across her face.

"Did you see that?" Cherene gasped.

"Sugar Sweet looks super scary now!" said Lauren.

"Either someone invented a Shady Shadow Caster Machine, or that girl just turned half-demon," Riley added.

"Shush, I want to hear the story," Kareisha said.

"But…" Riley started.

"Shush…" Katie and Kareisha said in unison.

Katie remembered how Sharylin's eyes shifted to dark steel marbles right before her eyes earlier.

I thought I was just seeing things again earlier. Now her whole face is dark, and everyone else sees it too. Maybe, she is evil.

Her rational side cut in.

Maybe it is just some special effects with the lighting.

It was as if a black gloom had covered the stage. All the light that had been reflecting off the snow had vanished. It seemed that the whole universe had faded away and the only thing left was a petite, young girl turned demon. Sharylin had everyone's attention as she began her story of the "Cavern Escapade."

"It was a dark and dreary night. The moon shone through the fog-filled evening sky. In fact, it was a night much like tonight. Two young girls snuck away from their cabins just before midnight. They wandered far into the woods in search of an adventure. They never knew what an adventure they were about to discover.

"The branches of the trees were heavy with snow. The storm from the previous night had left the trail completely covered by a blanket of snow. The girls tramped through the forest making their own path. The wind was howling, begging for them to follow it."

The wind was howling like that the day I first came to Salem. I wonder if they had the same bad feeling I did as they walked down the dark, snow-covered path.

"One of the girls came to an abrupt stop. There, before their eyes, was an entrance to an old cave. They ventured inside and were pleased to discover that the cave kept the chill at bay.

"One of the girls noticed a small opening to the right. They crawled through the opening, anxious about what they would find next. And do you know what they found?"

Sharylin scanned the group of entranced campers before continuing.

"They found a narrow passage that led them through a corridor. The girls followed the path through the cave to what appeared to be a dead end, but one of the girls noticed a glistening light coming from a small crack in the stone wall. She peeled away small pieces of the old stone, and the wall crumbled to pieces before her eyes.

"A beautiful room emerged with a sensational fountain in the middle of a dark pool of water. The pond was surrounded by an arbor. Mesmerized by the scene before them, they walked to the edge of the water. It was dark; the darkness drew them in and caused them to fall into a trance. The water lapped at the toes of their shoes. When the water receded, a golden shimmer was left on their shoes. One of the girls reached down to find out what it was. Tiny specs of gold glistened on her fingertips.

"'Is that what I think it is?' one girl asked.

"'If it is, we're going to be rich,' the other said.

"The girls embraced one another and jumped up and down at the prospect of finding a pool of gold.

"'How will we get it back to camp?'

"'We have to go back and get something to take this back to camp with us.'

"The two girls turned around, about to leave the room." The rhythm of Sharylin's speech slowed and her voice grew frighteningly hoarse.

"Before they could take a single step, a dark creature appeared before them. 'Just where do you think you are going, my dears?' the creature's question a veiled threat.

"Wide-eyed and horrified, the girls were paralyzed by fear. Neither spoke. The old crone raised her wrinkled, withered hands above her head and muttered words in a language unfamiliar to the girls. The girls closed their eyes and braced themselves for what the old witch had in store for them. As her incantation came to a slow end, the girls opened their eyes to see a beautiful, young, blonde-haired, blue-eyed woman standing before their eyes. Both girls breathed a sigh of relief. There could not possibly be anything scary about something so beautiful.

"One of the girls said, 'Oh thank goodness, we thought you were going to kill us.'

"The lovely young woman before them smiled, her midnight-blue eyes dancing in the dim light of the cavern.

"'What makes you so certain I am *not* going to kill you?' the creature said in a too sweet voice trying to mask the malice of her question. The girls embraced each other, steeling themselves for the worst. A maniacal cackle filled the cave.

"'Don't be such sillies. How would someone like little 'ole me hurt anyone?' Eerie laughter echoed throughout the cave, like the distant sounds of ethereal children long since departed from this world, their tiny voices laughing and singing in a meadow consumed by fog."

Sharylin stopped the story, letting the effect of the haunting laughter of the ghostlike children run through the campers' minds.

Katie could almost hear the sweet, yet spooky, hollow tones of the children's voices filling the night air. An unnerving feeling that someone was watching her flooded her being. She glanced around to see if Christy's crew was looking her way, but their eyes were fixed on Sharylin. Katie tried to shake off the feeling, but it tightened its grip, refusing to turn loose.

As a chill ran down Katie's spine; she wrapped her arms around herself and looked back in Sharylin's direction.

Blonde hair, blue eyes, sweet voice. Was the villain in the story, Sharylin? It's just a story, Katie. It's just a story. But there is something that is just not right about that girl. Shake it off, Katie. It's just a story.

Sharylin smiled sweetly at the crowd. Her blue eyes were dancing in the firelight. Her voice soft and spooky, she continued with her dark tale.

"The girls looked from one side of the cavern to the other trying to find the joyful yet lost little children. The beautiful creature's voice turned from eerily sweet to deep and hoarse. Her blue eyes narrowed as a daunting grin split her face. 'You will not find them dearies.'

"'But...why?' the girls cried out in unison, their eyes pleading for mercy.

"'Because...' she breathed the words as if there were fire in her throat, 'they're dead!'

"The word dead echoed throughout the cave. Each girl gasped, horrified at the sight before them. The sweet, blonde girl had morphed back into an old, withered crone. Her maniacal laughter reverberated off the moist walls of the cave.

"'Hahahahahahahahahahahahahahaha...they're dead, my dearies. Like you.'

"The dark creature flung her hands at the girls and a

black gust of air swept through their beings, devouring them in an instant. Their screams chilled the cavern."

The camp crowd gasped. Gooseflesh formed on Katie's arms and a shiver went up her spine. Her mind flashed back to the magical dreams that she had been having.

Could there be a connection? Could this place truly exist?

She peered through the crowd to see Sharylin perched on the edge of the stone stage. The dark shadow was still hiding two-thirds of her face. For a moment, Katie thought Sharylin looked straight into her eyes. A devilish smile crept over Sharylin's face, and the dark steel marbles that were her eyes seemed to peer deep into Katie.

Katie gasped. *What's happening to her?*

The gloom over Sharylin's face disappeared and was replaced by the light cast from the lamppost on the side of the stage. Her eyes were dancing with blue brilliance once again, and the night seemed to be set right as Sharylin continued her narrative.

"Some say that when the moon is high in the sky and there is a misty fog looming over the lake you can still hear the voices of the lost children. If you listen closely, you might even be able to hear the screams of the two campers that went looking for a little adventure in the middle of the dark night."

Sharylin stood up; the crowd of campers erupted into applause. Hoots and hollers from the audience filled the chilly evening air.

"Thank you. Thank you," Sharylin said. She bowed

and bounced off the stage in the direction from which she had come.

Oliver took center stage in his bear costume clapping his paws together. "See, I told you it would be a treat! Sharylin is quite the storyteller. Now it is time for the counselors' skits."

The counselors took the stage and performed for the eager crowd. Katie was mildly amused, but again, she felt as if someone was watching her. She did not even bother looking around. She knew her efforts would be fruitless.

Katie tried to focus on the skits, but her thoughts turned towards the story Sharylin had told.

It is as if she took a page straight out of my dreams: the cave, the fountain, the creature, and the eerie feeling that I can't seem to shake.

Katie's thoughts were interrupted by a strong hand on her shoulder. She gasped and turned abruptly to find her eyes locked with the familiar deep pools of blue.

"Brian, what…"

Brian's smile spread across his face. His eyes were dancing in the firelight. "Katie, they told me you were here, but I didn't believe it."

Katie was caught off guard. She was excited to see Brian, but she did not want him to know that.

What's the deal with this guy? Every time I see him, I get butterflies in my stomach, and I can't think straight. But he's part of their group; I can't let myself have feelings for him.

"Well, I would have a hard time believing them if I were you, too." Katie snapped back. "I guess that is what happens when you hang out with liars and bullies."

"Katie, I . . . Well, I just wanted to say hey. I'm glad you're here." Brian's smile faded as he turned on his heel and left.

"Who was that hot guy?" Lauren asked.

"You didn't tell us you had connections, Katie," Riley added, seeming not to notice the fact that Katie was still flustered from her encounter with Brian.

Cherene jumped in to deflect the overly excited girls. "Girls, girls, just chill! Katie doesn't want to talk about that guy. He's part of 'the group.'"

"Oh, scary," Sharylin chimed in.

"I guess you would know about scary; wouldn't you, Sharylin?" Katie added, raising an accusing eyebrow.

"What's that supposed to mean, Katie?" Sharylin asked with hurt bewilderment.

Katie's eyes shifted to each of the girls. They were staring at her as if she had just stabbed Sharylin in the back with a knife. "Oh, I didn't mean anything bad. I just meant that you know how to tell a good scary story, so you would know about scary stuff."

What she really meant was that she was totally suspicious of Sharylin and her eyes that were blue oceans one moment and dark storm clouds the next. She also knew that if she divulged her suspicions, she may never get to the bottom of what Sharylin was all about, not to mention the fact that she did not need more people against her here at camp. There were only so many places she could hide in the middle of nowhere in the middle of winter. She could not tick-off everyone at camp.

"Okay girls, let's get back to our cabin," Meagan insisted. "It gets really spooky out here when everyone disappears into their cabins."

Katie looked in Meagan's direction, startled by what she witnessed. Meagan's eyes turned dark and stormy, just like Sharylin's. The next instant, they were brown again.

Please don't let me start seeing things again. I must be frustrated because of Brian. Why am I letting him get to me like this? He's just a guy; a guy who is part of Christy's stupid group. But he looks so cute when he smiles, and he keeps talking to me. Get a grip, Katie.

Katie noticed that the whole group had advanced so far into the forest that she could not see them anymore.

"Hey guys, wait for me," Katie yelled into the freezing night air as she sprinted in the direction that her cabin mates had walked.

~ 16 ~

TOO GOOD TO BE TRUE

The next morning, amidst the smell of eggs and sausage in the mess hall, Oliver gave the campers a choice between going on a snowshoe hike to a neighboring camp or up to the old lodge to go skiing. Katie had spent a little too much time waiting for her cabin mates to make up their minds about which event they wanted to attend, so she had to run faster than was probably safe through the snowy woods to the pick-up site for the skiing expedition. As she hustled breathlessly around the last turn, Katie heard the rumbling of the bus engine and saw the black exhaust escaping from the back of the dilapidated, old school bus. A small line of students was assembled waiting for their turn to get on the bus. Katie was the last to arrive. When it was her turn, she made her way up the rubber-lined steps of the bus and scanned the almost empty rows of seats to determine where she should sit.

Her eyes locked with Brian's blue eyes. Time seemed to stop. Everything in her peripheries was blurred, as if she and Brian were only people on the bus. Katie half expected a sappy love song to start playing on the bus's outdated radio system. She shook her head to clear her thoughts. Brian, still smiling from ear to ear, was waving for her to sit by him. Without thinking, Katie walked towards Brian and sat in the row next to his.

I can't believe I just did that. He's with them. He's the enemy. How am I going to get out of this without being too obvious?

Katie looked around the bus for a reason to get up and move. There, towards the back of the bus, a girl was sitting all by herself. Katie started to get up. "I think I should go and sit by her; she's all alone."

Brian reached out quickly and grasped her hand. "Don't!" he said his voice loud and demanding.

Katie's eyes grew wide; she shifted her focus from his face to where his hand was gripping her arm tightly. Through her own shock, she managed to say, "What are you doing?"

Brian quickly removed his hand.

"Sorry. I meant to say, 'Please don't go. I really want to sit by you.'"

Katie sat back down and eyed him suspiciously.

"Why?" she asked.

"Why?"

"Why do you want to sit by me? You barely even

know me."

"Remember the first day you came to school, and I saw you in the hallway?"

"Yes," Katie said casting her eyes away from his stare. Her thoughts returned to that moment when they had first seen each other. There was something about his eyes that had drawn her to him.

"I thought to myself, 'Wow. There is someone that I would like to get to know.' You are beautiful, Katie."

"So, you want me to sit by you because you think I'm pretty?"

"That isn't all, Katie."

She looked at him shaking her head from side to side, her green eyes wide.

"Seriously, there is more. Stop looking at me crazy and I'll tell you."

"Crazy? You mean like this?" Katie bugged her eyes out and made a silly face.

Brian laughed and grabbed both of her hands in his. "Yes, exactly like that! That is what I like about you. You say and do whatever you want, and you don't seem to care what others think."

Katie looked at him and could not help but smile.

"That and the fact that you said your favorite book is *Pride and Prejudice*."

"Oh my goodness, you like *Pride and Prejudice* too?" Katie could not contain her excitement.

"I admit it; I am an English dork. I plan to major in

English Lit in college," Brian confessed. "Although, I do have to say that I am more of a *Wuthering Heights* fan."

"Oh, please tell me you're not brooding and foreboding like Heathcliff," Katie retorted.

"I said I like the book *Wuthering Heights* better. As far as me as a person, I guess you could compare me more to Mr. Darcy."

"What, the whole 'too good for the rest of the world, full of pride and personal prejudices' part? That explains your choice of friends," Katie blurted out and regretted it immediately.

Why did I say that? He's trying to be nice. And he looks so hot in his ski gear!

"Actually, I was thinking more along the lines of the highly educated, romantic, nice kind of guy that falls for a girl that—"

"He thinks he is too good for?" Katie interrupted.

"No, I was going to say he falls for a girl that won't give him the time of day."

"Oh. Sorry."

"Don't be sorry. It didn't end badly for Mr. Darcy and Elizabeth," he smiled and raised his eyebrows up and down daringly.

The sincerity of his gaze mesmerized her. She could not help herself; she smiled back as her cheeks turned a bright shade of red. She looked away, hoping he did not notice that she was blushing. They rode the rest of the small drive to the ski lodge listening to the music that was playing on the bus speaker system.

Was he just comparing us to Elizabeth and Mr. Darcy? Does he think we could be a couple?

Katie mulled the idea of it over in her mind. She was definitely attracted to Brian. He was smart, funny, and very cute. He had also showed he could be compassionate when his friends were trying to hurt her and Cherene. The thought of having a boyfriend again made her smile.

She cast her glance in his direction.

Oh goodness, he's looking at me.

Katie smiled and quickly turned away again.

He probably thinks I am crazy.

The bus came to a halt. Brian reached over and grabbed Katie's bag before she could grab it. She started to protest but decided to let him be a gentleman. They made their way off the bus and to the lodge.

The campers were divided into guys and girls and sent to two different small changing rooms, so they could make last minute adjustments to their clothes and leave their bags while they skied.

Katie made her way to the bottom of the slope to meet up with the other campers. A sun-tanned man who was dressed in all black professional grade ski attire was speaking.

"Okay, can I get your attention now? I will be your ski instructor. Everyone up at the lodge calls me Clyde. You can call me anything you like; just don't call me late for my tee time!" He laughed at his own joke. "Get it? Tee time? Golf?"

A few of the teens laughed, but most of them looked

around at each other, clearly not getting his joke.

Clyde shook his head and pointed to a short woman dressed in bright yellow ski gear. “This is my assistant, LaTonda,” he said.

Her kinky black hair was spilling out of her ski cap and brushing against her shoulders.

“We will be giving basic lessons on how to ski.”

LaTonda stepped forward. “Let’s start by having everyone who already knows how to ski step over to the left. I will give you a quick rundown of the rules of our ski lodge, so you can get started right way. Then I will come back and help with the new skiers.”

Most of the campers moved to the left with LaTonda. Katie found herself standing with three girls—the non-skiers.

Brian already knows how to ski. I should have known. That’s alright; I don’t need to spend any more time with him. With his group of friends, we wouldn’t last anyway.

“That means you ladies are with me,” Clyde said. “Let’s head over to the bunny hill and get started.”

Katie walked with the other girls towards a small, snow-covered hill.

As Clyde was giving instructions, Katie felt someone behind her. She glanced back to find Brian beaming at her. She tilted her head to the side and looked at him quizzically.

“I thought it would be more fun to brush up on my skills with you,” he whispered. Katie smiled and despite herself even let out a little giggle.

After the basic beginner’s lessons, Brian and Katie

held on to the rope tow and let it pull them to the top of the small hill. At the top of the hill, Katie was full of excitement. She could not wait to try her new skills.

Brian made a grand gesture with his arm. “Ladies first,” he said.

Katie smiled through gritted teeth. “Here I go! Wish me luck!” She pushed off with her poles and began her descent.

“Luck!” Brian yelled and set off down the hill after her. He could hear her screaming with excitement as she passed the first small tree that marked the halfway mark of the bunny hill.

Katie almost crashed into Clyde at the bottom of the hill. Stopping was harder than she realized, so she was grateful that he was there to break her fall. “Easy now, you’ve got to be smarter than the skis girl,” Clyde teased.

“Hey, I’m just glad I didn’t roll all the way down the hill!” Katie announced pumping her poles in the air like an Olympic skier after a record-breaking run.

Brian slid next to them and stopped like a pro. “I knew you could do it, Katie!” he said.

“We just have to work on her stopping technique,” Clyde said.

“I’ll help Katie,” Brian offered sliding closer to her.

“I think you’re in good hands then,” Clyde proclaimed as he skied off to help two other girls. His voice echoed through the hills, “Okay girls, I’ve got good news and bad news; which do you want first?”

Katie laughed at Clyde's silly ways and looked at Brian. He was looking down at her through serious blue eyes, his mouth turned up at the corners.

"Are you sure you wouldn't rather be on the slopes skiing than playing on the bunny hill with me?" Katie asked looking up at him trying to keep from showing her excitement.

"I am exactly where I want to be," Brian said and placed his arm around her waist to lead her back to the rope tow to try it again.

~ 17 ~

PRANKS

The bus arrived back at camp after the sun had disappeared and the moon was peeking through the tall pine trees. As they left the bus, they began to walk towards their cabins down the snow-dusted path that was lit only by moonlight and a few carefully placed black wrought-iron lampposts. Brian reached down and held Katie's hand.

"I'm glad I decided to go skiing today," Brian said, glancing down at Katie.

"Me too," Katie said, smiling up at Brian. "Although, I was a little curious as to why you weren't with your friends."

"I could ask you the same question," Brian teased.

"Well, my cabin mates wanted to check out the guys at the other camp. I have never been skiing, so I wanted to give it a try. Besides, I figured I could check out guys anytime," Katie said, raising her eyebrows up and down and smiling flirtatiously. "Now quit stalling and tell me why you didn't go with your friends today."

Brian chuckled and looked around the forest, scanning the tall, snowy pines.

Katie turned her head from side to side, surveying the woods. "What are you looking at?"

"The forest has eyes and ears, you know," Brian said trying to sound spooky.

"Don't say that; you're giving me the creeps," Katie scolded with a grin.

Brian laughed loudly. He stopped in the middle of the snowy trail and turned to face Katie. He grabbed hold of her other hand and held both in his.

"Do you want the truth or the reason I told my friends I wasn't going with them?" Brian asked.

"What do you think?" Katie responded, giving him an expectant look.

"Right, the truth," Brian said. "The truth is that I wanted to get away from Christy, Darrell, and Destiny for the afternoon."

"But they are your friends."

"Yes, but I can tolerate only so much of their senseless humor, especially when they direct it towards undeserving victims."

"So you *don't* approve of how mean they are to others?"

"Of course not."

"Then why do you hang out with them?"

"You know how it is at school, Katie. Everything at school is based on cliques. If you're not 'in,' you're 'out.' There is no middle ground."

"True," Katie said.

She thought back to when she was popular. Even when you were "in," a person was always one wrong move from being on the outside. Being on the outside for the last couple of years had taken its toll on Katie. There were so many times she wished she could be popular again. Katie wondered what she might be willing to do to keep her social standing.

Maybe I am being too tough on him. No, there is no excuse for being a bully. But then I have never actually witnessed Brian being a bully. Besides, what did Grandma used to say? "Don't judge a man until you have walked a mile in his shoes."

Brian continued, "I have always been 'in.' I don't want to know what it's like to be 'out.'"

"I know what you mean," she started.

"Is it like that with your group too?" Brian interrupted.

"No, but I wasn't always in the group I am now. When I was a freshman, I was part of the 'in-crowd' too."

"So you *do* get it then?"

"Yes and no," Katie said.

Brian furrowed his brows. "What do you mean?"

"I understand wanting to be in the popular group at school, but my friends were never bullies like your friends."

"Do you really think of them as bullies, Katie?"

"What do you call it, Brian?"

"I know Christy and Destiny can conjure up some insane plans, but most of them are harmless enough."

"Unless of course you are one of their victims, Brian," Katie said, disgust creeping into her tone.

Brian dropped Katie's hands. He ran his hands through his hair and held them at the back of his head. He stood solemnly watching Katie's expression.

Katie eyed him, trying to read his expression.

This just got way too serious.

Brian broke his silence, "I see your point, Katie."

Katie let out a short sigh of relief, and smiled as she nudged him with her shoulder. "I knew you would see it my way."

Brian reached down and grabbed her hand in his. "I better get you back to your cabin before campfire."

"Yes, we can continue our discussion about your bullies, I mean friends, later," Katie teased.

Brian shook his head and smirked. "I am going to quit while I am ahead."

"Who said you were ahead?" Katie asked, shooting him a cheesy grin.

They walked hand in hand until they arrived at her cabin. Standing at the bottom of the steps, Katie could hear her cabin mates inside, talking and laughing. She looked down at the ground, too shy to look Brian in the eye. It had been a long time since a boy walked Katie home.

"Well, thanks for everything today, Brian."

"No, thank you. I haven't had fun like that since, well,

ever."

Katie considered his words as she looked into his blue eyes.

Is he for real? What do I say to that? I feel the same way. What if this is some cruel joke?

"Um, I guess I don't know quite what to say to that," Katie said.

"Say you had the most fun ever, too," Brian offered.

A mischievous smile crept over Katie's face. "*You* had the most fun ever, too!"

He shook his head back and forth. "See…just like I said… you're crazy!"

Their laughter was interrupted by the sound of Riley flinging open the door of the cabin. Cherene and Riley stood side by side at the open entrance.

"I told you I heard voices," Cherene announced, looking back at the girls in the cabin. "Hey guys, Katie's back."

"And look what the cat dragged in," Lauren added, jumping up between Cherene and Riley so that she could be seen.

"Hot guy alert," said Riley.

"Katie, I—" Sharylin started to say.

"Hey, where's the fire?" Kareisha asked, pushing her way to the front of the crowd.

The whole group of girls broke out in knowing laughter as Cherene dragged Katie into the cabin by her arm. "Thanks for bringing our girl home, Brian," she shouted.

The door slammed shut on Brian, but the elated grin on his face remained.

Brian started on his way back to his own cabin.

As he approached his cabin, there was a small group of guys outside. They were surrounding a swirl of strawberry-blonde hair. As usual, Christy was holding council with as many male followers as she could gather.

Destiny's excited voice filled his ears, "Hey guys, Brian's back."

The guys who had previously been enthralled with Christy's tales turned to see their friend coming up the snowy path.

"Brian, what's up, dude?" Darrell asked.

"Hey man," another said.

Brian nodded his head in acknowledgement and answered, "What's up?"

One by one, the other guys said their goodbyes and broke away from the group, making their way up the hill towards their own cabin.

"How was skiing, man?" Darrell inquired.

"It was cool. I haven't skied yet this winter," Brian said careful not to betray his feelings about spending the day with Katie.

Christy stood next to Brian and slid her arm in his. Looking up at him with big brown eyes. "Did you miss us?"

"Uh, no!" Brian answered with a hint of sarcasm.

Christy looked at him in disbelief. "You know you did."

"Okay, you got me, Christy. And I missed *you* most of all."

"Hey, what about me?" Destiny asked, sounding hurt and needy.

"Come here you," Brian said. He wrapped his arm around Destiny and tussled her hair with his free hand.

"Stop it, Brian. I just did my hair," Destiny complained loudly and wiggled free from his grasp.

The group made their way inside the cabin and sat down on the bunks.

"You missed a great snowshoe hike, Bri," said Christy.

"Yeah, tell me about it."

"We came up with a killer plan to get back at our little friend, Katie Dumb-Dumb," Christy started.

Brian closed his eyes and breathed deeply. It was a moment before he responded. "Don't we have enough to do without torturing unsuspecting people?" he asked.

"Don't be such a goodie-goodie, Bri," Christy said.

"I thought we were here for a break from school. What's with all the drama?" he asked, sounding bored.

Then Darrell spoke up, "Christy, let's just forget it for now. We can fill him in later." He leaned over, grabbed his coat, and stood up to leave. "We have to get to the campfire."

Destiny grasped onto Darrell's hand and pulled him back down on the musty smelling bed. "Campfire is not for another thirty minutes," she informed him. "Go ahead Christy; tell Brian what we have planned for him."

"Planned for me? What do I have to do with your

plan?" Brian asked, worry invading his sarcastic tone. "Am I the only one seeing danger signs flashing through their mind right now?"

"Don't be such a wimp, Brian," Destiny said as she slapped Brian's knee. "Listen to Christy."

Darrell and Destiny leaned forward on the mattress to hear Christy's demented plan.

"Okay, well this is the plan we came up with. Katie thinks she is better than all of us. So we are going to show her that she can't get the best of Destiny and me," Christy began.

"How does this affect me?"

"Let me finish, Brian. I've seen the way she looks at you. She is so into you."

"I don't think so, Christy," Brian protested. His mouth turned up in a slight smile. "She has never even given me the time of day."

"Please, Brian. We're girls; we know when a girl likes a guy. She has been into you since her first day at school," Destiny assured him.

"So, we want you to pretend like you like her," Christy continued.

"How would that put her in her place?" Brian questioned.

A huge smile spread across Christy's face. She was about to reveal the cruelty of her plan. An evil light flickered in her eyes as she wove her arm through Brian's and leaned in so that her mouth was almost pressing against his ear.

"It would put her in her place because after you get

her to like you, you will break her little heart by letting her see us together once we all get back to school." Christy pursed her lips, her brown eyes wide and cold defying Brian to find a fault in the plan.

"So let me get this straight. You want me to pretend to like a girl, so that I can break her heart by pretending you and me are a couple after she becomes attached to me?"

Christy smiled and clapped her hands together. "It is brilliant! Don't you think?"

"Well, there is one major flaw with your plan," Brian said.

"What could be wrong with my plan?"

"You are just assuming that I can get Katie to like me," Brian explained, his tone too cool as he pushed the memory of Katie laughing and smiling up at him to the back of his mind so as not to betray his true feelings.

"Trust me Brian; she likes you."

Brian shook his head back and forth. "I don't see it. Besides, isn't messing with Katie getting boring?"

"Never. She deserves everything that is coming her way," Christy stated pronouncing each syllable as if it were its own word.

Her cruel tone gave Brian gooseflesh and sent a shiver down his spine. He narrowed his eyes at her, and stood still, as if he were silently screaming the words he did not dare to speak out loud.

"I will take that as a 'yes'!" Christy proclaimed triumphantly. She pulled Destiny to her feet. "Come on

Destiny, let's get back to our cabin and change for campfire."

Christy and Destiny bounded out of the door, leaving it wide open. Brian and Darrell sat inside the room and watched the girls as they walked briskly down the snowy path. Brian stood up and closed the door behind them.

"Christy is out there, man! I would hate to be on her bad side," Darrell said with a wry smile.

"I didn't want to say anything, but she is beginning to seem borderline unstable," Brian added. "I think someone should say something to her."

"Are you going to be that someone? Because I'm not," Darrell said.

"Her vendetta against Katie doesn't even make sense to me. What did Katie do to Christy anyway?"

"Beats me, man. You have to admit, Brian, some of the things Christy and Destiny come up with are pretty funny."

"I don't know. I think Katie is too smart to fall for an act; I would have to be an Academy Award winning actor to get her to believe this scheme that Christy cooked up."

"Man, you like her."

"What? No," he corrected.

"It's alright, Brian. You wouldn't be the first guy to think a Goth chick was hot."

"It's not like that. She's not like that. She's smart and funny."

Darrell jumped up and slapped Brian on the back. "I knew it. I knew you liked her."

"Yes. I like her," Brian admitted nodding his head in

agreement.

Darrell shook his head and laughed at his friend. “You better not let Christy know you like Katie, or *you* will be the object of her wrath. And definitely *do not* tell her I knew anything about this, man.”

“Ah, thanks, man. With friends like you, who needs enemies?”

“I’m just saying, Christy will go through the roof if she finds out you and Katie are legit into each other,” Darrell said.

“I didn’t say she was into me. Before today, she wouldn’t even give me the time of day.”

“And now?”

“She might be starting to like me, but Christy and Destiny are wrong. Katie has not been scoping me out for the past month.”

“Look man; just keep how you really feel about Katie to yourself. You know how Christy is. She toys with one victim and then moves on to another target after a while. Maybe she’ll get bored and move on to someone else before winter break is over.”

Brian looked past Darrell and nodded in agreement. “Yeah, you are probably right. Keep this between us, man.”

“You got it.” Darrell put his hand on Brian’s shoulder. “Come on, we had better head down to the campfire, too.”

“I’ll catch up with you. I need to change my socks; they’re still soaked from skiing this afternoon.”

“Alright, catch you later,” Darrell said, nodding his head. He left the cabin and headed for the campfire.

Brian sat down on his new, midnight-blue sleeping bag; he had to move to the other end of the bunk to avoid the metal springs from the underside of the bed that were poking through the thin mattress under his bag. He changed his socks and sat on the edge of the bed staring at the dirty floor. After several minutes, Brian got up and grabbed his coat off of the metal headboard and headed down to the campfire.

Brian approached the last row of wooden benches that were arranged in a half-moon shape around the cement stage. Someone had already started the bonfire; its flames were reaching for the snow-covered branches high above the fire pit.

Brian's eyes spied Christy, Darrell, and Destiny to his right. Christy and Destiny were smiling and pointing to the benches on the other side of the stage. Brian glanced to his left and saw Katie sitting with her cabin mates.

Katie had not seen him yet. She was involved in conversation, smiling, and laughing with the girls from her own cabin. He looked wearily towards his "friends." They were staring at him.

Christy pointed in Katie's direction and mouthed the word, "Go."

Darrell nodded his head in agreement, and Destiny was smiling like the cat that ate the canary. Brian headed towards Katie and her group. When he got close, their conversation stopped abruptly as each girl looked at him like he was wearing the opposing team's jersey in a playoff game.

"Hey girls, look who decided to grace us with his

presence," Lauren announced in a condescending tone.

"Is there room for one more over here?" he asked, looking to Katie for permission to join them.

Katie smiled shyly and squirmed in her seat, looking around uncomfortably. "Sure, have a seat."

Brian settled in beside Katie. Oliver announced the first skit of the evening. A moment later, Christy and Destiny sauntered across the stage. The beat of the music filled the cold night air. They began to sing.

"Where's an avalanche when you need one?" Cherene asked.

Katie gave a knowing grin, nodding her head in agreement.

Looking up into the night sky to the snow covering the trees, Katie closed her eyes and focused her mental energy on the branches above the stage. She imagined the snow falling swiftly from the limbs onto the duet. She could feel a warm sensation running through her body; Katie reached for her amethyst stone and concentrated with all her might on the snow falling. The audience gasped. She opened her eyes to see the snow crashing down on top of the singing duo.

A pile of snow enveloped Christy and Destiny. Christy's shrill screeches echoed throughout the mountains. She jumped around shaking her arms and legs trying to shake the snow from her hair and clothes.

Destiny had taken the bulk of the manmade avalanche; she was lying under the pile of snow, motionless. A low, guttural groaning was heard from beneath the pile of snow as

Destiny pushed herself up onto her hands and knees. Then, another growl as she used all her strength to stand up. She looked like a snow monster. The audience roared with laughter, drowning out the screeches of Christy and Destiny.

Cherene glanced quickly at Brian and back at Katie. She mouthed the words, “Did you do that?”

Katie grinned from ear to ear and looked away hoping Brian would not see the guilt that was written all over her face.

~ 18 ~

ICE BREAKERS

Katie flung open the latrine door and ran down the snowy path as fast as her flip-flops would allow. Thin strands of her black hair stuck to her tear-streaked face. As she ran to the bottom of the hill and started towards her cabin, she heard a familiar, yet unfriendly voice.

"Um, Um." It was Christy' shrill voice. Laughter erupted from the same direction as Christy's voice.

Katie wrapped the shower curtain tighter around her; steam floating from her hot, freshly showered body. She glanced back towards her cabin contemplating whether she should risk running around almost naked in the middle of winter with nothing but a shower curtain between her and the freezing elements.

"Oh Brian, won't you please help me with these skis? I can't seem to get them on my big feet," Christy continued to tease. Katie's curiosity was piqued. What were Christy and Brian doing down by the frozen lake at this time of night? She crept slowly towards the lake. As she drew nearer, the voices became crystal clear.

The heat from the shower water was beginning to fade. Katie felt a small shiver climb up her spine, causing her shoulders to shudder. She reached forward with her right hand, holding on to the shower curtain with the left. She made a small opening through the branches of a tall, pine tree and peered down at the spectacle on the lake.

Darrell and Destiny were standing on the wooden dock that was made slippery by a layer of ice that had formed over the old, porous wood. Christy was standing in a moonlit spot out on the icy lake just a few feet away. She was draped in clothes that looked too familiar to Katie.

Those are my clothes.

Just as she was about to move through the branches of the old tree, her foot caught on a root preventing her from going forward. Katie pulled and twisted her foot until it was finally free. She looked up to see Christy mimicking her.

"Kiss me, Brian," Christy teased. Her arms were wrapped around her own shoulders like she was hugging herself, and she was making a face like she was kissing at the air in front of her.

"Oh, Brian! Don't you just love my 'tar-black' hair color? It matches my 'oil-slick' nail polish perfectly!" she squealed. Destiny and Darrell were doubled over in two. Their laughter echoed throughout the mountains.

Katie began to shiver, but it was not from the cold. She was so angry she felt as if she might explode. She narrowed her eyes and focused on the light that exposed the imposter. Katie could feel her anger churning; she was not going to let Christy get away with taking her clothes and mimicking her.

It was bad enough that Christy and her friends had stolen Katie's clothes while she was showering, but to come out here and make such a scene was even more maddening.

Who does she think she is?

Katie considered her options. She wanted to hurt Christy. She wanted to punch her in her stupid, perfect face.

Then her mind wandered back to the feeling of watching the spider web of broken glass form on the bathroom mirror. A smile spread across Katie's face. Instinctively, she reached for her lilac gem, but her hand slipped down the slick, plastic shower curtain without making contact.

The stone. Where is my stone? How will I make her pay without the stone?

The thought of Christy getting away with her little charade infuriated Katie; it was almost more maddening that she would not be able to retaliate without her stone. The anger grew wildly out of control. She felt lethal. She furrowed her brows and glared at the image of the beastly girl on the slick ice.

Closing her eyes, she envisioned a thick black line cutting through the ice. She saw the blocks separating and moving apart. The view in her mind made a smile creep across her face.

Suddenly, there was a loud crack and a scream. Startled, Katie opened her eyes to see Christy jumping up and down on the ice.

"Help me!" Christy's earsplitting scream penetrated the cold, night air.

The block of ice that Christy was standing on had broken away from the ice connected to the dock. She was drifting slowly away from the safety of her friends. Even from the trees, Katie could see Christy's face was a mask of sheer terror.

How do you like the feeling of helplessness, Christy?

Katie mulled the question over in her mind. She let out a sigh of fulfillment and a small, self-satisfied cackle as she stood back and watched Christy panic and lose control. How many times had Christy and her clique caused someone else's heart and mind to be filled with fear, anxiety, and complete terror? Katie stood with one hand on her hip, and the other clutching her plastic makeshift towel as she watched the scene unfold before her eyes.

Katie stepped forward to get a better view. As she moved closer, she realized that Christy's ice island had traveled very far from the shore. Destiny had found canoe paddles in the old boat storage on the far end of the dock, and she was trying to toss them out to Christy. Darrell continued to throw a life preserver on a long rope in Christy's direction.

The ice that held his co-conspirator had drifted so far away from the dock that the life preserver was landing in the water just feet beyond Darrell. It splashed water all over him, but it would never be long enough to save his friend.

Christy's cries had become hysterical sobs; her hands were waving violently in the air. Her despair was becoming a complete panic. Katie knew Christy deserved this and more. So why was she feeling so guilty all of a sudden?

Katie became aware of the fact that half of the cabins had come out to see what was happening at the frozen lake. She looked down at herself and remembered that she was in a green plastic shower curtain.

She turned to run back to her cabin but was stopped dead in her tracks by a bloodcurdling scream and the frantic call for help. "She's in the lake; Christy fell in the lake! Help! Someone help!"

Katie turned abruptly and saw the terrible scene before her. She winced as she acknowledged to herself that she had been the cause of it. There were whistles blowing, and people were yelling and running all around the snow-covered shoreline.

"Call 911, and then call the ranger," Oliver ordered, his voice cutting through the chaos.

Katie stayed firmly planted were she stood for just a moment, contemplating the damage that she had caused. On the one hand, she knew she was right for causing Christy to feel the same helplessness that she made others feel every day. On the other hand, she knew her stunt had taken a terrible turn for the worse. Someone could end up dead, and it would be her fault.

She scanned the chaotic scene and focused in on

Christy. She was in the water, but she was hanging on to the edge of the ice. Katie closed her eyes tightly and imagined the elements of nature: earth, water, fire, wind.

Wind.

Wind would become her life preserver. She saw in her mind the branches of the trees moving slowly at first and then bending in one direction as a huge gust of wind forced its way through the branches of the trees. Then she felt it, the breeze blowing on her frozen legs and shoulders, pushing her hair away from her face.

"The wind is really picking up," a male camper announced.

"What's happening?" someone else asked.

"Darrell, look, it's moving her closer to the dock," Destiny shouted.

"Just hold on Christy. Mother nature is on your side," Oliver reassured her.

"Hang on just a little longer, Christy. You're almost safe," Darrell encouraged in a hopeful, but anxiety ridden voice.

"Christy, we're all here waiting for you. It's going to be okay," Brian added from the group of onlookers.

Katie's mental storm froze. She looked up to see Brian standing with Destiny and Darrell, hands outstretched, as if they were all holding on to an invisible rope that was pulling Christy towards them.

Where did Brain come from? What would he think if he knew I had caused this mess?

Just as quickly as it had started, the wind stopped. Although the wind ceased to move the ice, Christy was close enough to catch the life preserver. Darrell grabbed the round life preserver and tossed it to her. It landed on her right hand, but she refused to try to grasp ahold of it.

"Christy, hold on to the preserver!" Brian shouted over the noise of the fear-stricken crowd. Christy did not budge.

"What is she doing, Brian? Why won't she take it?" Destiny cried out.

Brian tried again, "Christy, take the preserver!" Christy stared off in the distance without making a move. Brian turned to Darrell and Destiny. "We have to do something. Without the wind blowing her towards the dock, she could freeze to death out there."

"Aren't you guys her friends? Aren't you going to help her?" Lauren asserted as she barged into their discussion.

"I don't see you coming up with any bright ideas," Destiny retorted.

"You don't have to be Einstein to know that she is either paralyzed by fear, or the icy water has taken its toll on her ability to move," Cherene added.

"Great, and with the wind stopped, she is not going to get any closer in time," Darrell complained in a panic.

"Christy, can you swim to us?" Oliver inquired.

Christy's teeth were chattering, and she was not able to speak. She had only been in the water a matter of minutes, but it had already caused her body to start to shut down.

I need to get her out of there; I am not having her

death on my hands.

Katie refocused her energy on the element of wind. She created a picture in her mind of trees bent in two from a powerful blast of wind. She stood, fixated on the wind, but she did not feel its familiar breeze against her skin.

The more she tried, the less she could concentrate. Images flooded her mind of a funeral procession, an open coffin, Christy's open coffin. She saw a graveside service. Brian was there. He was standing far away from Katie. When he looked in her direction, she saw a look of disgust and hatred through the tears that ran down his cheeks.

I have got to concentrate. Concentrate, Katie.

She imagined a gale coming from the ocean, attacking a nearby beach town. Still, there was no change in the weather.

Oh, forget this.

Katie hoisted the shower curtain up around her chest tightly and made a knot in it as she ran down the snowy mountain towards the lake. Just before she got to the shore, she heard Cherene say, "Hold these."

She was pulling off her boots and shoving her jacket in Lauren's hand. Before Katie could say a word, Cherene dove into the water. When Cherene surfaced, she let out a piercing scream. Katie stood, amazed at her friend's courage and completely horrified at the fact that it was her fault that all of this was happening.

Cherene swam to Christy and grabbed her under her arms and around her chest. Christy was dead weight, her head flopping forward like a rag doll as Cherene pulled her towards the safety of the dock. When the two girls arrived at the dock, Brian and Darrell pulled Christy out first.

The paramedics had arrived and put Christy in a special warming suit that looked like a giant aluminum burrito. Lights from the ambulance flashed on the icy shoreline. The ambulance was on standby to take the girls to the nearest hospital.

Brian turned back to pull Cherene from the frozen water, but she was not there. The two boys looked around frantically, searching for Cherene. Katie knew that her friend had not gotten out of the lake. She had watched in dismay as Cherene had simply sunk beneath the cold, black water without a cry for help. She had not even splashed at the surface of the freezing water in distress. One moment she was above water; the next, she had disappeared.

Katie's mind returned to the graveside, but this time the casket was not surrounded by Darrell, Destiny, or Brian. Seated beside the dark, cherry wood casket were Cherene's mother and father. The roses on top of the casket were black, with just a hint of red at the tips. Katie's eyes grew wide; she had to look away. When her gaze returned, her eyes focused on the horrific image before her. Cherene was standing in an all-white gown that clung to her wet body. She was standing in a pool of water one moment, and the next, it was tinged with red. When Katie glanced up to see Cherene's face, her beautiful grayish blue eyes had turned black, her face a pale, white mask, like a ghost. Her lips were stained black with red slashes that accentuated the sides of her mouth. Katie saw that Cherene was trying to tell her something. Katie drew closer and listened as Cherene's whisper revealed her truth.

"I know what you did," Cherene taunted. "I know what you did."

Katie opened her eyes in a flash and heard Brian and Lauren screaming Cherene's name.

Katie kicked off her flip-flops and ran barefooted down the length of the dock to the where Lauren, Brian, Darrell, and Destiny were standing. She pushed them aside and plunged face first into the icy, cold water. At first, she did not feel anything. Then she realized that the numbness she felt was caused by a thousand stinging ice needles penetrating her skin over and over. Katie opened her eyes to try and to see Cherene, but there was only darkness. She looked upward towards the surface; she could barely see the moonlight shining faintly through the void of night and freezing cold water. It felt as if her heart stopped for a moment. How would she find Cherene in the blackness?

She swam deeper, moving her arms from side to side, reaching out for her best friend in the blackness that surrounded her. She could tell that her breath was about to run out. She knew she would have to come up for more air, or she too would drown.

As she started back for the surface of the lake, she felt a warm hand grab ahold of her leg. She was shocked and frightened at first, but then the realization dawned on her that it might be Cherene begging for her help. She looked down hopeful that it might be Cherene, but even more fearful that it was not.

When she looked down, a soft white light filled her sight. Before her was a beautiful creature. Her hair was dark, with just a hint of red. It appeared to be flowing in all directions from her head and cascading down her back. Her body was iridescent, her eyes glowing and green. For a moment, Katie thought she must be having another vision. Was she dying from hypothermia imagining the beautiful creature that seemed to be calling for her to follow her into the misty light?

The panic to get air had dissipated. She no longer had the instinctive sensation that she needed to resurface for air. She felt the familiar tug of the warm hand on her foot. When she glanced down at the water creature again, she saw that she was motioning for her to follow her to the depths of the lake. No longer worried about air, Katie followed the being down, down through the tunnel of light, down to a still figure at the bottom of the lake.

Katie recognized instantly that it was Cherene lying lifeless at the bottom of the lake. She reached down intuitively and grasped Cherene around her chest, pushed off the hard lake bottom and swam towards the surface of the dim water. As she drew nearer to the breath of life, the water grew murkier. Katie glanced back to see if the beautiful creature had followed her up to the top, but she saw only a fading light and a huge tail descending into the depths of the lake.

The closer Katie came to the surface, the heavier

Cherene felt in her arms and the colder Katie became. The shock of the cold could not detour Katie from her mission. The intense need for air began to overtake her body once again. She swam with all her might as she burst through the surface of the water and let out a tremendous scream.

The first image she saw was Oliver standing with his arms outstretched holding a sleeping bag. Brian and Darrell reached for Cherene and pulled her lifeless body from Katie's arms. Oliver laid the thick sleeping bag on the dock. Once Cherene was laid on the bag, the paramedics placed a warming blanket on top of her and began checking her vitals. Katie held on, her numb fingers gripping the edge of the frozen wood of the dock, as she watched the tragic scene before her.

This is my fault. What am I going to do if she dies?

"Weak pulse, no breathing," one of the paramedics proclaimed. The other paramedic began blowing into Cherene's mouth trying to revive her.

Please save her, please. I'll do anything. Oh God, what have I done? Please save her, God. I'm so sorry!

Suddenly, Katie felt two strong hands grasp her wrists and pull her out of the water. She tried to stand on the dock, but she was unable to steady herself on her numb limbs. She crumbled into the arms of the person that had pulled her from the freezing lake. When she was certain he had a strong hold of her, she looked up. Brian's worried face was regarding her.

"We need another bag over here!" Oliver yelled with authority.

Meagan ran swiftly down the dock with an aluminum

bag in one hand and furry snow boots in the other. Oliver took the bag and wrapped it around Katie, quickly. As Meagan slid the boots on her feet for warmth, Katie realized that the shower curtain was still clinging to her frozen body; she pulled at it and let the plastic sheath fall to the icy dock beneath her.

Meagan started to lead Katie towards the second ambulance that had arrived, but Katie could not be moved.

"No, I have to stay," Katie pointed to Cherene's unresponsive body. "I have to know if she…"

Katie could not finish her sentence. The words would not come out of her mouth. It was just too terrible to imagine.

How could Cherene be dead? And how could it be at my hand? She was just standing here moments ago. I did not want to hurt anyone. I just wanted Christy to pay. I just wanted her to know what it felt like to feel helpless.

Her thoughts were interrupted by the shouting of one of the paramedics, "She's breathing! She's breathing! Get the stretcher over here, now!"

Relief filled Katie's body. The crowd, a silent mass a moment ago, let out a collective sigh of relief. As the paramedics closed the ambulance door, the campers started to retreat up the snowy mountain to their cabins.

Brian walked up behind Katie and Meagan and put his hand on Katie's shoulder.

"Are you okay, Katie?"

"I will be," Katie replied, her voice barely a whisper.

"What happened out here? Why were you all down

here to begin with?" Brian questioned.

"You do not even want to know, Brian." Katie tried, but she could not make her guilt-ridden eyes meet his.

"No, really, I do want to know," Brian insisted.

"Not tonight, Brian. Please, let's just get some rest," Katie said as she turned away from him and let Meagan lead her to the nurse's station.

As they walked, Katie thought back to her first paranormal event. It had seemed innocent enough. She had never imagined that she would be able to perform such a feat as she had tonight. She never thought her powers could be deadly.

Her thoughts returned to the light and the image beneath the water of the lake. The scene replayed in her mind like an old film. She saw the iridescent glow from the creature beneath the water and the light that led her straight to Cherene.

How could it have been real? I must have imagined it. But she touched my foot. I felt her touch my foot. Or did I? People in extreme situations often experience strange phenomenon. I read that somewhere, in a magazine. It must have been my mind playing tricks on me.

Katie saw a sign with a red cross on it and realized that they had arrived at the nurse's cabin. She turned to face Meagan. "Thank you so much for everything, Meagan. I'll be fine now. You can go back to the other girls at our cabin."

"No way, I am staying with you."

"Meagan, please. I've caused enough trouble for one night."

"Caused enough trouble?" Meagan said, almost exasperated. "How can you say saving someone's life is causing trouble?"

A sense of relief flowed through Katie's being.

That's right. No one knows I am the cause of this horrific chain of events. She would not be so nice to me if she knew the truth.

A smile started to form in the corners of Katie's mouth, masking the guilt that was trying to claw its way to the surface. She contemplated telling Meagan what happened. Then she thought of Cherene. She almost killed her best friend. How could she explain that to someone like Meagan? Meagan had probably never done harm to anyone in her life, even by accident.

But the guilt, the guilt was gnawing at her soul. Katie felt it would wear at her and wear at her until there was only a little sliver of her sanity left. She felt the loss of her amethyst rock was punishment for the harm she almost caused, but that was not enough. Katie knew she had to admit her secret to someone. She looked into Meagan's eyes. They were sad and solemn eyes tonight, not bright and lively like they usually were.

Meagan smiled and reached for the door. "Come on, let's get you inside."

Katie grasped ahold of Meagan's hand. "Honestly, I am fine. I would feel so much better if you would just go back to the cabin."

"Are you sure?" Meagan asked.

"I promise; I'm fine," Katie replied.

"Okay, but if you need anything, have them send someone to get me. I probably won't sleep much tonight after all this excitement," Meagan said. She smiled and turned on her heel to leave.

Katie watched as Meagan walked briskly up the snow-covered path towards their little cabin in the woods. She disappeared through the thick, snow-laden branches of the pine trees that Katie hid behind just an hour before. That moment when she first realized that Christy was making fun of her seemed like a lifetime ago.

More than anything, Katie wished she could turn back the hands of time and change how she had reacted. She never intended to hurt anyone.

Or did I?

Unable to fathom the possibility that evil could exist within her, Katie turned back towards the wooden door of the nurse's cabin. As she did, a light caught her eye. Katie focused her attention on the lake. In the distance, there was a shimmering image; it lasted only a moment, and then it disappeared.

~ 19 ~

LET THE GAMES BEGIN

The sun peered out from between the last of the remaining gray clouds that were stretched across the morning sky. It had snowed for three days after the frightening incident on the frozen lake. Oliver stood on the concrete stage before the blazing fire, waiting for the last of the groups of campers to make their way to the campfire before announcing the morning roll call and passing out the mail.

"Well campers, it has been three days since we've seen the sun. I think we have all had our share of arts and crafts and indoor games," he began speaking, and the crowd slowly started to calm down.

One by one, each camper directed their attention to the dynamic camp director on the stage. "Who is ready for some outdoor fun?" he asked jumping up and down on the concrete.

A few campers gave hoots and hollers, but mostly there was a quiet in the audience.

"I said…Who is ready for some outdoor fun?"

A few more people added their voices to the excitement, but still, most of the group just looked around and made comments under their breath.

"Geez, tough crowd," Oliver began again. "Okay, let's see if this will get you going. Let's welcome back two of our campers that I know you've been missing; Christy and Cherene come out and join me on stage."

All the campers jumped up whistling and cheering; everyone was on their feet clapping and welcoming the two girls back into the folds of camp life. Katie smiled from ear to ear when she saw Cherene walk out in front of Christy.

Cherene's hair was pulled up into a messy bun, and she wore warm winter snow pants and a black jacket to match.

Not to be outdone, Christy followed a few paces behind Cherene; her perfectly styled strawberry-blonde curls bounced behind her, revealing her flawless face. Her hot-pink snow suit accentuated her figure and her overly sexy walk flaunted the rest.

"Uh, it's not a fashion runway, Christy," Lauren chided, her words peppered with sarcasm.

Katie stifled a laugh, but Riley and Kareisha chortled loud enough to cause Christy to stop her silly walk and look in the direction of Meagan's cabin. Meagan shot the girls a sideways glance with big eyes as if to say, 'Be nice.'

When the clapping had died off, Christy and Cherene made their way off the stage and returned to the audience to sit with their cabin mates. Katie leaped from the cold wooden bench and wrapped both arms around her best friend.

"I'm so glad you're okay! I was so scared!"

"You think you were scared?" Cherene asked.

"I know it must have been horrible for you, but we were the ones standing around thinking you had died," Katie replied.

"Hello! What part of 'she's not breathing' did you not hear, Katie?" Lauren questioned. She looked around the group for approval. "Where I come from, 'not breathing' equals not alive."

"I know, right?" Riley agreed.

"Technically, if there is still a heartbeat, you are not dead," Kareisha inserted.

"Okay, Miss Know It All," Lauren retorted.

"I am simply saying that doctors do not call a time of death until the person flatlines," Kareisha continued.

"Kareisha's right," Riley added.

Meagan stood in the middle of girls and looked at each one, her expression a silent plea for their banter to stop. "Girls, seriously? We are lucky she is here. Can we just be grateful things did not go the other way?"

"Meagan's right, guys!" Riley agreed.

"According to you, everyone is right, Riley," Lauren said.

Riley furrowed her brow at Lauren and said through gritted teeth, "Let's just be happy everything turned out for the best."

"Theoretically, it would have been best if none of it had happened in the first place," Kareisha asserted.

"Kareisha!" the group of girls said loudly in exasperation. The silence that followed was deafening. The girls looked around to discover that the entire group of assembled campers was listening to their discord.

Meagan whispered, "Let's just sit down."
The girls complied and turned their attention to the stage.

"Well, now that that is settled, who wants to have some fun?" Oliver asked the group of campers as he waved his arms up and down encouraging a grand response.

This time the group's comeback was boisterous! "Now that is more like it," Oliver encouraged. "If you glance down by the lake, you will see that booths are being set up for the winter games that will take place this afternoon. Then, we will have a special treat for everyone this evening. If you look behind where you are sitting, you will discover that our staff has begun preparation for our annual Faery Ice Kingdom dance."

The crowd's excitement was palpable.

"I thought that would get your attention," Oliver said. "Your counselors have all the details. I am certain they will share them with you when you get back to your cabins. Now, let's get down to business. If I can have your attention, I have some mail to give out."

While Oliver handed out the mail, Katie's mind wandered back to the evening of the disaster on the lake. Images of Christy making fun of her, and Destiny and Darrell doubled over laughing at her expense flashed through her mind. Anger stirred within her. A picture of Cherene's lifeless body invaded her thoughts. Katie's anger was quickly surpassed by the guilty feelings that had plagued her heart and mind since the near-death incident on the ice had happened.

I almost killed my best friend and my worst enemy at the same time. What if they had both died? How would I live with myself? But they didn't die, Katie. Get a grip.

Katie tried to clear her mind, but the guilt refused to release its grip on her heart. *How am I going to live with all this guilt?*

"Are you okay?" Cherene asked as she nudged Katie.

Katie looked at Cherene and manufactured a smile. "I'm fine."

"You don't look fine to me. You know you can tell me anything, right?" Cherene said.

"I know. I am just relieved to have you back."

Cherene looked at Katie, her expression revealing that she knew Katie was not being completely honest. Cherene wrapped her arm around her friend. "When you decide you want to talk, I'm here. Okay?"

Katie leaned into her friend's hug. "Okay," Katie said and tried to smile as if the weight of what she had done was not crushing her spirit. She considered telling Cherene the truth but then quickly thought better of it.

* * * * *

"I didn't pack a dress. The brochure didn't say anything about a dance," Kareisha complained sourly as the girls closed the door to the cabin. Each girl sat on her own bunk. Katie and Cherene shared the bottom bunk of their bed.

"Oh, now that is what I am going to talk to you about," Meagan said excitedly.

"Don't worry, Kareisha. We are going to make our own gowns from frozen, old pinecones and blocks of ice we create from the snow," Lauren said with mock encouragement. She chuckled under her breath at her own sardonic reply.

Despite Lauren's instructions not to worry, Kareisha's face was in a state of uneasiness.

Meagan gave Lauren a disapproving look and tried to gently ease the tension in the room. "We are not going to make our own designs," Meagan said reassuring Kareisha. "The theme is a Faery Ice Kingdom, so the camp directors have rented winter-themed gowns that might have been worn at a celebration during the Renaissance time."

"You mean like during the times of lords and ladies?" Riley asked.

"And knights and fair maidens?" Katie added her face lit with excitement. While talking, she noticed a lump under the covers of her bunk. She pulled the covers back and saw the clothes that were stolen from the shower the night of the lake incident. She put her hands in the jeans pocket; the amethyst rock was still there. It warmed in her hand. Katie smiled and placed the stone in the pocket of her coat.

"Exactly!" Meagan exclaimed.

"Don't forget the dungeons and dragons," Lauren reminded.

Sharylin shook her head as if she were irritated with Lauren, but her blue eyes and soft smile betrayed not a hint of frustration. "Well, the times I have been to the winter dances the focus was more on the beauty and romance of whatever time period they were celebrating."

"Yes, it is about the splendor and chivalry of the time period," Meagan explained. "The boys will be dressed as knights or lords, and we will wear magical gowns with sequins and gems that sparkle."

Katie bounced up from her bunk and clapped her hands together joyfully. "It sounds wonderful! When can we pick out our dresses?" Katie was happy about the dresses, but the true source of her joy came from the return of the amethyst.

"Our time to view the costumes is in about ten minutes, but don't forget that we get to go to the lake area for winter games this afternoon too," Meagan reminded the girls.

"I can't wait!" Riley bounded up off her bunk and reached for her coat. "Let's get a head start."

Riley and Kareisha locked arms and led the procession out of the cabin. Katie was the last to pass through the threshold. She closed the cold, wooden door behind her and stood for a moment on the snowy porch. Reaching into her coat pocket, she pulled out the amethyst stone and watched it come to life in her hand. A soft lilac light began to pulse slowly from the tiny gems inside the stone. Katie felt a surge of warmth fill her entire being. She closed her fingers around the familiar ridges of the stone, gently closed her eyes, and let the enchantment envelop her.

~ 20 ~

A ROYAL DISASTER

When evening arrived, the campground had been transformed into a beautiful, magical kingdom. Tiny, twinkling lights were strung in the trees that lined the paths from each cabin to just beyond the campfire where they united into a single snow-covered walkway that led to an enchanted castle.

As Katie and her cabin mates rounded the bend of trees just before the campfire, they stopped dead in their tracks. One by one their mouths dropped open, wonder dancing in their eyes.

"Wow, they have outdone themselves this year," Meagan exclaimed as she gawked at the entrance and spun around to take in the full effect of all the lights leading up to the castle.

A large tent had been erected and shaped to resemble a castle; gray stones were painted on the sides of the tent to imitate the stone walls of an authentic, medieval castle. At the entrance, instead of two flaps held open by rope, the sides were rolled around two large columns with enormous turrets at the top of each post. The columns were draped with ferns and beautiful white and light purple flowers spiraled down the sides.

Inside the walls of the castle were huge ice sculptures of fountains and swans. At the far end of the hall stood the head table draped with gossamer covered lights and piled high with meats, cheeses, crackers, and fresh vegetables.

Circular tables lined the dance floor, which was an attraction all its own. The floor was made from an iridescent durable material that emitted a soft white light from within.

“This is more beautiful than prom,” Riley announced.

“I know, right?” Kareisha agreed without argument. The girls turned to face Kareisha.

“Well give the girl a cookie,” Lauren said. Riley cocked an eyebrow as if to question Lauren.

“What? That's the first time she hasn't argued since she has been here,” Lauren replied.

“Don't spoil the moment,” Meagan advised.

Kareisha opened her mouth to respond but stopped short when Meagan shot a wide-eyed warning stare in her direction.

"Hot guy alert!" Riley whispered quietly as she tapped

Katie on the shoulder and turned her towards a lord that was walking towards the group of girls.

Katie saw the handsomely dressed lord approaching and smiled in spite of herself. He was dressed in a gold royal doublet that had rhinestone buttons and dark purple thread stitched in a pattern of connected diamonds throughout the material. His doublet was cinched at the waist with a solid brown belt which matched his brown pants and boots. One of his hands was holding on to the mock sword that hung at his side.

"Brian," Katie said warmly.

"I didn't think it was possible," Brian said.

"What do you mean?" Katie asked, unable to stop smiling at her handsome suitor.

"I did not think it was possible for you to be more beautiful, but you are stunning tonight, Katie."

Katie glanced down at her full-length, purple velvet outer gown. It had lovely hanging sleeves that almost kissed the floor when she walked. The purple material was gathered at her midriff and opened from waist to floor revealing a golden satin inner gown and a formfitting, light purple bodice made of velvet. The bodice was embroidered with thread that looked like finely spun gold. Beautiful diamond and oval shaped ruby and rhinestone gems embellished the square neckline.

Katie smiled shyly. "Thank you, Brian. You look pretty handsome yourself."

Brian held out his hand. "Would you like to dance,

milady?" he asked, flashing her a daring smile.

Katie gave a slight courtesy, placed her hand in his, and the Renaissance pair walked to the softly illuminated dance floor. Brian took the lead and held on tight. Katie inhaled quickly; his forcefulness was unexpected. As she was very experienced at slow dancing, she welcomed his assertiveness on the dance floor.

"I'm surprised you and your cabin mates made it to the dance tonight. After all the damage you did at the winter games this afternoon, I thought for sure you would need an early bedtime."

"Are those words of regret I hear, Sir Brian?"

Brian threw his head back a little and laughed out loud. His eyes twinkled with amusement as he stared fondly at Katie. "Well, it is just that I did not know that a lady of your position would be so skilled at games generally reserved for men," he teased.

Katie turned her head and stared at him for a moment considering whether to keep up with the role play of the Renaissance period or say what she truly thought of his chauvinistic statement.

Her eyes wandered over the crowd and beheld the beauty that surrounded them. She decided that sticking to the theme of the evening was better than establishing her feminist position.

"Father, the King, has not any sons. He gave special permission for my sisters and me to participate in the tourney this afternoon, but…"

"But what, milady?"

"But, if it pleases you Sir, I shall try not to win so much at the next celebration," Katie said, batting her eyelashes.

"Indeed, milady."

Katie spied the girls from her cabin at the side of the dance floor. They were giggling and pointing at her and Brian. She noticed Riley motioning for Katie to come near.

Seriously?

Katie lifted her skirts gingerly and curtsied before Brian. "Now if you'll excuse me, Sir, I have something to attend to."

Before he could protest, she turned on her heel and rushed back to the group of girls that were anxiously watching her dance.

"What is it, Riley?" Katie asked, breathless. "This tight bodice is suffocating me," she said, shifting the material.

"Oh do tell, do tell," Riley begged. "How was it? What were you two talking about?"

"Well, we didn't have much time to talk; someone interrupted our dance," Katie said, looking at Riley with mock disapproval.

"I know. I'm sorry," Riley said. "But tell us what he said," she continued as mischief danced in her blue eyes.

"Nothing really. I think he was a little shocked that we did so well at the winter games earlier today," Katie answered as she looked around the room for a punch bowl. All the talking with Brian had made her thirsty. Or maybe it was from the nervousness she always felt in his company.

"These Renaissance costumes are very hot. How did they wear so many layers all the time?" Katie asked as she tugged at the bodice of her dress, trying to straighten the tight fabric.

"Speaking of very hot, I see a guy for me," Riley announced and grabbed Lauren and Kareisha's hands, dragging them along as she hurried in the direction of a huddle of boys that were standing by the meat and cheese trays at the head table.

Katie laughed at Riley and glanced back at Cherene, Sharylin, and Meagan.

"Aren't you going to dance?" Katie asked.

"A true lady does not ask a man to dance," Meagan replied.

"Oh, not you too!" Katie could not take any more of the women's roles of the time period, even if it was just for the evening. "You know we might be dressed like we're in the fifteenth century, but it is actually the twenty-first century. We wait for no man!" Katie proclaimed in a loud voice.

The girls looked at Katie with wide eyes. "But . . ." Sharylin started to protest.

"Come on, I want to dance!" Katie announced, tugging gently at the girls' arms.

Cherene, Sharylin, and Meagan followed her reluctantly to the middle of the lighted dance floor. Katie was surrounded by her friends, beautiful gowns, lights, and the hope that she and Brian might get to dance again later that evening. She glanced to her left and discovered Brian in a group of beautiful gowns and tendrils of curly hair, strawberry-blonde and dark black hair to be specific.

Well, there went that idea.

Although she was a little disappointed that she would not be able to dance with Brian again, she resolved not to let it spoil her fun. She turned her attention back to her small group of friends and enjoyed the rhythm of the upbeat music.

After several fast songs, the castle was once again filled with the soft music of a slow song. The girls left the dance floor quickly, finding themselves standing between a chocolate fountain and an ice sculpture of a swan. They were there only a moment before Brian stood in front of Katie again with his hand held out.

"Would you like to finish our dance, milady?" Brian said, raising one eyebrow and flashing his best persuasive smile.

Katie extended her arm and placed her hand in his. "Of course, milord," she responded, trying to sound calm.

As they walked away towards the dance floor, Katie could hear Lauren and Riley imitating their words and pretending to barf afterwards. She laughed to herself as she stared to her side and smiled sweetly at Brian.

As they swayed to the music, Katie thought about the fact that just moments ago she had given up the hope of dancing with Brian. He was brave going against his group. Katie remembered how hard it was to go against the "in-crowd." Once you were out, you did not get back in.

"What are you thinking about in that head of yours?" Brian asked brushing a loose curl behind her ear.

"You don't want to know."

"I wouldn't have asked if I didn't want to know."

"Well, I was just thinking that when I saw you with Christy and Destiny that we probably wouldn't be dancing again this evening," she admitted.

"Why would you think that?"

"I just know they don't like me."

"Well, I like you," Brian said with a confident smile. "A lot," he added.

Katie blushed and cast her eyes away from his stare.

"What? No witty comeback?"

Her shyness vanished at his challenge. "Actually, I was thinking of how to tell you I like you too, but now I don't know if I do," she said with a smirk, one eyebrow held high—a dare.

Brian looked down at Katie. Her green eyes sparkled.

"Well, I know I like you, Katie Ryan. You are not like any girl I have ever met."

"Ever? Really?" Katie questioned.

"Ever," Brian assured her.

Katie could not help but smile. She looked down for a moment, watching her velvet gown dusting the lit floor below. When she looked up, she saw that Brian was watching her, his brilliant blue eyes brimming with expectation.

Oh goodness. I think he wants me to say it back.

Katie took a deep breath. *Here goes nothing.*

"I like you too, Brian," she said.

The corners of his mouth started to turn up, but then his gaze shifted past Katie and his eyes grew wide.

That was not the response I was hoping for, Katie thought. *'I am so glad you return my feelings,' or 'I thought you would never say it too,' or even a simple 'Yes!' would be better than a look of shock.*

When Katie realized that his gaze was not returning to her, she looked over her shoulder in the direction of his stare. She saw Christy and Destiny approaching. Christy had a determined, menacing look on her face, and she was heading straight for the back of Katie. Before Katie could speak, Christy placed her arm on Katie's shoulder.

"Katie, you aren't going to keep this handsome guy all to yourself, are you?"

Katie stared at her, considering how to respond. She did not want to stop dancing with Brian, but she also did not want to start another battle. She wondered for a moment if the powers that she had could make a person disappear. She quickly dismissed the thought, remembering how the mere thought of making something happen seemed to make it a reality.

Katie breathed in deep and let it out, calming herself before she spoke. Holding her head high, she said, "Thank you for the dance, Brian." Katie batted her eyelashes at Brian and smiled sweetly over her shoulder at him as she turned on her heel to leave.

As she walked away, she felt a tug at the bottom of her

dress accompanied by the sound of material tearing. Katie stopped dead in her tracks. She glanced over her shoulder to see that the bottom half of the back of her gown laid in a pool beneath Christy's foot.

Katie gasped, no longer able to hold in her emotions. Her stare shifted from the torn dress to Christy. "You!" she bellowed, not caring who heard.

One by one, the couples surrounding her stopped dancing and stared at her newly exposed backside. Her embarrassment quickly turned to anger. Katie could feel the heat building inside of her, her mind searching for a way to make Christy pay.

Christy turned around feigning innocence. She looked down at the gown that was gathered around her feet. Christy looked up at Katie with exaggerated bewilderment. "Katie, I—I'm so sorry. I didn't realize I had stepped on your gown."

"Cut the innocent act, Christy," Katie said as she stormed towards her nemesis and Brian.

"Innocent act? What are you saying, Katie?" Christy asked in an overly confused tone.

"I think you know what I'm saying, Christy."

Brian stepped between the two girls trying to ease the tension that was building. "Katie, I am sure Christy did not mean to tear your dress." He looked at Christy with wide eyes, his expression and tone both insisting. "Right, Christy?"

Christy continued, her tone implying that she should be above suspicion. "I didn't mean to tear her dress." Christy stared innocently up at Brian. "You believe me, don't you?"

Katie shook her head in disbelief. She looked to Brian. When he did not respond, Katie glared at him. He opened his mouth, but still, he did not speak.

Her anger was burning her from the inside out. She felt exactly as she had the night on the lake, when she had almost killed Christy and Cherene. Katie breathed deeply knowing any powers she invoked would have terrible consequences when she was this full of emotion, this angry and out of control. She let go of the breath she had been holding.

"Figures," Katie said to Brian, rolling her eyes. She stormed out from the middle of the gawking couples and headed for the exit.

"Katie, wait!" Brian called out, but it was too late. Katie disappeared out of the castle doors; Cherene and two other girls from her cabin followed quickly behind. Brian looked over his shoulder at Christy and Destiny. They were trying to stifle their laughter. He shook his head in disbelief, his face a mask of disgust.

As he looked away and continued towards the door, Christy grasped Brian's shoulder from behind. "Let her go, Brian. Let's dance."

Brian wheeled around quickly and stared angrily at Christy. "You did it on purpose, didn't you?" he accused.

"Oh Brian, do you really have to ask?" Christy answered with self-satisfaction dripping from her every word. Brian shook loose from her grip. He stood firmly in place, hands folded in front of him glaring at the pair of mischievous girls.

Christy leaned into Brian and whispered, "Nice touch. Keep up the sullen boyfriend act. It is very convincing."

Christy and Destiny walked away quickly, laughing to themselves. They made their way to the chocolate fountain at the back of the castle.

Outside the castle, Cherene tried to console Katie. "Are you okay? I'm sure they can fix the dress."

"I am fine. I don't care about this stupid dress. I just can't stand that she got the best of me, again."

"Hey, I guess all those layers turned out to be a good thing, huh?" Lauren added. "The Renaissance bloomers are less revealing than the skinny jeans we wear today."

The girls laughed at Lauren's comment.

"We're all here, let's get back to the cabin," Cherene said.

"Wait, Riley is missing," Lauren announced. The girls returned to the castle entrance and scanned the room for Riley. "Look, there she is, by the chocolate fountain," Lauren proclaimed. "You guys wait here; I'll go and get her."

The girls watched as Lauren made her way through the crowded room to the chocolate fountain in the back of the castle. Riley was standing right next to Christy. As the girls watched from the entrance, they saw Riley take her whole hand and put it in the fountain.

"What is she doing?" Meagan asked.

"Making a chocolate-covered hand," Sharylin offered, unsure.

"I think she is up to something," Cherene suggested.

"Up to no good," Kareisha corrected.

The events happened so quickly; it was hard to say exactly what occurred. One moment, Riley's hand was in the chocolate fountain, and the next, she was lying on top of Christy.

Christy's scream could be heard throughout the castle. "What are you doing? You idiot!"

"Oh Christy, I am so sorry. Was that your face I slathered with chocolate?" Riley asked in an artificial tone.

"Don't even pretend you didn't mean to do it, you wretched—"

"Here, I will prove I did not mean to do it. Let me help you. You have some chocolate in your hair." Riley ran her own chocolate-covered hand over Christy's hair and face. "There, that's better."

"Augh, get off of me!"

Riley got off Christy and turned to walk away. She glanced back over her shoulder and smiled innocently at Christy, mouthing the words, "So sorry."

Destiny grabbed the back of Riley's dress and growled, "You're not sorry!"

Lauren stepped between Riley and Destiny and grasped a huge clump of Destiny's hair. Her face was an inch from Destiny's. "No, she's not sorry. But you will be if you don't let go…now."

Destiny let go of Riley's dress and grabbed hold of Lauren's hair. She raised her free hand in the air, readying to strike. She swung her hand to hit Lauren in the face. A moment before she made contact, Oliver grabbed ahold of Destiny's hand and held it back and away from Lauren.

"I wouldn't do that if I were you, young lady," Oliver warned. He looked at Lauren and Riley. Nodding his head in the direction of the castle entry he said, "I've got this, girls."

"Come on Lauren, let's get out of here," Riley said.

"Hold on, Riley," Lauren said as she took a strawberry from the nearby table. Lauren eyed the strawberry in her hand and the chocolate on Riley's arm, smiling mischievously.

Riley shook her head back and forth. "Go ahead," she said with a chortle.

Lauren dragged the strawberry through the excess chocolate on Riley's arm and shoved the entire chocolate-covered strawberry in her mouth at once.

"Yum. I always wondered what the big deal was with chocolate-covered strawberries," Lauren mumbled, her mouth overflowing with the chocolate-covered fruit.

Lauren and Riley walked briskly through the large banquet room to their friends that were waiting outside the great hall. The night air was chilly, but the sounds of the girls' laughter warmed them.

"That was crazy cool," Cherene said.

"I can't believe you did that," Katie said in disbelief, "but I'm so glad you did."

"Normally I wouldn't encourage unkind actions, but she really had that coming," Meagan admitted.

"I couldn't agree more," Sharylin chimed in. The girls turned to look at Kareisha.

"What?" Kareisha said, clearly confused.

"Aren't you going to tell us how wrong we are for laughing at someone else's misfortune?" Lauren queried with just a hint of sarcasm.

"No," Kareisha answered matter of fact.

The girls looked at her with surprised expressions.

"Wait for it," Lauren taunted.

"Well, I mean, it was rather hypocritical of all of you," Kareisha started to say.

"I knew it," Lauren announced pumping her fist in the air in triumph.

A few of the girls laughed at their banter.

"If you would let me finish, Lauren, I was going to say that it was hypocritical, but she definitely deserved it."

Lauren draped her arm over Kareisha's shoulder as she said, "I knew you would come around eventually."

"Let's get out of here," Meagan suggested.

The girls began their walk back to the cabin. The twinkling lights reflected off the snow and illuminated the way. The sound of snow crunching under footfalls diverted the group's attention to the image of a Renaissance man running towards them.

As he neared the group, Brian yelled, "Katie, wait!"

Katie looked at her friends. "You guys go on without me; I'll catch up."

"Don't be too long," Meagan warned.

"I won't."

The rest of her cabin mates continued down the path.

Brian slowed his gait and stopped in front of Katie. "I'm glad I caught you!"

"What do you want?" Katie asked, her tone colder than the winter air that surrounded them.

"So, we are back to that now?"

"Back to what? You taking Christy's side?"

"Katie, I really didn't think she meant to do it. I mean, it could have happened by accident. You see that, right?" Brian pleaded.

Katie considered his words.

Why does he have to be so cute?

She knew he was right, but she also knew that in this case, Christy meant to do it. But did she have to hold that against him? Was she really being fair?

"Yes, Brian. I can see that a person might accidentally step on someone's dress in a crowded room."

Brian let out a sigh of relief. "You aren't mad at me, then?"

Katie looked at him impishly. "I'm sorry. Did I say I wasn't mad at you? Because I thought I said that I could see that a person might—"

Brian wrapped an arm around Katie's back and pulled her to him. Before she had time to protest, he leaned forward and kissed her softly on the lips for just a moment. When he backed away from her; her face was still tilted towards his, her eyes were closed, and a sweet smile spread across her lips. Katie stood like that for a moment before she realized that he was no longer kissing her.

Oh no, I'm standing here enjoying a kiss that is no longer happening.

Katie opened her eyes and looked sheepishly at Brian.

Light from the snow was reflecting in his bright blue eyes. He was smiling from ear to ear.

Either he really enjoyed the kiss too, or he is laughing at me.

Not able to discern which, Katie tried to play it cool. "If you think that a kiss means that all is forgiven—"

"You were right, Katie," Brian interrupted, his voice plagued with sadness. "She all but admitted she did it on purpose."

"I see."

"Katie, let's not let them define who we are. I really like you. I would like to see where this might go."

"I would like that too, Brian."

He leaned down and kissed her lips once again. This time, he lingered just a little longer than the last.

Katie pulled away first. "I think I had better catch up with the rest of my cabin," she said with a satisfied smile.

"I could walk you," Brian offered.

But Katie was already walking backwards down the snow-covered path. "I'll see you tomorrow, Brian," Katie shouted.

When she was sure she was far enough away that he would not be able to see her torn dress and exposed backside, she turned and ran off through the moonlit woods.

Once she was safely behind the cover of the tall pine

trees, Katie stopped to catch her breath. She looked back to where Brian had been standing. Far off in the distance, Katie saw a deep purple light that glowed for a moment, and like the flame of a candle snuffed out by a sudden gust of wind, it vanished.

Katie wondered to herself what it could be. It reminded her of the image on the lake the evening that Cherene almost died. That light had shone only for a moment, but then it too disappeared into the dark night waters. That night she had simply thought she was exhausted and seeing things. But there was more to it than that; she was seeing something else.

She stood for a moment contemplating all that she had seen in the last couple of months. The fountain in the meadow, the dark shadows in Sharylin and Meagan's eyes, and now a second purple light that disappeared as soon as it appeared. Katie felt as if something was calling her to it. A strange sensation crept over her entire body as if an invisible string was attached to her, gently pulling her towards the light.

She stood staring into the distance hoping the light would reappear. When it did not, Katie turned and ran through the chilly forest to the safety of her cabin.

~ 21 ~

The Calm Before the Storm

Katie arrived back at her cabin to find the girls sleeping. She quickly took off her half-torn evening gown and replaced it with warm winter clothes and boots. She grabbed her backpack and stuffed snacks, a flashlight, two bottles of water, and an extra scarf, hat, and gloves into it. Katie grabbed an extra flashlight from Meagan's nightstand and shoved it in her coat pocket. She heard Cherene stir in the bunk above.

Cherene yawned and asked, "What are you doing, Katie?"

"I've got to get out of here," Katie whispered.

"Why? Did something happen with Brian?"

"No. Everything is great with Brian. I just need to go and check out some things."

"Let me go with you, Katie," Cherene offered as she pulled the top layer of her black sleeping bag back and peeled herself out of its warm embrace.

"I don't want to drag you into this, Cherene."

"What exactly is 'this'?" Cherene asked. She pulled on snow pants and a jacket over her pajamas.

"Let's go outside and talk about it. We don't want to wake up the other girls."

Katie shut the large, wooden cabin door as softly as she could. The two girls stood on the icy porch with their arms folded in front of them for warmth.

"Cherene, there is so much going on inside of me. I just can't explain it."

"Katie, there is not much you could tell me that would shock me after what you shared with me in the middle of the night in my parents' basement. Just tell me what is going on."

The familiar guilt that kept trying to take residence in her mind reared its ugly head. Katie thought about how she almost caused not one, but two people's deaths just a few nights ago. She was sick of the guilt.

"Would it shock you if you knew that the whole reason Christy was in the lake to begin with was my fault?"

Cherene closed her eyes and took a deep breath.

"I wondered how that whole situation had come about. But Katie, you may have started it, but I am sure you didn't mean for anything that serious to happen. Right?" Cherene asked searching Katie's eyes for the truth.

"Of course I didn't mean for anyone to get hurt. Especially you. I would never want to hurt you. You are my best friend, Cherene. You have to believe me."

Cherene put her hands on Katie's shoulders trying to calm her friend. "Katie…Katie… I don't blame you. I kind of figured that there was something else to the story."

"So, you let me have all this guilt for days, and you already knew?" Katie questioned in an accusing but playful tone.

Cherene loosed a breath. "You don't have to be a brain surgeon to figure out that a gust of wind doesn't just appear out of nowhere and suddenly disappear with no other effects but to move a huge plate of ice that just so happened to have your arch nemesis holding on to it for dear life."

"Oh. I guess I wasn't that slick, huh?"

Cherene shook her head back and forth, wrapping her arms tightly around her for warmth.

"Even if you already knew, I am still sorry. Do you forgive me, Cherene?"

"I forgive you. I know you would never hurt anyone on purpose, Katie."

Katie's mouth turned up slightly as she nodded. Keeping her eyes cast down so Cherene could not see the guilt that was pooling in her green eyes.

"Alright, now that that is settled, can we please go in? It is freezing out here and I need to sleep," Cherene said through a yawn.

Katie looked at Cherene suddenly feeling as if she did not deserve a friend like her. If she were honest, she *had* meant to hurt someone on purpose. She wanted to make Christy and her friends pay for all the hateful things they had done to Katie and Cherene—to so many others.

As she watched Cherene step towards the door, Katie blurted out, "You can go back in, Cherene, but there is more that I have to figure out."

Cherene turned to face Katie cocking her head and squinting her eyes as if she could not quite see the person standing two feet in front of her. "Like what?"

"I keep getting this sense that there is something calling me to the woods, like a magical energy that is drawing me to it."

"That sounds creepy," Cherene said. "In fact, it sounds like something you should avoid, not run towards."

"Cherene, I need to find out what it is. It's more than just a feeling. The cave story that Sharylin told, I've seen those images before."

"Seen them before? You mean like in a movie or a book?"

"No, I mean that I have actually seen the fountain she described, and I have dreamt about the cave," Katie explained.

Gooseflesh started to form on Cherene's arms. "Now you're really starting to freak me out, Katie." She turned towards the cabin and placed her hand on the doorknob.

"Well, you can go back inside, but I have to find out what this is all about," Katie declared sternly. "I'm going to try to find the cave."

Cherene looked over her shoulder at Katie. "But—"

"Cherene, if I don't find anything I'll come back," Katie reassured her best friend.

Cherene let out an exasperated sigh. “Just wait here.” She went into the cabin and returned with both of their sleeping bags.

Katie grabbed Cherene and hugged her tightly. She took a step back. “I knew I could count on you!” Katie boasted. “You’re the best! Now let’s get out of here before anyone else wakes up!”

The two girls walked briskly down the hill towards the south end of the forest; the area where Katie last saw the purple light. Just before they made it to the campfire amphitheater, Cherene stopped abruptly and grabbed on to Katie’s arm. She whispered in her ear, “Look, someone is over there. Let’s go back; I’m scared.”

Katie looked in the direction Cherene was pointing; there was a lone image standing sentinel beside the lake. The night sky was dark, and a light mist filled the air above the lake.

“He looks familiar,” Katie said, intrigued.

“Katie, please. Let’s just go back. I don’t want to end up in the lake again. That guy looks creepy.”

Cherene turned on her heel and started to retreat up the hill.

“Wait Cherene, I think I know that creepy guy.” Katie strode quickly in the direction of the lake. Cherene followed reluctantly.

“Brian, is that you?” Katie asked as she drew nearer.

Surprised, Brian turned around. “Katie, Cherene, what are you two doing out here?” he asked, sounding pleased to see the two girls.

"We could ask you the same thing, Brian," Cherene replied.

"I was just getting some air. What's your excuse?"

"Katie is on a mission to find the cave from Sharylin's story," Cherene said with just a hint of sarcasm.

Katie turned on her friend. "Cherene, seriously?"

"What?"

Katie shook her head in dismay.

How could Cherene betray me like this? What will she say next? 'Oh, by the way, Katie is a paranormal freak.'

"We thought it would be cool to see if that cave actually exists," Katie offered quickly before Cherene could give away more details.

"Well, why don't I go with you?" Brian asked.

Katie fumbled for a response. "No, we'll probably be gone half the night." Katie grabbed Cherene's hand and pulled her towards the dark forest. As they walked away, Katie shouted over her shoulder, "We'll see you in the morning, Brian."

Brian caught up with the girls and wrapped his arm around Katie's shoulder. "You didn't really think you could get rid of me that easily, did you?" he asked, grinning from ear to ear.

An impish smile spread across Katie's face. "I guess I'm not that lucky," she said as she nudged Brian.

He reached down and held on to her hand. The trio trudged through the dark forest guided only by the moonlight streaming through the still branches. The woods were silent, except for the sound of the snow crunching beneath their feet.

Cherene looked up towards the night sky. "It is so calm and serene out here."

"It could be the calm before the storm," Brian suggested.

Katie took in her surroundings. The sky was dark, but the moon shone brightly through the tall pine trees, casting shadows along the path. "I was just thinking how it felt ominous out here," Katie said with a hint of dread in her voice.

"Ominous? Are you scared?" Brian asked.

"I wouldn't say scared, but it feels like something bad is about to happen."

"Katie, you are seriously starting to freak me out," Cherene exclaimed, her eyes wide with fear.

Katie pulled Cherene to the side. She whispered so that Brian could not hear. "The farther we get into the woods, the feeling that something is drawing me towards it is more intense."

"Is this supposed to make me feel better, Katie? Because it's not!" Cherene yelled.

"Shush. I don't want Brian to hear. I think we are getting close to that cave Sharylin described."

Cherene pleaded with her friend, "Katie, please, let's just go back. I am really scared now."

"You can go back with Brian; I have to finish this," Katie said in a cold tone.

Cherene shrunk back from Katie's harsh words; her face displaying a look of shock.

"Well, what if IT finishes you?" Cherene questioned. Her voice was riddled with fear.

Katie turned towards Brian. "Brian, can you please walk Cherene back to the camp?"

"Where are you going?" he asked, confused.

"I am going to find that cave. Cherene wants to go back," Katie explained.

Brian glanced from Katie to Cherene and back to Katie again. "Katie, if you are going on, we will go with you, right Cherene?" he said.

Brian and Katie continued down the snowy path; Cherene followed a few paces behind mumbling under her breath. They walked on like that for what seemed like forever.

As they walked, a gentle wind stirred the branches above. Katie and Brian stopped to look up at the moving branches overhead. Cherene, not realizing they had stopped, bumped into them. "Hey," she said taking a step back.

A gust of wind blew Katie's hat from her head. She turned around to see Cherene holding her own hat on her head with one hand and clasping Katie's in the other.

"See, the calm before the storm," Brian said. He grabbed the hat from Cherene's outstretched hand and gave it back to Katie. "Good catch, Cherene."

The next moment, the wind whipped through the forest. Tiny flakes of snow swirled around Katie, Brian, and Cherene. In seconds, large snowflakes were pouring from the darkened sky above. Soon, even the moon was veiled by the snowstorm.

"I told you we should have gone back, Katie. Now what are we going to do?" Cherene cried out. Her voice was a concoction of accusation and fear.

"Like I knew there would be a snowstorm!"

"Hey," Brian yelled, "we need to find shelter." Brian shifted his sight from one girl to the other. They were too caught up in their banter to hear him. He shouted, "Now!"

Katie and Cherene stopped arguing and looked at Brian, stunned by his sudden outburst. Katie opened her mouth to protest, but she was quickly interrupted by Brian's insistence.

"We need to find shelter now. Come on."

"Where are we going, Brian? We're in the middle of nowhere in the middle of a storm," Cherene pointed out.

"There is a big boulder over there with a ledge we can hide under until this storm passes," he explained.

They trudged through the mounting snow and ducked under the rock. It offered protection from the falling snow, but it did not stop the wind from biting at the exposed skin on their faces. They turned away from the wind to face the wall of the boulder.

Katie glanced to the outside of the rock that was sheltering her from the harsh storm. She saw a hint of purple light in the distance. Katie felt the familiar pull of its energy and began walking slowly towards the light.

This must be where it has been coming from.

Katie moved in the direction of the warm, purple light. She reached into her front pocket to feel the amethyst rock. It felt warm inside her pocket. A calm sensation rushed through her whole body. She moved methodically towards the entrance of what looked to be a cave. As she drew closer, she could tell that the energy was coming from deep within the cavern.

Her eyes were entranced by the light; its energy tugging at her. She could hear Cherene and Brian in the background yelling for her to return, but she could not stop even if she had wanted to.

The entrance of the cave was dark and foreboding, yet it called to her, insisting that she enter. The shadowy forest became light around the perimeter of the darkened cave entrance. In a trance, Katie walked towards the cavern, still feeling the pull of the purple light within. It was as if she had waited her whole life for what was about to happen.

~ 22 ~

LITTLE LOCKED BOX

"Katie, wait for us!" Brian shouted. Suddenly, the purple light vanished and the white light that illuminated the outside of the cavern disappeared. Katie turned around to see Brian and Cherene running towards her; the snowstorm raged all around.

"Katie, you found a cave. Let's get in, quick. This storm is becoming a severe blizzard," Cherene said.

Katie, Brian, and Cherene ran into the opening of the cave. A huge snowdrift had accumulated at the entrance that carried on for several feet into the open cavern. They plodded through the snow, making it a few feet into the halls of the cave. The blackness enveloped them.

Katie stopped first, then Cherene, and then Brian.

"I can't see my hand in front of my face," Cherene announced, alarmed.

Katie fumbled for the flashlight she tucked into her

coat pocket earlier and turned it on. "There, that should help."

"Do you think this is the cave in Sharylin's story, Katie?" Cherene asked.

Katie did not answer Cherene's question. She was busy looking all around her new discovery. Brian answered Cherene instead.

"I don't know if it is 'the cave,' but it is 'a cave,' which means we will be safe from the storm tonight," Brian said with cool confidence.

Katie's heart was beating rapidly. She knew this was the cave; it called to her. She belonged here. She did not know how or why, but she knew it. She could feel it deep within her being.

"Since we are going to be here all night, we may as well explore a little. What do you think?" Katie asked, flashing Cherene a cheesy grin that reached all the way to her eyes.

"I think you are lucky you are my best friend, or I would kill you, Katie Ryan," Cherene stated in a tone more full of fear and frustration than anger as she stomped the snow from her boots.

Katie and Cherene looked at Brian.

"What do you say, Brian?" Katie asked batting her eyelashes.

Brian looked down at Katie through tired eyes. He let out a breath as a smile tugged at the corners of his mouth. "I think I'm a sucker for a pretty girl," he said, shaking his head back and forth, "and I think you know it, Katie Ryan."

Katie raised her eyebrows up and down and smiled impishly at Brian.

He threw his head back and laughed. “Count me in.”

The walls were damp; a light mist filled the corridors of the mysterious cave. With only a single, narrow ray of light from the flashlight to guide them, the trio walked watching each step they took through the eerie cavern.

“This is scarier than Sharylin’s description in the story,” Cherene complained.

They turned down one tunnel and then another. Before they realized it, they had gone deep into the cave. At the end of the corridor, there was a shimmer of white light. Even before Katie saw the light, she sensed it. A warm sensation filled her body, and the now familiar tug of energy drew her to the end of the corridor. To her left, she saw the soft illumination.

“Guys, check this out,” Katie said.

The three stood at the entrance to a small room that was bathed in a soft white and pale-lilac light. They entered the room. It was colder in the small room than in the larger area, but their fascination outweighed their need for warmth, convincing them to remain in the cool, dimly lit room.

“Where is that glow coming from?” Cherene asked no one as she turned around in search of the source of the light.

“I don’t know, but if we’re going to stay in here for the night, we’re going to need a fire and a place to sleep,” Brian said.

Brian searched the perimeter of the room for small

twigs. As he was gathering the sticks, he stumbled upon what looked to be an old fire pit. He dug deep into the hole and pulled out a flint stone. After piling the twigs in a pyramid, he beat the charcoal stone against another stone; a miniscule spark ignited allowing him to create a small fire with a slip of paper from his pocket. He tucked it into the base of the pyramid of sticks and fanned it gently. A small fire began to grow; before long, Brian, Cherene, and Katie were warming their bodies by the fire he created.

Katie opened the two sleeping bags and made a makeshift bed for them to keep warm.

She leaned back against the cool cavern wall and turned to look at Brian. He was sitting next to the wall with both hands held behind his head.

"You look like you're enjoying this, Brian," she commented.

"I used to be a Boy Scout, so the outdoors is like my second home."

"Your pack leader would be proud," Cherene teased.

"Funny, Cherene. So Katie, what exactly are you hoping to find here?"

Katie shot Cherene a warning look before explaining. "I just wanted to see if this place was real."

"Be real, Katie," Brian said, staring at her through suspicious eyes.

Katie knew Brian did not believe her, but what was she supposed to do? She could not very well tell him that she was a paranormal freak. He would go running straight back to

Christy and her crew, and then Katie would be dead as a doornail when they returned to school after winter break.

She smirked at Brian and said, "I am being real. Plus, anytime I can get away from your buddies is a bonus for me."

Brian sighed deeply and nodded his head in exasperation. "Got it." He turned away from Katie and closed his eyes.

"Are you mad at me, Brian?" Katie asked and nudged his arm gently. He shook his head no and continued to rest his head against the cave wall.

"Awkward," Cherene said. "You can cut the tension in here with a knife, guys."

Katie looked sideways at Cherene and rolled her eyes as she mouthed the words, "Right?"

"Come on Brian don't be mad. I thought we weren't going to let them define us," Katie said leaning over him trying to get his attention.

Brian was silent. He stared at the fire for what seemed like forever to Katie. Finally, he said, "I am not mad, Katie, but is the topic of Christy always going to be a sore subject for us?"

"I guess that depends on her," Katie said.

Brian sat up and faced Katie. "Maybe it would help if you could tell me what the problem is with Christy. I know you guys don't like each other. My question is, why?"

"Actually, I was hoping you could tell me what her problem is," Katie answered.

"She wasn't always this bad. When we first started

going out, she was nice."

I knew they had dated.

She cut her eyes at him.

"What?" he asked shrugging his shoulders and raising his hands, his palms open and facing up.

Cherene laughed out loud. "You just told your 'new' girlfriend that her arch enemy was your 'old' girlfriend. That's what!"

"Cherene, stop!" Katie demanded. The fact that Brian and Christy dated was maddening; it made her despise Christy even more, but she wanted to play it cool. "Brian, go ahead; I'm listening," she said.

"We only went out for a couple of weeks. Then she had a big family tragedy that took up all her time, so we decided just to be friends," Brian's voice trailed off, and he looked away for a moment in deep thought.

"What is it, Brian?" Katie asked.

"Why didn't I realize this before?" Brian said as he shook his head back and forth, his mouth open in surprise.

"What? What is it, Brian? The suspense is killing us!" Cherene announced.

"Her dad was a banker. He had stayed late one night at the bank. When he went home, he left the building out the back door that led to an alleyway; there was a gang of thugs waiting outside. They beat him up and left him for dead. He was rushed to County General Hospital and spent a week in intensive care before they lost him."

"He died?" Katie asked, horrified.

"Yes. Christy just wasn't the same after he died," Brian said.

"So, she actually used to be nice?" Katie inquired.

"I wouldn't say nice, but she was not evil like she is now," Brian responded.

"Brian, I feel sad for Christy. Losing a parent is a difficult thing, but that doesn't explain why she seems to target me with her cruel pranks."

"It would if you knew that the thugs that beat him up were a gang of gothic punks. They never caught them, but video footage from the alley showed a bunch of guys and two girls. All of them had jet-black hair, dark leather clothes, and various tattoos and piercings; anyway, you get the picture."

"You think she's picking on us because we look like the type of people that hurt her father? Don't you think that's a stretch, Brian?"

"They didn't just hurt her father, Katie; they killed him. I am not saying I know for sure, but you asked what I thought. I think that might be the reason she picks on you."

Katie considered his reasoning. She knew how much losing her own father had affected her life, and he was not even dead. He chose to leave. How would she have felt if someone took him from her?

"I guess anything is possible, Brian," Katie said. She was not convinced of his theory, but she did not want to fight with him either.

Cherene, always the peacemaker, tried to calm the situation. "Yeah, you never know how someone is going to respond to tragedy, Katie. She could have just snapped."

Katie did not know how to respond to this new information. Christy had targeted her since her first day at school. Katie had become accustomed to thinking badly of her. This new information changed things…a little.

Katie remembered the horrible note that Christy had thrown at her in class. She thought about its contents. It read, "It should have been you. DEATH is too good for you. You'll pay!"

Katie had not understood what could have prompted such a malicious note from someone she barely knew. This new information would explain the contents of the note.

Maybe Brian was right, but she did not want to talk about it anymore. It still did not excuse Christy's cruelty. Katie turned her back towards Brian and covered herself with the sleeping bag.

* * * * *

Brian lay against the wall of the cave; the red-orange light from the small fire barely a flicker in the darkness. The girls were sleeping, but he was wide awake. He turned to tap Katie on her shoulder and froze.

He rubbed his tired eyes to clear the fog, but he was not seeing things. Something was glowing on the other side of the dark room, its essence growing with every facet of darkness it enveloped. Brian stood up and walked slowly towards the light. As he drew closer, he could see that it had originated from a small, wooden box that was inserted into the cavern wall.

He ran his finger along the smooth, wooden surface careful not to damage the box that had been hidden away for who knew how many years. He grasped the latch, but it would not open. There was a hole in the front; he put his finger inside to try and trip the lock. When that did not work, he pulled out his pocketknife and slipped different gadgets into the hole. One by one he tried each of the tools contained within the small red Swiss Army knife. None of them worked.

Brian glanced back at Katie and Cherene. They were both snuggled together in the warm sleeping bag.

"Katie, Cherene, check this out," he yelled across the room, his voice cracking.

"What?" Cherene said groggily, her head still tucked under the blanket. "We're trying to sleep."

Katie sat up halfway and blinked her eyes to adjust to the change in lighting. There was something strange about the tone in his voice. "What is happening, Brian?" Katie asked.

She got up and ambled towards him. As she got closer, she saw that he was standing next to a small, wooden box that was in the wall of the cave. A faint light was coming from within the box and radiating out slowly filling the room with its brightness. As she approached, the white light began to pulse with a purple radiance.

Katie started to get that pulling feeling inside of her again, the feeling that she was being drawn towards an unseen energy.

That light. Could it be the same light I saw from the cave earlier this evening, the same one from the lake?

She cocked her head to the side and regarded the wooden box.

"What's inside?" she asked.

"I don't know yet. I can't get it open," Brian responded through gritted teeth as he tried again to pry open the box.

"Maybe it takes a key," Cherene suggested as she meandered up behind Katie and Brian.

The wooden box was completely bathed in a lilac and white light. Katie probed the hole in the front of the box.

"There is something hard inside of the hole. It feels like it is lined with stone."

The contrast between the smoothness of the surface and the rough ridges within was very familiar to Katie. As if by instinct, she reached into her own pocket and pulled out her amethyst gem.

Katie gently pulled the box from its home inside the wall of the cave and set it on the rock next to her. She kneeled in front of the treasure. Carefully, she inserted her stone into the hole of the little, locked box. Nothing happened.

"Try the other way," Cherene encouraged anxiously.

Katie flipped the jewel over in her hand and cautiously slid it into the makeshift lock. The stone slipped easily into place like the last piece of the puzzle. A soft click filled their ears.

Katie felt warmth surge through her body. The three friends waited in silence. After a few moments, Katie shrugged her shoulders. "Guess it didn't work, huh?" she said.

Brian's gaze was fixed upon the box. He reached out both hands to grab hold of the girls. "Wait, it's moving," he said in a startled whisper.

The box was vibrating softly on the rock. A steady hum was building from the base of the locked box. Katie, Brian, and Cherene watched wide-eyed as the mysterious box seemed to be revving its engine in preparation for a colossal race.

When it seemed that the wooden chest could not hum any louder, the lid burst open; it flipped back, banging itself on the back of the wooden chest. The motion of the lid slamming back startled Katie, Brian, and Cherene; they fell back and scurried across the ground to the perimeter of the small room, trying desperately to get as far away from the magical box as possible.

They stood up with their backs pressed against the damp cavern wall and watched in awe as an intense stream of white and lilac mist spilled out over the floor of the cave.

~ 23 ~

A FAIRYTALE TO REMEMBER

A vision of a beautiful, delicate woman appeared before their eyes. Her hair was soft and flowing, dark with red highlights. Her green catlike eyes gleamed through the darkness that enveloped her image. She was thin and looked fragile. The white translucent sheath she wore spilled delicately over a soft, lilac-colored silk slip.

The light shone from within her being and radiated outward from her image. Her appearance filled the cavern, making it impossible to see anything but her. Her long fingers were calling them near; her smile welcoming their presence.

Katie, Brian, and Cherene were her captive audience. As if someone had magically pressed play at just the right moment, she began her oratory. Her voice was soft and sad. She looked off in the distance as if she were reminiscing about a time long ago. She seemed compelled to divulge her secret and most personal tale to virtual strangers.

She began, "Our dearest Katheena, it is time for you to know the story of your birth. It is your very own personal fairytale of sorts. Of course, a fairytale would not be a good one without seemingly impossible obstacles to overcome and evil lurking around every corner.

"Your story starts just a few months after I turned eighteen. Although I was still young, I imagined many versions of the fairytale life that I planned on living.

"I fell in love with a man from another realm. At the time, I was unaware of his identity. He was a magical creature, handsome and witty. He stole my heart with his good looks and his charms.

"Little did I know, he was promised to another, one of his own kind. When she discovered that we had already been married, her rage was unquenchable. She brought us to this cave and held us captive until you were born.

"Many days, I sat and wondered to myself, 'Is this really what my life has become? Did I truly deserve to be held captive and threatened with death for being naive?' No matter which way I looked at the dire circumstances, my punishment did not fit the crime.

"On the morning of your birth, I glanced wearily around the icy prison that held your father and me captive. Your father sat slouched over with his head buried in his hands. When he looked up at me, I almost did not recognize his face. His once youthful and spirited countenance was dark. His face was covered in filth, and his eyes overflowed with sadness. He looked like a lost soul awaiting judgment for a crime he could not help but commit.

"I stood slowly, the weight from my pregnancy slowing my movements. It was then that my labor pains began. The intensity increased as each hour crept by. Eventually, the extreme pain caused me to lose consciousness.

"When I came to, your father was still there with me. It had been months since I had discovered his secret, the nature of his true identity. I was so angry at him for his lies and the anguish that they caused. I had not spoken to him but a handful of times during the many months we were imprisoned in the cave.

"When I looked into your eyes, my dearest Katheena, none of that mattered anymore. I knew I could not stay angry with him forever. For nine months we waited for the moment of your birth; once you arrived, our joy was immeasurable.

"You, Katheena, were the most beautiful baby girl. Despite the conditions of our imprisonment, you were born healthy; you were perfect, and you were all ours.

"I cradled you in my arms and glanced toward your father. Seeing the joy and love in his eyes melted my heart, and I knew it had all been worth it. The lies and the cover-up, they were for my protection. He really did not have any other choice. I could forgive him his secrecy because it was for our family, our perfect, happily ever after family. No matter what the future brings, our dearest Katheena, always know that you were loved. Whatever we did, we did because of our deep love for you.

"One day, you will know your true identity. When that day comes, you must—"

Her speech stopped abruptly. As she tried to resume speaking, her words became static like a channel that is out of tune. Katie could not make out what she was trying to say. She strained to hear the last of the message.

"When… eighteen…will—"

The light surrounding the delicate image sputtered and began to fade. It was nearly extinguished like the last flicker of a flame in the wind. The light raced towards the box, gaining speed as it lost its luster until finally it disappeared completely within the box and burned no more. The lid slammed shut loudly.

The force of the lid crashing down was so intense that it sent vibrations throughout the cave. The small tremors intensified until the walls of the cave shook violently. Katie ran to the wooden chest and retrieved her amethyst gem from the hole in the front of the enchanted box. The ground beneath their feet trembled, rocks dislodged from the sides and roof of the cave. Stones were falling all around Katie and her friends.

"Run this way," Katie shouted to Cherene and Brian. They dashed towards the opening of the room they were in and followed Katie's lead as the cave crumbled down around them. Debris was flying and falling, it seemed like they would never make it to the entryway that led out of the room. Once Katie passed the threshold, a huge booming sound echoed, and a loud crash thundered from behind. She turned to see the entrance sealed. She made it out, but Brian and Cherene vanished behind the wall of fallen stones. The cave above Katie started to give way; she had to run further away from the entrance or be crushed by the falling stones. She ran as far as she could until the sounds of the crashing boulders seemed far away.

Katie stopped to catch her breath. Could Cherene and Brian have made it out, maybe through another corridor in the cave that she did not see? Were they trapped inside the room or worse . . . were they buried alive?

Katie knew she would have to find help if she were going to save Cherene and Brian. First, she had to find her way out of the enchanted cave and back to camp. Then she could find someone to help her save her friends. Katie turned around in the narrow corridor of the cave, trying to decide which way to go next, the weight of knowing that her friends' lives were in her hands almost crushing her spirit.

~ 24 ~

REVELATIONS

Katie glanced from side to side and saw an opening. The space beyond was dark and filled with a thick mist, but beyond the darkness, there was light trying to break through the fog covering.

Katie walked towards the image. For a moment, she thought that it might just be a mirage. Like people see mirages of water in the desert, maybe she was seeing a mirage of light. The mind has a funny way of playing tricks on a person; it lets one see what they need to see, until that person can handle reality. Katie stopped, not wanting to be disappointed by her own mind games.

She shook off the apprehension and continued towards the light that was breaking through the dark fog that loomed before her. She stood within the dark, wet cave. The thick gray fog rolled towards her. A dark figure advanced from the grayness towards Katie.

The mysterious creature moved gracefully over the loose stones on the ground, but the being held the stench of death. Katie saw the form of a woman. Her long black robes trailed behind her as she advanced swiftly and without hesitation.

Katie's breath caught as the woman's appearance was revealed. Her wrinkled face a twisted and grotesque mass. Strands of her long black hair blew wildly about. Her glowing black eyes bore through Katie.

"Ah, I have finally found you. I knew you would come eventually," she taunted. Her words gave way to her menacing laugh.

Katie shivered from the cold and the fear that overtook her body. Although she was frightened, she was also intrigued. Her anticipation almost outweighed the fear. Katie drew nearer to the woman but quickly wished she had not. The intense being's black eyes began to glow and a blazing, red-hot heat burrowed into Katie's chest.

"What are you doing to me?"

"Nothing that will hurt you, my dear," her breath was ragged, almost forced. "As I said, I have waited for this moment for so very long."

"What do you want from me?" Katie asked, trying not to show the fear that was building inside.

"What I want from you can wait. I have something to share with you first."

"Wait a minute, can you help me? My friends, they are

stuck in . . ."

She waved her hand and dismissed Katie's questions. "Never mind your friends and all your silly questions. All will be revealed soon enough."

"But—"

"Silence!" the being bellowed.

Katie closed her eyes and took a deep breath. The creature's voice turned soft and overly sweet as she spoke, "Everything has its own time. Now is the time for you to know my story."

"You want to tell me a story?" Katie asked with disbelief and exasperation. "I don't have time for this. My friends have been trapped within this cave. I must help them."

In one swift move, the dark creature was upon her. The crone's acrid breath heated Katie's face; as her crooked fingers yanked her hair, forcing her head back. Katie choked on the pungent stench.

"Listen," the dark creature enunciated slowly with a snake-like hiss.

"Alright, alright, I will listen," Katie said. She would have to worry about finding Cherene and Brian later.

The old woman's grip on Katie's hair loosened and Katie shuffled backwards, standing close to the damp wall of the cave. She listened as the ancient crone began her oratory.

"I am the Unseelie queen, the ruler of the Otherworld. I was once the most beautiful woman in the Shadow Lands. I was betrothed to the most handsome of all Seelie Fae, my sweet, sweet Daniel."

Is she for real?

She mulled over the woman's words. Katie had read about the Seelie and Unseelie Fae. They were beautiful, magical creatures but very dangerous, especially those of the Unseelie court.

The Unseelie queen continued, "Have you ever known what it is to experience true love, my dear?"

"I am only sixteen. I don't think so."

"Well, it is everything you read about in the fairytales, no pun intended, of course," the queen said; her laughter filled the cavern. Her voice became sweet, almost endearing, "Our parents had tried in vain to arrange a marriage between Daniel and me, but I would have none of their scheming. Little did I know that the Fae I had fallen for was in fact, the Seelie Prince. It was love at first sight. The wedding was planned. Our families were elated. We were destined to rule the Kingdom of Faery together, forever. I have felt no greater joy than in those few months before my world was shattered."

Katie knew a little something about having her own world shattered. She started to feel a little sympathy for the frightening creature.

"What happened? Did he die?"

"Oh, he was destined to die all right, but not by honorable means."

Her black eyes glowed—orbs of evil and revenge.

"It was the night before we were to be wed. Daniel did not return from his trip to your realm. My father sent out a search party for him, but he was nowhere to be found. I had a sickening feeling in the pit of my stomach. I knew something was amiss.

"I went right away to the land of humans. I sensed his presence the moment I entered this world. He was sitting on a park bench, near the lake with a fountain. He was holding hands with a beautiful woman, though her beauty could not be compared to mine."

The dark queen morphed into the beautiful being she had been long ago. Katie's eyes grew wide at the sight of the stunning creature. Her hair was golden, her eyes a striking midnight blue. The image lasted only a moment, then she transformed back to the hideous evil queen.

"I knew the moment that I saw them that there was more to them than met the eye. I joined their party and decided to steal her joy just as she had stolen mine.

"I remember the look on her face when she discovered that the man she was consorting with was not human. He was a wolf in sheep's clothing playing at being human in order to win her affections.

"Then the most gruesome discovery was made. The human woman was with child. They had stolen away and had a secret wedding. It had been two moon cycles since their blissful union. I could not bear the pain of the betrayal. My one true love was professing his love for another."

Katie stood still, dumbfounded by her revelation. She did not know what to say. "I'm so sorry. That would be very hurtful," she managed.

The old crone waved her hand dismissing the very idea

of the old pain.

"Oh, never you mind with 'I'm sorry.' I'm sorry never fixed anything in my world. But I fixed the two of them," she said maniacally. Wringing her hands in front of her in triumph, the Unseelie queen cackled.

Wide-eyed, Katie asked, "What did you do?"

"I found this cave and imprisoned them here. They stayed here for months until she gave birth. She was so shattered by his betrayal that she would not even speak to him until she gave birth to the sniveling brat. I thought maybe there would be hope for him and me. I thought she would leave him, and then I could have my love back.

"The idiot he was, he swore his undying love to her. He swore to stand by her even if she refused to speak to him forever. He told me he never loved me. I had been played for a fool. Thinking that our meeting was by chance, when it had been the result of our parents' scheme to join the power of the Seelie and Unseelie courts. Daniel had agreed to go along with their plan leaving me to play the ignorant jester."

"I can see why you were so angry," Katie said.

"I would show them to make a fool out of me. They would see bloodshed yet."

"Bloodshed," Katie whispered.

"After the baby was born, the two of them were so enthralled with one another again. They could not take their eyes off each other. That miserable wench took what was most precious to me, so I swore to take what was most precious to her.

"I plotted to steal the baby and watch them suffer. I knew that eventually I would grow tired of their weeping. When that day came, I would kill Daniel and his beloved wife, Scarlett. Daniel's father, the Seelie king, caught wind of my ploy and made a deal with my father, the Unseelie king, to make a trade. Daniel's life would be spared, so that he and I could be married, and the original arrangement fulfilled. In exchange, his beloved wench, Scarlett, would die by my hand and the sniveling little brat, Katheena, would be raised in the human realm."

Katheena. That name is familiar.

The Unseelie queen continued her tale. "Daniel even helped his stupid little wench to make a hologram, a little fairytale of sorts, a message from a new mother to her precious daughter detailing her birth. They hid the box in the cavern. The box was enchanted with a spell; it could only be opened with a special stone."

The wooden box. The beautiful woman that shared the story with us. Oh my. Could this all be real?

"They thought it was a perfect plan, but then they did not know I was watching them."

"What did you do?" Katie asked, mesmerized by the queen's story.

"The day came when I was to lift the ice bars that imprisoned them. They thought I could be so easily assuaged. They thought I could be appeased with a marriage to Daniel, a man that clearly loved another. Little did they know, it was all a ruse. My intentions had not been altered by their little arrangement. I still planned to steal the baby and kill Daniel and Scarlett."

Katie gasped. "So, you killed them all?" Katie asked, her tone betraying her fear.

"If only I could have exacted my revenge. It all happened so quickly. The instant I showed my true self and raised the ice bars that hideous Scarlett threw herself into the black water, and Daniel disappeared before my very eyes. The Seelie queen had the baby spirited away by a human woman. I unleashed my fury on the Seelie king. He was the only one man enough to face me, but I was no match for his powers. I was but a princess then. But now… now I am the Unseelie queen, ruler of the Otherworld."

The old crone's speech stopped. She turned from Katie and walked slowly to the edge of the water. Although a thick fog loomed over the middle of the pond, Katie was sure she could see the outline of a fountain.

Her glare returned to the old woman at the water's edge; she watched the queen's back rising and falling with each deep breath she took. The Unseelie queen turned slowly and glowered at Katie.

"I lost everything that evening in this dark cavern. I lost my one true love and the hope of a child for myself."

"But you could still have a child," Katie offered.

"Daniel's mother put a curse on me that made my womb barren. I searched and searched for the child that my beloved sired. When I realized that I could no longer have children, I wanted to raise her as my own."

"Did you ever find out what happened to the baby girl?"

"My sources told me that Daniel's mother left her with an old human woman; Lucille was her name."

"I see."

"Do you? I mean, do you really see, my dear?"

Actually, I don't see at all, but you are seriously starting to creep me out, you old bat!

Katie was completely unaware of what the dark being was hinting at, but she could not let the queen know she did not have a clue of what she was trying to suggest.

"Yes, I think I do. Why didn't you go and see the baby girl if you knew who had her?"

"I said I knew *who* had her, not *where* she was," she hissed, years of anger filling her tone. "His wretched mother placed a spell on the baby that would protect her from me as long as she stayed within a one-hundred-mile radius of Lucille."

"I'm so very sorry to hear of your pain," Katie said. She thought it best to appear to be sympathetic.

This woman has two switches, saccharine or lethal.

Katie's mind wandered back to Brian and Cherene and their predicament.

I've got to change the subject. This woman will go on forever about these people from her past.

She decided now was as good a time as any to bring the conversation back to her troubles. "Okay, I've heard your story; now can you help me find my friends?"

"Come closer, my dear," the Unseelie Queen's voice cracked as she spoke, giving her tone an eerie sense.

Why are you talking like that?

She walked a little closer. She could not imagine what it was that caused the Queen to speak in such a curious tone. "What do you need?" Katie questioned.

"I want to show you the powers that the black water can bestow upon you." Katie looked ahead, curious and cautious at the same time.

She went on. "I know what you want. I was once a young girl just like you. Tell me now, what is it that you desire most?"

Katie felt that was really a personal question.

Is she for real? Just because she told me her story, doesn't mean I want to share mine.

What was it that Katie wanted? She could go with her old standby: world peace. She could wish for a boyfriend. Maybe she wanted money. They say it can't buy you love, but it can buy a whole lot of other things. Money might buy her mom the freedom to not have a husband. Wait, why was she even considering this question?

"I…well…I don't really know what I want," she stuttered in response.

"Nonsense, you and I both know what it is that you want," she insisted. "Come here and I will show you."

Reluctantly, Katie walked towards her. She looked different, darker almost. Not in the way that one becomes suntanned after staying in the sun too long, but she was definitely darker. It was as if her spirit were black. The moment Katie got within arm's distance of the being; the queen reached for her and grabbed her arm near the shoulder.

Suddenly, it was as if the world had shifted. Katie saw blackness, and from the center of the darkness, a white orb began to clear the dark region from the middle outward. It left a black rim with a light that glowed around the inner edges. In the middle of the sphere, Katie could see a scene unfold before her. She saw a girl with dark brown hair and red highlights that shimmered in the sun. She was smiling, laughing. She was surrounded by girls that looked at her in an adoring manner.

Then the scene shifted, and the surrounding girls were separating to let someone near the girl.

Oh, he is cute.

He was tall, dark, and handsome. As he came very close, Katie recognized him. It was Sean. His green eyes were dazzling in the sunlight. His eyes matched the eyes of the girl. In fact, the girl's eyes matched Katie's eyes perfectly.

Katie struggled to see it clearly. It couldn't be. It was. The girl was her. The girl was Katie, and the boy was Sean. It had been so long since Katie saw herself with anything but black hair, she did not recognize herself at first.

The people surrounding them were their friends, Katie's friends. They were her friends from her first high school; the vision was of Katie during her freshman year. It was all playing out before her very eyes. What she wanted most. It was what she had once possessed.

The queen was right; Katie wanted her old life back.

She wanted the life she had led before her father left and the parade of men came in and out of her mother's life and in and out of Katie's life too. But how could the queen possibly know this? How did an evil queen know what was in her heart?

"I can see what you desire most in your heart," she answered.

"Wait a minute, I didn't say that out loud," Katie insisted, fear seeping into the back of her mind.

"You did not have to. I can see into your soul. It is the black water," she replied. "The dark water gives immeasurable power to those who drink of it. I want to offer that power to you, Katie. The power would give you anything your heart desires. Come, drink from the black water."

"Why do you want me to have the power?"

"I want you to be the daughter I never had. We could rule the Otherworld together, my dear. Come, all you must do is drink from the black water."

Katie thought about it. Could she really be telling the truth? Could Katie have her old life back? How many times had she wished and hoped and prayed to have her old life back: a mom and dad in the same home, friends that adored her?

"So, you're saying that all I have to do is drink from the black water, and everything I once had would be mine again?"

"Tempting, isn't it, my dear? You would never want for anything again."

"But, what about the friends I have now? What would

happen to them?

"Why, it would be as if they never existed."

The thought of her old life sounded pleasant. No Phil, no Christy, no Darrell, no Destiny. Poof, they would simply be gone from her life. Who could ask for more than that? Then her thoughts turned to the good things in her life now: Cherene, Brian, and the new girls she met at camp. Could she take them with her?

"They would be gone as well, my dear. It is a small price to pay, don't you think?"

She did that mind reading thing again.

"When you say gone, what exactly do you mean?" she dared to ask. Something in the back of her mind did not feel right.

"Why, they would cease to exist of course," she said sibilantly.

Her tone sounded frightening, evil, and full of retribution. While Katie pondered her words, the queen dipped a pitcher into the dark waters and let it fill slowly, careful not to touch the waters herself.

"What, what are you doing?" Katie inquired, unable to keep the panicked tone from her voice.

"I am bringing to you everything that you always wanted. Come Katie, it is time to drink."

Katie backed away from her slowly like a man trying not to startle a wild animal.

"So, before I do this, when you say cease to exist, you mean that they will cease to exist in my life, right?" she asked but it was almost like a hopeful request. Deep down, she was afraid she knew the answer to her own question.

The evil being moved quickly toward Katie, causing the water to splash from the pitcher.

"Enough! Enough of this wasting of my time. I have what you want. Drink from the black water and you will have it all."

"But I have to know first, what do you mean by cease to exist?"

The queen's eyes blazed with anger, and her voice echoed through the cavern, "You stupid little fool, don't be so melodramatic. You know what I mean! It will be as if they never existed in *your* life!"

In an instant the demonic beast was upon her. "Now drink!"

Katie gasped in horror as the evil one pulled Katie's head back by her hair with her free hand. A million thoughts ran through Katie's mind all at once. She was not ready to give up the good along with the bad. Her old life was wonderful, but it was just that. It was her old life. She liked her new life.

Did I really just think that?

Suddenly, she realized that she had spent so much of the last two years wishing for a life she could no longer have, she did not realize that her new life was not so bad. In fact, it was pretty awesome. It hit her like a ton of bricks. She did not want her old life back anymore. She wanted to see what this life had to offer her.

Katie wondered if life was truly that cruel. Once she made the amazing realization that she wanted to keep her life, the life she always complained about, she might not have a choice. This demonic beast was about to make her drink the black water that would automatically put her back into her old life.

Her mind flashed to that old life. The late night fights her parents had, the childish jealousy that the girls in her group showed and fighting to keep Sean as her boyfriend when the other girls wanted him. Making sure she wore the right clothes and did her hair just right. It all came rushing back. The terrible pressure she felt at trying so hard to fit in.

She really did not want her old life back. It was not as great as she remembered after all. This crazy being was forcing a life on her that she now knew for certain she did not want anymore. The thought of not getting a choice in the matter made Katie angry. “Wait, what if I don’t want it anymore?” she stammered.

The evil queen’s eyes burned into Katie. She felt the heat from her eyes from inches away. Katie did not wait for the answer. She reached in her pocket with her free hand, palming the stone. She was going to use it to strike the queen on her temple.

It had worked for David with Goliath.

Instantly, she felt a heat like no other radiating from the amethyst stone. The power of it unsteadied her stance and sent a surge of power to her head. She had to close her eyes to bear the pressure. Katie saw a lilac color glowing behind her eyes; it grew warmer and stronger.

Suddenly, as if she had struck the Unseelie queen with a powerful blow, her grip was broken and the queen flew across the cave, hitting the wet wall. Her body slid down slowly, lifeless. Katie did not stop to assess the queen's injuries. She bolted from the water's edge and ran through the tunnels.

I must find Cherene and Brian.

The cave was so dark and wet; she fumbled through its narrow corridors with both hands upon the walls trying to feel her way out. The only light was a faint glow dispersed from the water fountain room behind her. She was almost certain she did not sense the evil being following her, but she was too afraid to look back to be sure.

She wanted to get as far away as she could as quickly as she could. The farther she ran, the blacker the cave became. As she inched along, a fear rose in her. What if the black water gave the Unseelie queen the power to see in the darkness? Katie was going so slowly now; the queen would surely catch up with her in no time.

When Katie rounded the third bend, she remembered the flashlight she had stowed in her backpack before leaving on this awful journey. She hoisted the pack to the front of her, still creeping along slowly. The zipper opened easily, and she fumbled through the supplies at the top of the pack. She heard a small clink as something on the top of the pack fell to the cavern floor. She wondered to herself what it might have been, but she knew she would never find it in the dark.

She reached deep into the bag and found the flashlight. “Please work, please work,” she whispered to herself. Click. A small stream of light illuminated the floor of the cave. “*Yes,*” she whispered.

She ran the light from side to side to see what had fallen to the floor of the cave, but whatever it was, it evaded her sight. She did not have time to scavenge on the ground with the Unseelie queen hot on her trail. She gave up her search for the lost item and continued through the tunnels of the cave.

Guided by the light, running quickly became easier. She searched tunnel after tunnel, but she felt she was going in circles.

How am I ever going to find Cherene and Brian like this?

The adrenaline rush was diminishing, and she was getting very sleepy. It must have been morning by now, but she was so deep in the cave she could not see a spot of daylight.

She surveyed her surroundings trying to think of what to do next. To her right was a crevice in the wall. The opening was just big enough for Katie to slip through. She shimmied her way through the crevice and found that there was a tiny room on the other side of it. The room was dark, but Katie felt safely hidden from the eyes of the Unseelie queen there.

Katie made herself comfortable against the cool cavern wall. She closed her eyes and immediately fell fast asleep.

~ 25 ~

MIND GAMES

Katie heard a soft tapping against the wall of the cave. She sat straight up and looked toward the small crevice. There was a light shining through from the other side. She squeezed herself through the small opening and emerged on the other side. Looking over her shoulder, she saw a tall, lanky figure standing to her left. He was dark, but there was a soft glow emanating around his entire being. For a moment, his silhouette looked familiar to her, but his identity escaped her.

Katie pulled the flashlight from her pocket and turned it on to reveal the face of the dark figure. He was dressed all in black, but he was wearing a welcoming smile. He motioned to Katie with his arm. "Come with me now," he said slowly, methodically.

She knew in her mind that it was not smart to follow a stranger through the dark corridors of a hidden cave, especially a man that was wearing a coat of supernatural light around his being. Katie's mind said, "Run, don't walk; run away as fast as you can." But in her heart, in her gut, everything in her down to the core of her being said that he was part of her. He would not lead her astray.

Katie followed him through one tunnel of the cavern, then another. At the end of the second tunnel, the dark man turned into a room. As she turned the corner, she saw that a thick mist filled the chamber. In the middle of the room, the man stood staring blankly at Katie. For a moment, she got the feeling again that she knew him from somewhere.

Then he spoke. His voice was deep, yet warm. He spoke with such authority; it was the kind of voice that made a person want to hear what he would say next.

"I have waited many years for this moment, Katie."

Katie gasped, "You know me?"

"I have known you all of your life. Now, it is time that you know who you are," he stated matter-of-factly.

"I guess I am confused, Sir. Who exactly are you?"

"Who I am is not important. I have come—"

"I remember you now. You came to me before. You came to me in one of my bizarre dreams about fountains and flying faeries."

"Yes, that was me. I am here to finish what I started that evening. I am here to teach you the ways of the Fae," he said.

"The Fae?"

"Surely by now, you have discerned that you are

special, Katie. I have seen you use a small fraction of your powers. I am here to teach you how to use all of them."

"You mean there is still more that I can do?" Katie asked hopefully.

"You have only begun to tap into the depth of your true powers; you are the daughter of a Seelie prince after all."

Katie thought about what he was saying. She was the daughter of a Seelie prince. She had already met a creature that called herself the Unseelie queen. Part of her wanted to dismiss the information as impossible, but another part of her, the part that had been drawn to the cave to begin with, knew that he was telling her the truth.

"Are you some sort of Master Faery or something?" she asked teasingly.

"I like to think of myself as a Faery Godfather," he explained, "but that is not important. We have wasted enough time talking. I must teach you about your powers. I have seen you move and break objects, and you were able to use the element of fire without a second thought. I was most impressed when you called on the element of wind. Moving the ice on the lake was a brilliant move, until that Brian character distracted your thoughts, that is," her Faery Godfather said. His irritation at the thought of Brian was evident.

"You saw all of that?"

Katie was a little worried about what else he had witnessed. "This could get embarrassing," she thought.

"Don't worry, I only watch when you are invoking your powers," he said reassuringly.

Katie looked at him quizzically.

"Did he just read my mind? He's like the Unseelie queen," Katie thought woefully.

"I am the exact opposite of the Unseelie queen!" he bellowed. He breathed deeply, trying to calm his anger. "Yes, we can read minds." His voice returned to its normal state. "So can you, my dear Katie," he said with an admiring smile on his face.

"You can teach me how to read minds?" she asked excitedly. Katie thought of all the things she could do with a skill like that. She could know what Christy was going to say before she even said it. Maybe then she would not stumble over her comebacks every time the snotty girl tried to embarrass her. Better still, she would know for certain what Brian thought of her. A mischievous smile formed on her face.

"All in good time, Katie. Last time we met, I started to teach you how to transport your body. Let's start with the transport. Do you remember the steps?"

Katie's mind wandered back to the dream, but she could not recall his instructions. "Can you refresh my memory?"

He smiled affectionately and stood in front of Katie, pointing at the far wall. "Focus on the opposite end of the room. Do you have a spot in your mind?" he asked.

"Yes."

"Now, let the warmth of your powers wash over your whole body. Imagine your whole being vanishing from where you are now and reappearing in the place in which you have

focused all your energy."

Katie held her eyes shut tightly imagining the now familiar warmth of her powers rushing throughout her body. She envisioned herself vanishing in thin air and making her body reappear across the room. The warm sensation enveloped her entire being. For a moment, she ceased to exist. She had no thoughts, no awareness; she felt... nothingness. The next moment, the warmth returned to her. Her thoughts resumed, and she was very aware of the fact that she had shifted. She opened her eyes to discover that she had transported from one end of the room to the other.

"I did it! I did it! Did you see me?" she said enthusiastically turning to face her Faery Godfather.

He nodded in agreement and grinned sheepishly. "I knew you would be amazing. After all, you are my—"

Katie glanced sideways at him. "I am your what?"

He hesitated for a moment as if he were contemplating whether to reveal a deep, dark secret. "You are my Faery Goddaughter, of course," he said calmly.

"Can I try it again?" Katie asked excitedly.

At her request, he smiled from ear to ear and let out a chuckle. "Katie, you performed the transport seamlessly. I think our time will be better spent learning a new skill. It is only a matter of time before the Unseelie queen finds you."

Katie's thoughts returned to the image of the evil queen. The memory of the stench of her acrid breath made Katie want to throw up. She knew she would need every power imaginable to fight off the maniacal being.

"Okay. What's next?"

"When you face the queen again, it may not only be necessary for you to transport, but to shoot her as well."

Katie considered his words. She had never handled a gun. She did not feel good about the idea of shooting someone, even if that someone was an evil queen.

"I don't think I want to use a gun. My dad was never really in favor of them, and I guess his ideas kind of rubbed off on me," Katie wearily stated her feelings to the supernatural being. She hoped he would understand her position on weapons.

The light from his body flickered and disappeared quickly, but only for a moment. In the next instant, a huge flash of light radiated out from his fingertips and struck a rock several feet away. The rock was reduced to rubble.

"What was that?" Katie asked, shocked but very impressed.

He chortled loudly. "That is how our kind shoots. We use blasts of energy, not bullets, my dear child," he said with his laughter continuing to fill the dim cavern.

Katie shrugged her shoulders and gave him a disapproving look. "You could have just said that from the start. You don't have to make fun of me. I'm new at this, remember?"

"There is no time for hurt feelings, Katie Ryan. You are a Seelie princess. You must use your mind and your powers to control your environment. Feelings only get in the way. Come to me, now," he demanded.

Katie walked slowly towards him and stood by his side.

"Now, hold your arm out in the direction that you want the energy to hit. Hold your hand palm down. Center the force of your energy on your hand, and as you turn your hand over, envision the energy flowing out of your hand through your fingertips and striking your target."

He stood with his arm extended; a stream of light shot out from his fingertips and blasted a hole in the wall of the cave.

"Wow, that's incredible! Can I try?"

He turned slowly towards Katie.

"Yes, now it is your turn, my dear," he said methodically, smiling at his apprentice, his green eyes gleaming with pride. "Remember, your success depends on your ability to envision in your mind the energy transferring from your body and striking the object," he added.

Katie nodded her head to show her Faery Godfather that she understood his instructions. She closed her eyes and tried to purge the images that were flooding her mind. A million and one thoughts were tugging at her trying to pull her in one direction or another.

Katie breathed deeply and opened her eyes. She cast her focus upon a dark spot across the room in the cave. She followed his directions carefully. She envisioned her energy flowing from her body and out through her fingertips.

Without intending, she thought of her friends, Cherene and Brian. The idea that she may never find them again filled her mind for a moment. She tried to transfer her energy back to the task of shooting the wall in front of her. Through squinted eyes, she concentrated on the energy. Nothing happened.

"Why isn't it working?"

"Your head is full of rubbish," he scolded.

"My friends are not rubbish!" she corrected quickly.

"When you are at war, you must forget all else, Katie."

"Even my friends?"

"Especially your friends. War is no time for feelings or friends."

"That is cold."

"No. Strategy is not cold, Katie. Dead bodies are cold," his chilly tone echoed through the small room of the cave.

"Now, clear your head and start again."

Katie tried to concentrate, but a familiar voice seeped into her mind. She tried to silence the voice, but its existence persisted, prohibiting her from shutting it out. The next instant, the voice revealed its identity to Katie. It was Meagan.

"Katie? Cherene? Brian? Can you hear me?" Meagan shouted through the cool cave.

Katie's eyelids fluttered and then opened. She looked around and surveyed the small space that she occupied trying to remember how she arrived in such a tight spot. Her mind recalled the fact that she had sought this hole in the cave as refuge from the Unseelie queen. She had fallen asleep. A stream of artificial light moved back and forth outside her refuge.

"Katie? Cherene? Brian? Where are you?"

"Meagan, is that you?" Katie asked tentatively, fumbling for her flashlight.

"Yes," the voice from beyond the wall replied quickly. "Where are you?" she asked in the sweet voice that Katie had come to appreciate.

Even though her time at camp had been brief, Katie felt that Meagan was a source of security and safety. Meagan was the voice of reason whenever everyone else around her was being unpredictable and difficult.

"I'm in here, Meagan," Katie said as she stood up from the cold cavern floor. She brushed dust and small pieces of stone debris from her pants and squeezed herself through the slit in the cave wall.

As Katie emerged, she grabbed hold of Meagan's outstretched hand allowing Meagan to help her up.

Katie wrapped her arms around Meagan. "Oh Meagan, I'm so glad you came. I lost Brian and Cherene in another part of the cave. There is a—"

Katie stopped herself and loosened her grip on Meagan. Eyeing Meagan cautiously, Katie thought, *I can't very well tell Meagan that there was an Unseelie queen from the Otherworld with magical faery powers trying to take over my life.*

"I mean, there has to be a way to find them," Katie said finishing her sentence.

"Come with me. We'll find them together," Meagan

offered as she grabbed Katie's hand and pulled her through the dark tunnels. They turned down one short hall and then down another one, longer this time.

Meagan seems to know these halls.

"Meagan, do you know where Brian and Cherene are?" Katie asked suspiciously.

Meagan stopped abruptly. She turned to Katie and smiled her sweetest smile.

"No, silly. How would I know where they are?" she asked. Her lashes fluttered rapidly as she smiled innocently at Katie. As she stared at Katie, Meagan's eyes became shadowed by a dark film.

Katie cocked her head to the side, disquieted. Katie saw the blackness take over Meagan's eyes for only a moment, but just as soon as she thought she saw it, the image disappeared.

Oh, please, not now. I don't have time for my mind to play tricks on me again. I need to find my friends and get out of this creepy cave. Everything is okay. You are just seeing things because you are sleep deprived. Plus, it is seriously dark in here; everything looks black in a dark cave.

Katie talked herself out of her worry. "It just seemed like you knew where you were going," she explained.

"This is the way I came through before I found you. I was just trying to go back to where I started and see if we could find them together."

That makes sense. See Katie, get all the facts before you jump to conclusions.

Katie nodded in agreement. "That sounds like a good plan."

Meagan and Katie walked side by side through the dark, cold cave until they found a ray of morning light streaming down one of the long tunnels.

"There, over there!" Katie said excitedly pointing in the direction of the light. "There is the entrance of the cave."

~ 26 ~

A CASE OF MISTAKEN IDENTITY

Meagan and Katie raced toward the light. Both girls stopped running abruptly. The light was streaming through a tiny hole in the stone wall. Katie tried to peer inside. She saw a ray of light surrounded by darkness. She strained her eyes, desperately trying to see what was beyond the wall.

"It's a dead end," Meagan said. "Let's go back and try another tunnel."

Katie remained focused on the room beyond the wall. A small twinkle of purple light caught her eye. "Wait, I think I can see something. There is something in the middle of the room," Katie said excitedly.

"Let me see," Meagan said.

She pushed Katie aside and stood on the tips of her toes to see what was in the room.

"You're right, Katie. There is something in the room!"

Meagan shouted excitedly, craning her neck so that she could still see through the crack. Katie rushed over and tried to peek through the gap in the cavern wall with Meagan.

"I knew I saw something!" Katie said. She gently nudged Meagan aside so she could get a good view. A purple light winked at her. Warmth flowed through her being.

"How do we get in?" Meagan asked.

"I don't know; I was about to ask you the same question."

Their conversation was interrupted suddenly by the sound of footfalls. Katie and Meagan quickly turned their heads in the direction of the noise.

"Katie, oh my goodness! Thank God we found you," Sharylin's voice echoed through the dark hall.

Sharylin was carrying a flashlight, heading straight for them. Brian followed after Sharylin, pulling a reluctant Cherene close behind.

Katie rushed forward and hugged all three of her friends at once. Cherene and Sharylin stepped back and rested against the moist cavern wall, but Brian refused to break away from Katie. Finally, Katie stepped back and held his hands in hers, smiling at him. She turned her gaze from Brian and said to Cherene, "I can't believe you're safe! How did you get out?"

"Sharylin found us!" Cherene explained excitedly.

"Thank you, Sharylin. I was so afraid that I would never see them again."

Sharylin smiled softly and said, "Of course. I could not

let them stay trapped forever."

Her tone gave Katie an unnerving sensation. She said it as if she were the one holding Brian and Cherene captive. Katie remembered her grandmother's words, "Look into their eyes; the eyes cannot lie."

Katie regarded Sharylin's eyes. At first glance, Katie could not discern their color. They looked dark, not the bright blue color they should have been. But then again, the cave was dark too.

Just stay calm, Katie. Remember, don't make a judgment until you have all of the facts.

Katie fumbled for her flashlight. She raised it up slowly trying not to look too obvious.

"So, how did you know where to look, Sharylin?"

"I didn't really. I followed Meagan out here, but I lost her when she went into the cave. One or two wrong turns later and I heard scratching and crying."

"Let me guess, the scratching was Brian trying to dig his way out," Katie suggested. She glanced at Cherene and said, "And the crying was . . ."

"This brave girl over here," Brian said sarcastically, pointing his finger at Cherene.

Cherene shrugged her shoulders and shot Katie a cheesy grin. "I never said I was Pocahontas, you know."

Katie shook her head back and forth and giggled a little. Then she remembered her mission. As she continued to raise the beam of the flashlight, she asked Sharylin, "So how did you get them out?"

Sharylin twisted her mouth; she seemed to be contemplating her answer. The beam of light traveled from Sharylin's mouth, up to her eyes.

"No!" Katie yelled reflexively.

Sharylin's eyes were black pits.

It can't be. Get control, Katie. You are going to give it away.

"I didn't say anything yet, Katie," Sharylin said, shooting Katie an overly perplexed look.

Katie breathed deeply and considered her next move. Should she challenge Sharylin right now? Or would that cause a bigger problem?

I really need to get out of here.

Katie shook her head and tried to laugh off her mistake. "No, not you Sharylin. I snagged my fingernail on my coat zipper," she said as she sucked on her finger trying to make her tale more believable.

Katie peered into the darkness at Sharylin. A small ray of light was cast across her face.

She looks like she did the night of the cave story. Katie surveyed her mind for explanations of Sharylin's dark being.

"So," Sharylin broke the awkward silence, "what were you and Meagan looking at in the wall?" She turned around to see the hole that had a thin ray of light streaming through it.

"We think there may be a way out through there. We thought we saw a purple light," Katie said as she advanced towards Sharylin. Sharylin turned abruptly and held her hand out signaling for Katie to stop.

"Let me look," Sharylin insisted harshly.

Katie stared at her with a look of shock. *Sharylin would never be that harsh.*

Then, as if she realized just how severe she had been, Sharylin added with a smile and a giggle, "I don't think this hole is big enough for both of us."

Katie eyed Sharylin suspiciously. Brian came up behind Katie and turned her so that she was facing him. He wrapped his arms around her tightly. For a moment, Katie forgot her dilemma and gave in to his hug. She looked up at his face and smiled. "Miss me much?" she asked flirtatiously.

"You will never know just how much, Katie Ryan."

The seriousness of his tone took her back. "Are you okay, Brian?" Katie asked, concerned.

"Yeah. I'm fine. I just thought I would never see you again. Let's just say that I had a small taste of what it would be like to be without you, and I know I do not want to feel that way again."

He pulled her close to him again. As they stood holding one another, Sharylin ran both of her hands along the moist cavern wall, her fingers searching in the dark for the crevices that were so familiar to her.

She stepped back slightly with both hands firmly clutching the minuscule fractures in the wall. She closed her eyes and breathed in deeply. The rocks holding the wall together shifted slightly. A low rumbling echoed through the tunnel.

Startled, Cherene grabbed on to Meagan and Katie;

Brian turned in Sharylin's direction. Sharylin dropped her hands quickly to her sides.

"What was that?" Sharylin asked, sounding baffled.

"I think we should get out of here," Meagan suggested; the fear in her voice was considerable.

Cherene held on to Meagan with one hand and grabbed Katie's arm with the other. "Please, let's get out of here, now!" Cherene uttered through quivering lips.

Katie looked up at Brian, her eyes wide.

"What is it, Katie?"

"What should we do?" she whispered.

"You are usually the one with the plan, Katie," Brian said. He reached for her hand. "Katie, you are shaking." His expression revealing he was starting register the seriousness of the situation.

"You are the guy, Brian. Don't you think you should take charge?" Cherene asked.

Brian looked at Katie. "Are you going to let her get away with that kind of chauvinistic statement?" he asked, trying to lighten the mood.

Katie's mind sifted through her options. *We can turn and run as fast as we can, but if Sharylin is what I think she is, she'll catch us in a heartbeat. I can use my powers to smash her in to the wall again so we can get a head start. But then Brian would know what I am.*

Katie's mental list was interrupted by Cherene's voice. "It's only chauvinistic if a man says it."

"That sounds like reverse chauvinism to me, Cherene,"

Brian said.

"Brian, just do something," Cherene cried.

Brian peered past Sharylin. He tugged on Katie's coat sleeve and pointed down the long corridor. "Let's try this direction," he offered.

Sharylin stood in front of Brian and the other girls. "No," she insisted.

"No? Are you saying you won't *let* us go?" Cherene asked. She stepped forward, wide-eyed and stood defiantly in front of Sharylin.

Katie grabbed the back of Cherene's coat and pulled her back a step. "What are you doing?" Katie whispered to her best friend.

"I am not going to let her get away with talking to us like that," Cherene said.

"She's not acting like her normal self," Katie suggested.

Sharylin spoke up, "No. I meant that I think we should go in the direction that Brian and Cherene and I came from."

Katie held the light on Sharylin's face; her eyes weren't as dark as before, but they were definitely not the brilliant blue that Katie had remembered from their first meeting.

"Why do you think we should go that way, Sharylin?" Katie inquired suspicion rearing its ugly head again.

"Brian's way will only get us more lost," Sharylin scoffed as if Katie were a fool to even question her.

I know that cannot be Sharylin. Her words are always

sugar sweet.

"Really? That is your reasoning?" Katie said.

Sharylin stood for a moment. She rolled her shoulders back and stood up, fixing her eyes on the group that stood in her way. "I came in from that direction before I found Brian and Cherene," she said, pointing beyond the group in front of her. "It makes sense that the way out would be the way that I came in," she added.

Katie looked at Brian. He shrugged his shoulders and said, "Sounds reasonable to me."

Maybe I am jumping to conclusions again. People do react differently under stress.

She looked over at her best friend.

I mean, who knew Cherene would be such a basket case in the face of adversity. She always seemed so levelheaded back home.

"Okay, if no one disagrees, we'll follow Sharylin then," Katie said.

Meagan and Cherene looked at each other with a hint of skepticism between them. After a moment of contemplation, they shrugged their shoulders and agreed to follow.

The group of campers walked slowly through the gloomy corridors of the dark cavern. Low moans could be heard as they made their way down the halls. Sharylin took the lead. They hiked down one tunnel and then another. Each time they made a turn, they turned to the right.

After the third right turn, Katie whispered to Brian,

"Why do I get the feeling we are going in circles?"

Brian chuckled softly. "More like a square, but I was just thinking the same thing."

"I am starting to get a really bad feeling, Brian," Katie said.

"Yeah, something is not right. I don't think she knows where she is going."

Katie held on to Brian's arm tighter. When she stepped down with her left foot, she heard a loud crack.

Cherene whirled around and asked in a panic, "What was that?"

"It felt like I stepped on something and broke it," Katie answered, puzzled.

Brian shined his light on the ground. It was the thing Katie had dropped earlier when she was running away from the fountain room and away from the Unseelie queen.

"Sharylin, I really don't think this is the way," Katie said.

"Of course it is," Sharylin insisted.

"What makes you so sure," Brian inquired with doubt in his tone.

"Because this is the way I came in, so it must be the way out," Sharylin asserted.

Katie shined her flashlight in Sharylin's face. Dark shadows masked her expression; a grim smile spread over Sharylin's face. Her voice was sugar sweet for just a moment longer.

"Okay, Katie. You are too smart for me." Her speech

stopped. A low, guttural growl emanated from Sharylin's warped mouth. Her beautiful blonde hair began twisting and turning like the vines of an old, gnarled tree in a haunted forest. Her spine contorted and forced her back into a huge hump. With a wave of her warped fingers, Sharylin's body fell limp to the ground beneath the old crone's feet. The wretched witch stepped off Sharylin's corpse and kicked it aside.

~ 27 ~

CHECK MATE

Katie, Brian, Cherene, and Meagan watched in dismay as Sharylin's lifeless body hit the wall and fell in a heap on the cold cavern floor. Katie rushed to her friend's body.

"Leave her!" the evil being that emerged from Sharylin's body ordered.

Katie looked at the demented creature in front of her. She shook her head in disbelief. "Why did you have to hurt her?" Katie said through gritted teeth.

"Katie, Katie, Katie," the Unseelie queen cackled. "One way or another, I always get what I want."

Brian looked at Katie, his expression puzzled. He glanced back at the witch. "How do you know Katie?" he asked.

She moved slowly. A long black drape trailed behind her as she approached Brian. "Maybe the question you should be asking is, 'How well do *you* know Katie?'"

Brian shifted his stare from the withered, old woman fixing his eyes on Katie. "Katie, what is she talking about?"

Cherene walked and stood at Brian's side. She wove her arm through his, hoping he would protect her from whatever was happening around them.

"Katie?" Cherene questioned, worry plaguing her voice. Her eyes grew wide, begging for Katie to tell her something that would make all of this make sense.

Katie glared at the Unseelie queen. She narrowed her eyes, trying to will her to vanish. The old hag cackled and turned swiftly from Brian. In an instant, she appeared in front of Katie. Her maniacal laughter continued as she stood toe to toe with Katie.

"You silly little fool, you lack the training to make that happen."

The queen whirled around to face Brian, Cherene, and Meagan. Meagan gasped at the creature's warped features.

"Ask your precious Katie who she is."

Katie looked at her friends, wishing more than anything that she would not have to reveal her dark secret. Her eyes locked with Cherene's, pleading for support. Cherene's mouth opened slightly, realization dawning. She rushed to Katie's side.

"It's okay, Katie. They will understand. Tell them what you are," Cherene said, nudging her best friend forward gently, encouraging her to come clean.

"I . . . I don't know how to say it," Katie fumbled with

her words.

"Go ahead, Katie. I will be right here beside you," Cherene offered as she placed her arm around Katie for support.

Katie took a deep breath. She never thought it would come to this. She never imagined having to tell anyone but Cherene what she was.

"I . . . I . . . Well, I . . ."

"Enough of your nonsense, Katie Ryan!" the queen bellowed. The walls of the cave echoed and shook with each word she spoke. "Your precious Katie is a Seelie princess, and I am the one true and powerful Queen of the Unseelie Fae."

Cherene held Katie tightly, as if clutching Katie to her would prevent anything bad from happening. "What do you want with Katie?" Cherene stuttered, fear impeding her speech.

"She wants me to rule the Otherworld with her," Katie interrupted, suddenly finding the courage to speak.

Brian stepped forward and reached for Katie's hand. "But why you, Katie?"

"She can't have children. A curse was put on her long ago. She has been looking for the daughter of her one true love, but she has not been able to find her all these years, so she wants me to rule with her."

The dark being threw her hands up in exasperation. "You sniveling fool, how do you not understand this? *You* are the daughter of my beloved. *You* are the one I have been looking for all these years."

"But you said you wanted me to drink from the dark water and rule the Otherworld with you. You said you wanted me to be the daughter you could never have."

"You are already half Fae; you already hold the powers of the Fae, and you are the next in line to rule over the Seelie Court."

"Then why would you ask me to drink from the water? Were you simply trying to test my loyalty?" Katie asked, exasperated.

"The human side of you must be very idiotic and gullible. I wanted to destroy you; the way that I wanted to destroy you sixteen years ago, Katheena."

The words rang in Katie's ears. *Katheena. Oh my goodness. Oh my goodness. I am Katheena? I was the baby born to Scarlett and Daniel sixteen years ago?*

Katie shook her head, trying to wrap her mind around the unbelievable details that the Unseelie queen revealed to her.

My powers, the documents in Phil's desk, the enchanted box, and the magical dreams. Could she be telling the truth? Could I be the Seelie princess?

She glared at the evil being, her mind riddled with disbelief. "Then why let me drink from dark waters that would give me power that I already possess?" Katie challenged.

"Any Fae, Seelie or Unseelie, who drinks from the dark water by their own hand, will die instantly. I have waited sixteen years to finish what I started. It is time for you to die."

The evil queen cast her twisted fingers towards the top

of the cave and waved her hands in a grand gesture. The walls surrounding the group crumbled to the ground. Debris flew all around and thunder rolled through the dark cavern. Katie, Brian, Cherene, and Meagan huddled together and covered their heads to keep the falling rocks from striking them.

When the debris cleared, they were awed by what lay before their eyes. The dark cavern was dark no more. The gloom that had surrounded them was replaced by a bright room; lilac mist swirled around them as if a light wind were blowing it about the chamber.

As Katie glanced to her right, she discovered that beyond the beautiful haze was a cobbled path that led to a small pond. Surrounding it were reeds and Calla lilies. Poised in the middle of the pond was a spectacular stone fountain embellished with alternating amethyst and quartz stones that created a ring around the upper ridge of the fountain.

An immense, gray stone arbor jutted out from the edge of the water encircling the entire pond. It was supported by Roman pillars.

Katie walked slowly towards the pillars.

It is the same one I saw at school and in my dream. How can this be?

She reached up to touch the cracks in the structure.

"Katie, the black water," Brian yelled. He bolted forward and grabbed Katie around her waist. He pulled her away from the deathly waters.

The ghastly queen's cackling emanated from high above the water. The campers' eyes shifted upwards. Standing sentinel at the top of one of the turrets was the Unseelie queen.

"Oh Brian, it is so nice to see that chivalry is indeed not dead," the queen cackled. She flew down from the tower and hovered over her prey. "Unfortunately for you, it will take more than that to stop me from killing Katie. And when she is gone, there will be no use for any of you either."

She flew away, circling the room as she laughed a triumphant laugh. A trail of dark mist followed the evil creature as she made her way around the room. Soon, the beautiful purple swirls disappeared and were replaced by dark streams of black fog.

Katie stepped forward. She extended her arm in the direction of the turret closest to her and closed her eyes to focus. In the next instant, a bolt of energy shot out from her fingers. As the Unseelie queen tried to fly past it, the shot crashed into the tower. Huge pieces of stone flew through the air and struck the queen midflight.

Caught unaware, the queen was thrown back across the pond and went sailing into the opposite wall with her long clothes trailing through the dark water.

The evil queen stood up and shook off the powerful blow that Katie had dealt her. She looked straight into Katie's eyes and sneered as she spoke, "I see someone has been practicing her skills." She chuckled quickly and gave a deep sigh. "Never mind. You are no match for me, Katie Ryan."

"We'll see about that," Katie taunted.

Enraged by Katie's arrogance, the queen flew at campers. Katie bolted away from her friends to divert the queen's wrath. As the evil being changed course and honed in on her alone, Katie closed her eyes. In an instant, Katie transported to the opposite shore of the pond, leaving the airborne creature to smash headfirst into the cavern wall.

The ground shook, causing Brian and Cherene to fall on top of Meagan. Without warning, the Unseelie queen swarmed down upon Katie's friends. She held them captive with her powers. Unable to move, Brian, Cherene, and Meagan stood still, awaiting the queen's next move.

From the far end of the cavern, Katie refocused her mind. She sent two quick blasts. They struck the queen in the back of the head, but they did not seem to have an effect on her. Katie discharged another shot and watched carefully.

The energy ricocheted off of an invisible force field. Katie remembered the man in her dreams. He too had told Katie she was the Seelie princess. He had called himself her Faery Godfather. The dream must have been real, because she was able to shoot and transport herself just as he had said she would.

Something larger than a blast of energy was needed to break through the dark creature's defenses. Katie focused on the huge ball that was positioned at the top of one of the remaining turrets. She fixated on the huge boulder, envisioning it crashing down on the queen. Katie concentrated, knowing her aim would have to be precise if she was going to keep her friends out of the crossfire.

Katie closed her eyes and opened them again. A force of energy filtered through her body and extended to the gigantic rock that topped the tower. The next moment, the rock plunged down upon the queen.

Katie could hear Meagan and Cherene screaming. Brian made a low groaning noise as he grabbed both girls around the waist and leapt away from the exploding force field. The impact of the gigantic rock broke the queen's shield, leaving the queen lying under the massive boulder, motionless.

Katie transported herself across the dark, black waters to take her place next to her friends. Spinning around quickly, she realized that the evil creature was no longer lying beneath the oversized boulder. Katie looked frantically for the Unseelie queen, but there was no sign of the beastly woman. She was not atop the tower, hovering above the fountain, or on the opposite side of the pond.

Katie's voice was frantic. "Where could she be?" she yelled as she spun around to face her friends. She gasped in horror at what was before her eyes.

Brian, Cherene, and Meagan were trapped between the cave wall and an invisible shield. Their arms were held high above their heads, as if they were trussed by an unseen wire. Their bodies thrashed back and forth while they beat their hands violently against the transparent wall that imprisoned them.

Katie rushed to the barrier that separated her from her friends. She never imagined that her powers would lead to her own death, let alone the death of people she cared for so deeply.

In a panic, Katie turned around like a mad woman and screamed into the darkness of the chamber that surrounded her, to the queen she could no longer see.

"I give up! I will do anything you ask. Tell me what you want from me, and you can have it. Just please, let them go."

Brian banged on the force field, seeming desperate to stop Katie's bargain before it became a covenant she could not break.

"Katie, no. Run. Save yourself," he shouted.

Katie shook her head back and forth. "No, I won't leave you."

"She's going to kill us no matter what you do. Katie, please save yourself," he pleaded.

A gust of wind swept past Katie. She turned her head to see the Unseelie queen hovering over her hostages. The ends of her long black robe dangling in the ebony-stained fog that enveloped them all. Her evil chortle gnashed at Katie's ears. Katie placed her hands over her ears and shouted, "Okay, you have me now. Let them go."

The queen laughed her menacing laugh.

"Katie, no. Get out while you still can," Brian begged. He had stopped banging on his prison wall, but his hands remained plastered against it.

Katie moved slowly towards the wall and placed her hand against the invisible force field as if she could touch his hand. She smiled sweetly at him then squinted at Cherene. They exchanged one of their knowing looks. Katie looked at each friend and spoke a few last words before the queen could exact her revenge.

"It's okay. I have to do this, Brian. Cherene, I know you will understand. Meagan, I am so sorry you got dragged into this mess." Katie shook her head and drew a deep breath in as she regarded her three friends. "You must believe that I never meant for this to happen. Please forgive me."

Cherene's chest heaved as tears streamed down her mocha-colored face. Brian shook his head back and forth mouthing the word 'no' over and over again. Meagan simply looked away as if she were unable to stand what was about to happen to Katie.

In the blink of an eye, Brian, Cherene, and Meagan vanished from the fog-filled cavern. Katie surrendered to her captor, fearful of her own demise, yet hopeful for her friends' survival.

One moment the Unseelie queen was hovering over Katie, in her most demonic, dark state. In the next, she transformed herself into the beautiful creature that Katie had seen during their initial encounter. Her long golden hair flowed down her back; her striking midnight-blue eyes focused fiercely on Katie.

Although it had only been a matter of hours, their first meeting seemed like a lifetime ago to Katie. She was so naïve then. She did not even have a clue about her true identity, her parentage, the scope of her powers, or this demonic being's true intentions. Well, she had a clue. But she did not truly know the depths of the insanity with which she was now faced.

If this woman was to be believed, Katie was about to breathe her last breath. Without ever knowing true love, graduating high school, attending college, or getting married. What about her career? Why had she worked so hard in school if this was how it was to end? She had her whole life ahead of her. She was not ready to die.

Katie regarded the Unseelie queen's instant transformation. Her skin was no longer withered and wrinkled. Her face was as smooth as silk. Her golden hair was long and flowing, her eyes the color of the midnight sky. Her tattered and torn robes were replaced by a black satin robe that tapered to the floor and fanned out two feet in all directions. She truly looked like a queen.

With one giant gesture, the Unseelie creature shoved Katie to the hard cavern floor. Katie looked up to see the black mist swirling around the face of her predator. She held Katie's throat with one hand. Even with her two hands, Katie could not pry free of the Unseelie queen's intense grip. Katie scanned the room frantically, hoping to see a way out of the dismal situation. What she saw horrified her.

In her free hand, the Unseelie queen was holding a silver cup of dark liquid.

It must be the black water.

Panic besieged her entire body.

"Now, now Katie. I knew you would see things my way," the queen's maniacal voice filled Katie's ears.

She kneeled on one knee, bringing herself closer to her

prey. The cup was just inches from Katie's face.

I don't want to die. I don't want to die. I really don't want to die.

"It will only take a moment, my dear." The queen grabbed hold of one of Katie's hands, forcing her to take hold of the cup. The evil being wrapped her hand around Katie's. She lowered the silver cup to Katie's lips. "Now drink, dearie."

Katie turned her face. "Do not fight the inevitable, Katie. I can still find your friends and make them pay."

Katie considered her threat. She did not want her friends to pay the price for her birthright.

"Katie, drink and the nightmare will all be over."

Nightmare. The word rang in Katie's ears. Her mind flashed back to her most recent dream. Though it was not a nightmare, it certainly was a peculiar dream.

The man had taught her about her powers. Everything he showed her how to do, Katie had done. Katie pondered the force field that the queen had used to try to thwart the falling boulder, and the invisible wall that held her friends captive.

Would she be able to create one as well? Katie focused all her energies and channeled her fear, imagining a protective shield.

The air in the chamber became stagnant, the fog loomed in dark clouds above rather than swirling in ominous black streams. A gloom settled overhead, threatening to envelop Katie in its darkness.

The queen slipped her hand from Katie's neck and

grabbed the back of her hair trying to hold her steady.

Katie took a deep breath in. Aware that the queen's mission was all but complete. She closed her eyes and imagined a barrier to keep the cup of dark water from touching her lips. Katie felt the familiar rush of warmth envelop her.

When Katie opened her eyes, she saw the dark creature's eyes brimming with years of resentment and pain. The Unseelie queen lowered the silver cup but stopped just short of Katie's lips. Katie's eyes grew wide in disbelief.

The evil being banged the cup over and over above Katie's head but to no avail. The force field prevented the queen from making Katie drink.

The Unseelie queen glowered at Katie; her eyes grew wide and filled with anger. In a fit of rage, the queen morphed from her beautiful state back to her evil, grotesque being. She stood slowly and threw the cup at the invisible barrier with her gnarled fingers. Katie watched in awe as the cup bounced off her force field and rolled to the sandy shore by the small pond.

Katie's attention was diverted by the sound of Brian, Cherene, and Meagan running back through the tunnels of the cave towards the hidden, dark chamber of the cavern that held the fountain, the dark water, and the lives of Katie and Sharylin within its walls.

"Katie, we're coming to help you!" Cherene shouted.

Without a second thought, Katie jumped up and sent a blast of energy towards the gigantic boulder that was sitting atop the left tower of the entrance to the fountain room where Katie and the Unseelie queen were facing off in a deathly battle. The huge rock crashed down, sealing off the entryway of the chamber, keeping her friends out and safe for the moment.

Without warning, the Unseelie queen was upon her. She grabbed Katie with both hands and dragged her to the edge of the black water.

"You will drink, Katie Ryan. If it is the last thing I do, I will see you dead. I deserve at least that much!"

"That's funny, where I come from, good triumphs over evil, you old hag!"

A guttural sound filled the cavern as the queen lifted Katie's face close to her own decrepit, decaying face.

"You will drink the water now," she ordered, grabbing the cup with one hand and holding Katie down with the other.

Katie closed her eyes tightly and channeled her energy so that she could transport herself from the clutches of the Unseelie queen. She opened her eyes to discover that her attempt had failed. The beast still had her in her clutches.

An amused smile spread across the dark face of the queen. A slow low chuckle began from deep within growing louder with each moment. "You thought you could get away from me, you wretched little fool. Did you forget that I can read your mind? It takes a tremendous amount of energy and focus to vanish right in front of me. You are not strong enough, my dear Katie."

In the middle of her arrogant laughter, the queen stopped suddenly. The ground beneath them shook and the walls shifted.

"What? What are you doing?" she asked as she looked around frantically searching for the source of the vibrations.

Katie glowered at her abductor. Now it was her turn to smile maniacally.

"What? What are you doing, you sniveling little brat?" the Unseelie queen demanded, suddenly her voice did not sound as if she were so sure of herself. She looked around in a panic and unintentionally loosened her grip on her hostage, which allowed Katie the break she needed to slip from her clutches.

No longer bound by the beastly creature, Katie vanished and reappeared near the far corner of the cave. Katie focused her mental powers on the stones that formed the roof of the cavern. One after the other, she compelled the huge boulders to tumble to the floor of the cave, creating an enormous earthquake-like shaking. The boulders crashed down into the middle of the black water, causing a huge wave of the dark water to splash over the walls of the stone chamber. Katie created another force field to keep the water from touching her. The sands along the shoreline of where the pond had once existed absorbed the deathly water.

A hideous wailing ensued, "My water! My water! What have you done to my water?"

Katie surveyed the room looking for the Unseelie queen. At first, she did not see the evil being. Then, as if she were taunting her, the queen showed herself to Katie. She was hovering over the fountain; the ancient structure had withstood the explosion of falling stones.

Katie knew instinctively that waiting to make her next move would mean certain death. She sent an intense blast to the fountain and then another. The fountain exploded, sending enormous masses of rock into the air. One by one, Katie used the rocks as weapons, hurling each at the Unseelie queen.

"You can't beat me!" the queen's foreboding voice echoed throughout the cave. She raised her gnarled fingers to send a powerful blast to Katie. Before the evil being could strike at her, Katie hurled a huge boulder from the fountain and struck the Unseelie queen's outstretched hand.

The queen stared, horrified at her deformed hand. The impact of the boulder left bloody stumps where her twisted fingers had been. Streams of blood ran down her arm and fell to the bottom of the cavern. She wailed and screamed maniacally, "You! You will pay!"

Her image flickered; a huge clap of thunder sounded.

Katie continued to bombard her with the stones until the queen's image began to flicker off and on over and over again. Katie watched her presence fading as each stone missile struck her being. She continued the blast of hurling rocks until the Unseelie queen's form disappeared completely. The only thing that remained of the evil creature was the echo of her maniacal laughter and her sinister warning.

"I'll be back for you, Katheena! I'll be back!"

Katie waited for several minutes, crouched down in the corner of the cave, fearful of even breathing. She surveyed the damage. There was nothing left of the chamber within the cave. The fountain that was so beautiful had been leveled to a pile of rocks. Katie turned and saw Sharylin's lifeless body against the damp stone wall.

Cradling Sharylin's head in her arms, Katie slunk down and began bawling. How could Sharylin be dead? How could she have ever doubted her? All the times she thought Sharylin was possessed; she was, but not because she was inherently bad. She was possessed by the Unseelie queen. That beast had used her for her own purposes and cast her aside as if she were worthless. She laid her head on Sharylin's chest.

"I am so sorry Sharylin. I never meant for anyone to be hurt."

She lay perfectly still for a moment. The faint thump, thump of a heartbeat against Katie's ear. Katie pulled away from her friend and looked at her closely, placing her forefinger and middle finger over the arteries in Sharylin's neck. There was a pulse. It was a slight pulse, but it was a pulse.

Out of the corner of her eye, Katie saw a soft light and purple mist swirling at the base of what used to be the waterfall. She laid Sharylin down taking care not to do further damage to her near lifeless body and walked slowly towards the light. It was the same purple light that she saw at the lake when Cherene almost drowned. The same light that drew her here, to the cave.

She looked down to see a small puddle of the black water. Katie gasped and took a step backwards.

What if the Unseelie queen has come back to finish me off?

"Come closer, dearest Katheena. It is I," an angelic voice rose from the black water.

Stepping to the edge of the darkness, Katie peered through the water and discovered the water nymph from the lake. Although the water was only a few inches deep, the beautiful green-eyed creature looked as if she were in a body of water without end.

"Use the stone, Katie. Your friend will be all right. Use the stone."

And just as quickly as she arrived, the water nymph retreated into the depths of her pool of dark water and swam away taking with her the lilac light.

Katie reached into her pocket and found the familiar stone. A rush of calm flooded through her body. She ran her fingers over the smooth surfaces and rough edges as she raced back to Sharylin.

What am I supposed to do with the stone? She couldn't give me more direction than 'use the stone'? That is almost as useful as 'May the force be with you.'

Katie knelt beside Sharylin.

Use the stone.

She fumbled with the stone, turning it over and over in her hand.

Okay, I'm using the stone.

First, she placed it on Sharylin's mouth; nothing happened. She set it gingerly by her nose; still, nothing happened.

Third time's a charm, right?

She placed the stone on Sharylin's chest above her heart. The amethyst stone glowed purple and began pulsating with every beat of Sharylin's heart. The longer the stone lay on her chest, the faster and more intensely the stone pulsed.

After what felt like an eternity to Katie, Sharylin's eyes fluttered, and she took a deep breath. "Katie, what happened?"

She hugged Sharylin and helped her to her feet. "Would you believe me if I said you were possessed by an evil Unseelie queen that tried to kill all of us?"

Rubbing her temples with her fingers, Sharylin stood silent, contemplating the information. "Wow. That was real? I thought I was dreaming," Sharylin said, still seeming baffled. She looked at Katie for reassurance.

"I know it is crazy, but I promise it is true," Katie said, bracing herself for Sharylin to become unreceptive.

Sharylin's incredulous look slowly turned to one of acceptance. "I had heard the stories for years; I used to dream about finding the old crone in the cave." She paused and stared off in the distance. "All these years, it was real."

Sharylin shook off her dazed expression. She grabbed Katie's hands and said, "You have to tell me everything!"

Feelings of relief filled her being; Katie summarized the events to Sharylin as they walked to what used to be the entrance of the hidden chamber of the cave.

"How are we going to get out?" Sharylin asked in dismay, staring at the wall of rocks that had sealed the entrance.

"Stand back," Katie instructed. A crafty smile split her face and a gleam in her green eyes eased the tension. One by one, she moved the rocks with her mind and some with her hands. Within a couple of minutes the voices of Brian, Cherene, and Meagan could be heard from the other side.

"Hey, did someone have a party and forget to invite us?" Katie asked.

"Katie!" they shouted in unison.

"Who is 'us'?" Meagan asked. "Who is with you?"

"It's just me, guys," Sharylin announced in her bubbly voice.

The buzz of excitement over the news that Sharylin was alive drifted through the remaining barrier. Katie moved the biggest boulder. Cherene burrowed through the small opening and embraced her best friend as if Katie had been lost at sea for many months and finally rescued. After she hugged Katie, she gave Sharylin a huge bear hug, too. Meagan made her way through the debris next and barreled into the girls.

Brian tugged at a few rocks that were obstructing his ability to squeeze through the small gap and practically fell to the ground in front of Katie. He stood up quickly, picked her up in his arms and swung her around. When he stopped spinning, she slid down so that her feet were barely touching the ground.

"Aren't you going to say hello to Sharylin, too?" Katie asked.

Brian grinned from ear to ear. He mouthed the words, "Hi Sharylin," to Sharylin as he pulled Katie to him closely.

The warmth of his affection wrapped around her like a cloak. She could hear Meagan and Cherene making a fuss over Sharylin nearby.

Cherene tapped Katie on the shoulder. “Hello, trapped people over here. Can you two stop your public displays of affection and help us get out of here?”

Brian stood back from Katie and smiled roguishly. “Hey, can’t you just transport us back to camp?”

Katie pulled her head back and shot Brian a smirk laced with mock disapproval. She wiggled free from his grasp and squeezed through the hole they had made in the rubble. “Sorry babe, you’re going to have to walk!” Katie replied playfully, looking over her shoulder at Brian as she started to walk back down the long tunnel.

Brian, who had poked his head halfway through the hole to watch Katie retreating, looked back at the girls and laughed at Katie’s boldness. Brian stood by as each girl shimmied through the hole in the wall to join Katie on the other side. Brian was the last to get through. He jogged to catch up with Katie and the other girls, joining their quest to find the way out of the enchanted cave.

~ 28 ~

IGNORANCE IS BLISS

Still high from the battle with the Unseelie queen and amazed at the miracle of seeing Sharylin lifeless one moment and alive and kicking the next, the group of friends made their way anxiously towards the camp.

"Katie, that battle was crazy! But I don't understand why you didn't tell us you had powers before," Meagan said.

"I just barely figured out what I am myself. Besides, where I come from, people who claim they have powers are either high or mentally unstable," Katie replied.

"Well, not *everyone* will be as accepting as us. You may still want to keep it under wraps," Sharylin advised.

"That's true. It is easy for us to believe because we saw it with our own eyes," Cherene added.

"Don't worry; your secret is safe with us," Meagan reassured Katie. Meagan looked around at the others. "Right?"

One at a time, each of the girls agreed to keep the secret of what had happened in the cave between them. Katie was relieved that she did not have to beg for their loyalty or their silence.

Katie shifted her gaze to Brian. "I didn't hear you promise, Brian," she said, staring at him expectantly.

Brian glanced down at Katie, his blue eyes gleaming with amusement. Taking ahold of her hand, he laced his fingers with hers. "You know you can trust me, Katie," he said, his voice wrapped in sincerity.

Katie gave him an approving smirk. "I know. I just wanted to hear you say it," she said and leaned in close to him as they walked hand in hand towards the camp.

The group climbed the small hill that led to their safety. From the top of the hill, the lake and the outdoor amphitheater were visible. Seeing that the camp was in sight, the friends raced down the hill. Their quest to get back to the comforts of their cabins was stopped short by the presence of Christy, Darrell, and Destiny. Christy stood in front of them with her hands placed on her hips, a mask of attitude and disgust covered her usually flawless features. Darrell and Destiny stood sentinel behind her, sunglasses on, and their arms crossed over their chests looking like wannabe "Men in Black."

Katie stopped a few feet in front of Christy. "Now what?" she asked, rolling her eyes at her.

Christy walked straight up to Katie and spat on the ground in front of her. "That's what, Katie. What are you going to do about it?" Christy challenged.

"Christy," Brian scolded. He started to step towards Christy, but Katie pulled him back.

"I've got this, Brian."

Katie could not believe Christy just spat on the ground. *That is such a mannish thing to do.*

Everything in her wanted to grab the snotty girl by the hair and rub her stupid face in her own saliva. Katie looked past her to see Darrell and Destiny laughing at Christy's nerve. Katie's eyes were daggers of anger. She felt the familiar rage boiling within her.

Given what she had just been through, she knew she could do some serious damage to Christy, to all of them for that matter. Her options were endless. She could raise Christy a few feet off the ground and throw her into a tree. She could smash her face into a nearby rock or drown her in the icy lake. No, that was too harsh. Maybe she should just toss her in the lake and smear her mascara. Katie thought of a million unkind things she could say and do to Christy. Then she remembered the last time she used her powers with Christy out on the lake.

At that moment, the vision of the evil queen flashed into Katie's mind. She did not want to use her powers to hurt others; that would make her no better than the Unseelie queen.

Katie pondered the idea of thinking of something witty and hurtful, something that would utterly embarrass this chick who thought she was untouchable. But then she would be no better than Christy.

She decided to keep it short and to the point.

"You're no better than that spit you just spewed on the ground, Christy." Katie shook her head in disgust and turned to walk away.

Christy looked from one side of the campers that were assembled around her to the other side. The crowd stood with their mouths gaped open and eyes wide. Christy had never experienced this before. No one ever stood up to her. She usually had the upper hand.

"Seriously, that's all you've got?" she stuttered, trying to save face. "See, I told you she's afraid of us," Christy said as she looked around for approval from the crowd that had collected to watch the fight.

Katie stopped for a moment and considered her next move. Christy was really making this difficult; the urge to hurt or embarrass her was almost unbearable. Katie's mom's infamous words, "Two wrongs don't make a right," ran through her mind.

No, but it would feel good to hurt her the way she is trying to hurt me. Or would it?

Katie kind of felt sorry for Christy at that point. She was trying so hard to be noticed and liked. She must be miserable. Even with all of Katie's moves, the pain of her father's abandonment, and her mother's instability, she never felt so bad that she wanted someone else to hurt for no reason at all. She had not done anything to provoke Christy or her friends.

Then she remembered Brian's words in the cave. Christy's loss of her father was far worse than anything Katie had experienced. She did not want to make things worse for Christy, but she was not going to let her continue to be out of control and malicious towards her. Katie decided that honesty was the best policy.

"Christy, I am not afraid of you. I feel sorry for you. You need to get a life and then maybe you wouldn't worry so much about mine. Stay away from me." With that, Katie turned on her heel, determined to leave Christy and the drama behind her. She and Brian walked hand in hand down the snow-lined path.

"Bri, Bri, you can stop acting now," Christy shouted after them. "Brian, I said you can stop acting like you like her now."

Katie turned to look at Brian. "What is she talking about, Brian?"

"Let's just keep walking; she's getting desperate," Brian replied. He took Katie's arm and tried to guide her away from Christy and the rest of the campers.

"Come on Brian, you don't have to keep pretending. It's over; the plan didn't work," Christy taunted.

Katie stopped and faced Brian. "Do you have something you want to tell me, or should I ask Christy?"

"Go ahead Brian," Christy goaded, "tell her about our plan to make her think you liked her. She thinks she's so big and bad; she can take it! Right Katie, you're so big on the truth; give her the truth, Brian."

Brian stared at the ground; shame was written all over his face. Katie stared at him and shook her head in disbelief.

She opened her mouth to speak but shut it quickly. Her mind shuffled through the memories she and Brian made in such a short amount of time.

Katie remembered skiing for the first time while Brian cheered her on, the winter games, and the dance that followed. She thought of how they laughed, and bantered back and forth, and even kissed. Brian was the one that had pulled her from the lake and begged her to save herself when his own life was threatened by the Unseelie queen.

Even after he found out I am a paranormal freak, he still liked me. At least I thought he did. It was all just a cruel ploy to humiliate me.

"I see," Katie said, her voice barely a whisper.

"Katie, it's not like that."

"Brian, don't make it worse."

"You don't understand. It was her plan. I never actually agreed to it," he explained.

"Oh Bri, Bri, don't lose your nerve now. Remember, Katie is all about the truth. You know you agreed."

"Shut up, Christy," Brian demanded. He looked to be losing his cool. "Katie, even if I did agree, I never intended to go through with it."

Katie closed her eyes, wishing he would just disappear, but he continued to ramble.

"Katie, I liked you from the beginning. I never wanted them to pick on you. I only went along with the plan so they wouldn't make me a target. I never planned on pretending anything. I didn't have to. By the time she came up with the plan, I was already falling for you. Everything was real, Katie. Katie, please believe me."

"Find someone else to be the target of your childish games, Brian. I am done being made to look like a fool." Katie pushed past Brian and started off towards her cabin.

He grabbed her arm and turned her so that they were facing one another.

"Katie, I've fallen for you. Please, please believe me."

"Goodbye Bri, Bri," Katie said in the most saccharine voice she could muster as she jerked her arm away from him and headed towards her cabin. She walked away from the crowd as fast as she could without looking like she was trying to flee. Once she was out of the sight of the other campers, she began jogging through the forest path that led to the cabin. Tears stung her face; her heart was pounding.

How stupid can one person be? I should have known it was too good to be true.

Katie blamed herself for the ridiculous scene with Christy and the humiliation of having Brian reveal his true intentions.

Why didn't I just follow my instincts? I knew he was part of their clique. I should have steered clear of Brian and none of this would have happened.

As the cabin came into sight, Katie quickened her pace. She barreled into the cabin door and shoved it open. Katie threw herself on her bed, pulled her pillow over her head, and began sobbing uncontrollably.

What am I doing? All of this…over a boy?

She could not be that upset about Brian. They had barely even met a month ago. She considered Grandma Ceil's words of wisdom. "This too shall pass, dear."

The pounding of footsteps interrupted her thoughts. She quickly dried her eyes on her shirt and turned toward the door. "Brian, I said—" her words trailed off as she realized it was not Brian in the doorway. It was Cherene.

"Are you all right, Katie?"

"Cherene, I'm glad it's you and not him."

"Katie, I don't even know what to say. Christy's plan was just cruel."

"I wish I would have figured it out before I let him make a fool out of me," Katie said.

"Honestly, you don't look like a fool. Brian really set it straight."

"You think because he half-heartedly professed his 'fake love' for me that set it straight? Cherene, I thought you were on my side."

"I am on your side. Apparently, so is Brian."

"What do you mean?"

"When you left, Brian told off Christy and her crew."

"He did?" Katie asked and sat up straight.

"Let's just say there is no doubt in my mind about how he feels about you, Katie."

"Details, I need details, girl!"

Cherene snorted and laughed at the same time.

"That's the Katie I know and love!"

"Cherene…details!"

"Well, when you left Brian just kind of stood there for a moment, dumbstruck with his hands held behind his head. Christy laughed and called for Darrell and Destiny to follow her. Brian raced after them. He caught up with them and stopped them from going any further. He gave quite a speech in your honor," Cherene said and smiled proudly, seeming pleased with her news.

Katie sat on the edge of her bed and stared at Cherene for what felt like forever. "Well?"

"Oh yeah, as I was saying. He said, 'Christy, for as long as I have known you, you have been miserable and hateful towards anyone that was a little different than you. You have gone too far with this. Now the whole world knows about your insecurities. I was an idiot for listening to you, and I don't know why I ever worried about what you thought of me. If being your friend means I have to treat people like Katie and Cherene badly, then I don't need your friendship. Katie has more going for her than you could ever hope to have. I meant what I said. I love Katie, and your little tricks won't change how I feel.'" Cherene took a breath and gave Katie a cheesy grin.

Katie grabbed both of Cherene's hands in her own. "He really said all that?"

"That's not all. He had some words for Destiny and Darrell too."

"Well, don't stop now; tell me the rest, Cherene," Katie insisted as she clapped her hands together, her green eyes dancing with delight.

"Okay, okay. I can't remember it word for word, but he said something like, 'As for you, Destiny and Darrell, I've been where you are. So worried about what everyone would think that I stopped thinking for myself. My advice, get a life!' "

"Well good for him, but that doesn't change the fact that he pretended to like me to make a fool out of me."

"Weren't you listening, Katie? He said by the time Christy made that plan, he was already falling for you."

"Well, that is what he said. If you ask me, anyone that would agree to her little scheme in the first place is not someone I want to put my trust in."

Cherene rolled her eyes. She looked at Katie and shook her head back and forth. "I seem to remember a girl who told me once about how hard it was to be accepted by the 'in-crowd.' Something about changing who she was, even though she knew she shouldn't, just to fit in."

"All right, all right, I get the point."

Katie sighed in exasperation. This was a lot to take in. She did not know what to believe. She knew what she wanted to believe. She wanted to believe that Brian had not fooled her. She wanted to believe that his feelings were real. More than anything, she just wished that Christy had not opened her big mouth. Then Katie would not have to deal with any of this.

What is it that people say? Oh yeah, ignorance is bliss.

Katie thought she was quite blissful when she was unaware of the truth. No, it was better this way. She had to deal with what was real. She just had to figure out if Brian was for real or not.

"Katie, you'll make the best choice for you. Despite how you are feeling right now, you are not a fool."

"Thanks, Cherene. Let's get this stuff packed up. I've had enough camping to last me a lifetime."

"But there is still the final night of campfire. Everyone is going to present their skits. You don't want to leave yet, do you?"

"Cherene, so much has happened. I don't know if I can face everyone."

"You can't give them the satisfaction of knowing they won. Come on, let's get back to the group and show them that they didn't get the best of you."

"When did you become so wise?" Katie asked.

"I had a lot of time to think when I thought I was going to die in the cave. While you were off fighting evil, I had ample time to ponder life's big questions. This much I know for sure; you're coming with me to the last campfire tonight, even if I have to drag you there by your hair!"

Cherene laughed a maniacal laugh and grabbed Katie's hands and pulled her off the bed.

Together they ventured through the snow-covered path and joined the rest of their cabin mates. They were all getting ready to go into the mess hall for one final dinner together.

Dinner was not as bad as Katie thought it would be. Everyone included her in their conversations. She heard through the grapevine that Christy was sent home for behavior unbecoming of a camper. Destiny and Darrell looked like outcasts, sitting in the far corner by themselves. Katie almost felt sorry for them… almost.

The final campfire was a huge success. The fire burned bright; its light reflected off the surrounding snow and made the stage look like there was a spotlight hitting it. Each cabin presented the skits they had been practicing. Katie's cabin's production got the most applause. Before the clapping could die down, the counselors jumped on the stage, and someone blasted the song, "We're Glad You Came," from a boom box. The entire camp leapt from their seats and danced and sang along with the counselors.

Katie glanced from the wild group of campers to the perimeter of the frozen lake. Moonlight was dancing off the snowy hills that surrounded the water.

From the corner of her eye, Katie saw Brian staring at her from just beyond the stage. She held his gaze a moment too long because then he started to walk over to her. Katie was not ready for a conversation with Brian yet. She had not figured out if she believed him or not. Quickly, she turned away from him and joined the group of girls and guys that were dancing near her.

A moment later, she looked past the group she was dancing with and saw Brian retreating up the snow-covered path in the direction of his cabin.

Katie exhaled her disappointment and looked up to see Riley and Lauren cutting through the middle of the group, dancing like chickens in Katie's direction. She gave a half-hearted giggle at the spectacle. Glancing across the group at

Cherene, Katie mouthed the words, “I’m leaving,” and turned slowly to walk away from the group.

Just as Katie pushed her way through the last of the campers near the fire, Cherene sprang from behind and threaded an arm through Katie’s. They walked arm-in-arm through the forest to spend the last night of their winter camp adventure in the quiet of their small cabin.

~ 29 ~

FINALLY, HOME

The next morning, the campers emerged from their cabins to find that it had snowed during the night. A fluffy white blanket of snow was tucked snugly around the camp. The trees had turned silver as they slept. Some of the girls were running and sliding on the snow-dusted path on their way down to meet their parents.

Katie was not excited; her heart felt a little heavy. She had slept well but woke up thinking about Brian and the uncertainty that surrounded their relationship. After saying goodbye to the girls in her cabin, Katie's thoughts turned to her mom and Phil. They would be picking her up this morning; there was so much that Katie wanted to ask, but she was afraid they might not tell her the truth.

"Katie, Katie, over here! We're over here!" Katie's mom was waving her arms frantically.

Definitely overdoing it.

Mom could not possibly have missed her that much; she was only gone for two weeks. Mom tromped through the snowbank that had accumulated throughout the winter, too excited to walk the normal path the other parents were venturing down to pick up their kids. Katie felt a flush of red creep over her face.

"Seriously, Mom?" Katie blurted out as her mother almost tackled her. Mom held Katie as if she were the lone survivor in the middle of a natural disaster. "Mom, Mom, what's up with all the hugs?"

"Oh honey, I am just so glad to see you!" Her mom pulled back, still holding on to Katie's shoulders as if her life depended on it. "The rangers called in the morning yesterday and said you were missing in the snowy mountains."

"Didn't they call back and tell you I was found?"

"Well, of course, but the thought of you being lost out in the wilderness was just too much for me to bear. What if something had happened to you?"

Something had happened to Katie. In fact, a lot had happened. She had found out the identity of her real mother and father, suffered the painful realization that the boy she really liked had deceived her, and as if all that were not enough, she had battled the Unseelie queen.

I had better keep that one to myself.

"Actually Mom, a lot did happen to me. I have a lot of questions for you. Can we talk?"

"Sure honey, we'll have plenty of time to talk on the

way home in the car. Let me look at you once more."

Her mom hugged her firmly and kissed her forehead and cheeks a million times, then wrapped her arm around Katie's shoulder and led her towards Phil and the car.

Phil. Katie was not ready to deal with Phil yet. As Katie and her mom approached, a huge smile spread across Phil's face. Katie thought that he actually looked pleased to see her. He reached out and hugged Katie.

Well, that's a first.

It was not a generic little tap on the back. He grabbed her in a real bear hug and held on for longer than was necessary. If she had not just undergone the battle of her life, she might have even said it was awkward. As it was, she appreciated the affection, even if it was from Phil.

Katie smiled tentatively, unsure of how to take his newfound kindness. It seemed as if he had only ever been mean to her in the past. They had not really interacted very much before, and when they did, it was mostly when Phil was trying to teach her a lesson that she did not want to learn.

Mom jumped in the front seat and pulled down the vanity mirror to fix her hair and makeup. Katie helped Phil put her sleeping bag and duffle bag in the trunk of his car. A tornado of dark curls swept past Phil and barreled into Katie. Cherene threw her arms around Katie and gave her a ginormous hug.

What is with people and their hugs today?

The girls separated and laughed at one another. "I will let the two of you say goodbye," Phil said, still smiling as he walked to driver's side door.

"Thanks Phil. I will only be a minute," Katie said. She turned and looked at Cherene with sadness in her eyes. She was almost on the verge of crying.

What in the world is wrong with me? Crying was not Katie's thing, especially not in front of others.

"Hey, it's not like we're not going to see each other on Monday," Cherene assured her.

"I know. It's just…It's just been a *really* long two weeks," Katie said, trying to justify her emotions.

She wondered what exactly it was that she was feeling so down about. Yes, she had found out some devastating truths: her biological mom was most likely dead, and her real father was a creature from another dimension, also probably dead. A crazy queen wanted to send her to the land of the dead as well, and oh yeah, her "boyfriend" was a scheming liar. That was the part that really hurt.

Oddly, she could handle the part about her real mom and dad. After all, it explained so much. Besides, she had not even known they existed until twenty-four hours ago. The Unseelie queen was gone, at least for now.

The part that made Katie's heart hurt was Brian. She had trusted him. She had known she shouldn't, but she did it anyway. Brian had drawn her in. He made her believe in him and in the idea that they could be a couple. Then he pulled the rug out from under her. Maybe it was her pride that hurt the most.

"Earth to Katie!" Cherene said as she waved her hand

in front of Katie's face, trying to bring her out of her daze. Katie smiled at her friend. She decided she would think about it all another day. It was just too much to process right now.

Out of nowhere, two hands covered Katie's eyes.

"Guess who?"

"Seriously, Brian?" Katie said in exasperation as she turned to face him. "Do you think this is all a joke now?"

"No. I was just trying to break the ice. I want to talk to you," he said.

"I don't think so, Brian. Not right now. Maybe never," she added, her tone cold and dismissive.

"I knew you would probably say that, Katie. That is why I wrote you this letter." He brought an envelope out of the pocket of his jacket.

He looked so hopeful. Katie did not know what to say.

"I was hoping you would at least read this letter that I wrote to you. It explains a lot," Brian said.

"You mean it's full of excuses for why you made a fool out of me?"

"No, they're not excuses. They are my…" he paused. Katie gave him a sidelong look and raised an eyebrow

"Katie, please just read it." He looked down at her with big, blue pleading eyes. "Please."

Katie could feel herself getting weak. She wanted to throw her arms around his neck and pretend that nothing bad had ever happened between the two of them, but she knew the truth. If she had learned anything from the experience with the Unseelie queen, it was that she would not be phony. She wouldn't pretend to be something or someone she wasn't ever again. Reluctantly, she reached for the envelope.

"Thank you, Katie. You won't regret it; I promise." He flashed his cutest grin.

"We'll see, Brian," Katie said with a sly, almost flirty smile.

What am I doing? He's public enemy number one.

Katie watched as he turned and walked away. She counted three times that he looked back at her before he disappeared around the bend.

Katie turned and realized that Cherene had witnessed the whole scene. Cherene stared at Katie like the cat that ate the canary.

"What?" Katie said innocently.

"You've got it bad, girl."

"What? No I don't. I was just saying…"

"You were just saying what, Katie? You've got it bad?" Cherene shouted as she turned and ran off towards her parents.

"But…Cherene…wait…I can explain…" Katie shouted to her best friend.

"Yeah, yeah, I know. See you on Monday!" Cherene replied.

Katie laughed to herself as she got into the back of the car.

"All set?" Phil asked.

"Yes."

Katie glanced out the window and started to think

about all that happened in the last couple of weeks. She felt like so much had changed. Then the thought struck her: what had really changed? Her "real" mom and dad, two people she never met, died or disappeared the day she was born. How could she miss people she never even knew? The only dad she had ever known was still out of the picture, which was something that she was surprised to realize she had actually gotten used to over the last two years. The mother that raised her was still here, as loving as ever. Then there was Phil. Looking back, she could not think of anything that he had actually *done* to her, besides be an annoying adult. And have some anger management issues. And…Yep, Phil was still Phil. She would worry about him another day.

Katie glanced at Mom and Phil, sitting in the front seat, completely oblivious of her new awareness. What would she accomplish by forcing her mom to explain why she never told Katie she was adopted? Maybe her mom was planning to tell Katie when she turned eighteen. On the other hand, her mom might have thought that there was no need to ever tell Katie she was adopted since her "real" parents were completely out of the picture. It would almost seem cruel to tell a child such news. That settled it; Katie decided to keep the fact that she knew she was adopted to herself. She felt good about the decision to spare her mother's feelings, wishing to herself that the Unseelie queen had given her the same courtesy.

Katie remembered the letter she had stuffed in the front pocket of her jacket. Reaching in, she pulled out Brian's letter.

Staring at it for a moment, she contemplated whether she should even read it. What could he have to say? "I know I lied to you and schemed against you with your archrival, but do you still want to date me?"

Not!

The problem was that she really did want to date Brian. When she was with him, she was always smiling. He was funny and smart, and he was not afraid to act like a fool in front of her. Best of all, she could be herself with him too. She did not feel like she needed to pretend to like things she didn't just to make him like her.

Her mind wandered to the myriad of times she pretended to like football just so Sean would think she was cool. In truth, it was so boring to her. She thought the games took forever and she could not understand why anyone would want to play a game where they ended up on the bottom of a dog pile on the ground.

Brian was different, or maybe she was different now. Being around Brian was easy.

Maybe I should just read the letter.

* * * * *

Dear Katie,

I am writing this letter because there is a lot I think you should know. I know you will never let me say everything that I need to say without interrupting me like you like to do when my speech offends you, so I am writing down what I need for you to know. Hopefully you haven't already put down the letter after reading the first sentence.

I think you should know that I am sorry for what has happened. I really, really do care for you. You are the sweetest, funniest, most beautiful girl I've ever known. My feelings for you have been genuine since the first day I saw you. I was afraid to let you know this due in part to peer pressure. But now that you know, I would like to open my heart up to you. If you take this chance on me, I promise I will never let you down again.

Yours truly,
Brian

* * * * *

Katie clutched the letter to her heart, closed her eyes, and let out a deep sigh. She had been prepared for his letter to be riddled with contrite words, but she never imagined the depths of his sincerity. His words touched her heart and left the romantic part of her wondering what kind of fool she had been to ever doubt that his feelings for her were anything but genuine.

The skeptical part of her thought he probably copied it off the Internet from a website with a title like, "A Playa's Guide to Love Letters." The rational part of her brain put Skeptical Girl in check. . . there were no computers at camp which ruled out the Internet form letter option.

Maybe Brian is for real. Maybe, just maybe, he was

simply caught up in the pressure of fitting in—just like I used to be.

She had a lot to consider. Assuring herself she would deal with it later, she folded Brian's letter and placed it back in the envelope so she could read it again.

Katie listened to music on her cell phone and answered text messages from Cherene, which made the rest of the drive home seem to fly by. Before she knew it, Phil was making the turn down Maple Drive. It must have snowed the night before at home too because the snow covered the ground and rested on the branches of the tall pine trees that lined the road to their home. As he made the familiar left turn down their driveway, Katie had the sense of belonging, a feeling she had not felt since before her father left.

Katie reached into her pocket to feel the amethyst stone. She pulled it out and considered the beautiful gems tucked perfectly inside the tiny crevices. She sighed deeply and raised her eyes to regard the old colonial house that had become her home.

In the driveway, to the right of the house, Brian stood, leaning against the back of his black car, holding a bouquet of red roses. Despite herself, Katie beamed with joy and reached for his letter. She opened it gingerly; her gaze fixed on the last line of the letter. It read, "I promise I will never let you down again." Her mind wandered through the brief but remarkable memories they had already created together.

She stuffed the letter into her coat pocket, along with her amethyst stone, and shoved open the car door. Her first instinct was to run into his arms.

Once outside the car though, Katie made herself stand still a moment. She watched impatiently until Mom and Phil had exited the car and closed the front door of the house. Mom pulled the lace window covering to one side and peeked out the side window. A knowing smile showed on Mom's face. She gave Katie an approving nod and let the sheer curtain fall back into place, giving Katie and Brian privacy.

Katie let out a deep breath and walked slowly towards Brian. He met her halfway down the snow-covered driveway.

"Did you read my letter, Katie?" he asked.

Oh, why does he have to be so cute? How am I supposed to pretend I am mad when all I want to do is hug him?

"I did," Katie said as cool as possible. She made herself look away from him to seem more disinterested.

Brian took a step towards Katie. "So, I know we are not in a misty, hillside meadow with the sun rising behind us, but I was sort of hoping this would have turned out a little more along those lines."

Katie knew exactly what he was referring to: the love scene in the movie, *Pride and Prejudice.*

"So, you thought you would just write a sappy letter and all would be forgiven then?" she snapped. Instantly, she regretted the harshness of her words.

"No. Well, maybe something like that," Brian mumbled. He looked down at the snow-covered driveway and back up at Katie. He smiled roguishly and raised his eyebrows up and down, trying to soften her tough exterior.

Katie could not resist his smile. "You know, who needs meadows and sunrises?" Katie offered with an impish smile of her own. "That is a classic love story. In modern love stories the guy usually just grabs the girl, and they spin around until they get terribly dizzy and fall to the ground, giggling and picking grass from each other's hair."

Brian cocked his eyebrow. "Really, that sounds kind of like an eighties love story to me."

"Eighties, huh?"

"Yeah, definitely old school."

"So how would you see the ending of a modern-day love story?" Katie asked.

"Well, nowadays, girls seem to think the worst of guys. In the end of the modern-day love stories *I've* seen, the girl usually realizes just how wrong she was about the guy. After begging for undeserved forgiveness, the girl jumps into the guy's arms and lays a big kiss on him," Brian said with a hint of persuasion.

Katie laughed out loud.

"If you think I'm going to beg for forgiveness for something *you* did, you have another thing coming, Brian. Not in this lifetime buddy. There is no way—"

Brian dropped the flowers he had been holding and pulled Katie close to him. He held her tightly in his embrace and swung her around until they both fell onto the fresh snow, laughing hysterically. They rested flat on their backs and looked up at the snow-kissed branches of the pine trees above them as they tried to catch their breath.

Katie turned her head towards Brian. He was already staring at her. A contented smile spread across her face as she regarded Brian. Realizing just how silly the moment was, Katie giggled to herself.

In the distance, at the end of the drive, Katie spotted a tall, dark figure. She gasped out loud and sat up straight, eyes wide open, trying to discern what it was that had moved in the distance.

Brian sat up immediately, craning his head in the direction Katie had been looking.

"What is it?" he asked, a hint of worry creeping into his voice as he reached over to put a protective hand on her arm.

Katie knew that it was in fact something, but she did not want to ruin the moment she just experienced with Brian. Her mind flipped through the mental shots of him throwing down the flowers and scooping her up in his arms.

Those scenes are like a mushy, teenage love story from an afterschool special with a title like, "Your First Love." Cliché or not, it's our moment. There is no way I am spoiling it by saying, "Uh, I think the freaky man from my crazy dreams is at the end of the drive." Or worse, "You know that demon faery that tried to kill all of us? I think she may be here to finish the job."

"Katie, what are you looking at?" he questioned again, getting up and brushing the snow off of his clothes.

"It's nothing Brian. I just thought I saw Cherene's

mom's car drive by."

Katie reached up and took Brian's extended hand and let him help her up. "I think I should get inside. My parents said something about making a big welcome home dinner."

"Yeah, I should get home too," Brian said, his voice betraying his disappointment.

The couple walked arm in arm towards Brian's car; Katie's brisk pace urging him to walk faster to the vehicle. Brian turned to face Katie and placed his hands on her hips.

Great, he's going to want a kiss, a real goodbye kiss. I don't have time for this.

She looked over her shoulder to see if the mysterious being was still in the wooded area nearby.

Brian cocked his head to the side and narrowed his eyes at Katie. "Are you sure you are okay, Katie?"

"Yeah, yeah, I couldn't be better," Katie said as innocently as her anxiety ridden tone would allow. Katie stood on her tip-toes and gave him a quick peck on the cheek, a kiss she would give to her uncle or grandfather before leaving a family holiday meal. She smiled sweetly and turned to walk away.

"Can I call you later?" she heard Brian yell.

"Sure!" she answered back. A moment later, she heard his car door slam shut as she rushed towards her front door, anxiety creeping through her body. Her brisk walk became a run. She could hear tires crunching on the snow as the car made its way down the snow-covered drive. Katie peered over her shoulder to make certain it was in fact Brian's car she was hearing behind her.

Katie's eyes scanned the wooded area around her house once more. Satisfied that whatever was there had vanished, she pushed open the large, wooden door and disappeared as quick as she could inside of the old colonial home.

* * * * *

Later that evening, Katie secured the latches on her bedroom windows. She leaned back and rested her head against the cool brick wall that framed the window seat of the bay window in her room. Freezing air pushed against the thin-paned window, grappling to get inside. An eerie, yet familiar shrill howling sound plagued the evening air.

Deep in the woods, a small frozen pond covered the frigid ground. The forest was dark, except for the edge of the icy water, which was illuminated, as if the moon had decided to turn its spotlight on it so that Katie could see.

Katie peered through the window, trying to make out what was at the edge of the ice. A faint lilac light began to glow softly and grew in intensity. The mist flowed over a dark rock near the edge of the pond, encircling it.

The rock shifted slightly revealing a figure crouched down beside the pond. Katie was certain that she saw the image of a hand brushing through the lilac light.

The amethyst stone in her pocket began radiating heat. Katie reached inside and pulled out her stone. Tiny crystals in the rock's surface glowed emitting a deep purple light from within. Katie regarded it oddly. She looked up towards the pond again. The lilac mist had grown; it was the size of a small woman now. Katie's breath caught. Beside the growing lilac light, was the image of a tall, thin man in a dark trench coat floating above the ground.

Katie reached out, placing her hand gingerly on the frozen window. She watched for a moment, unsure at first, but then all at once she knew. Her mouth opened slightly. The warmth of her breath made a fog on the window as she whispered, "Dad?"

Made in the USA
Middletown, DE
23 August 2023